D0182961

KNEE DEEP IN DISHONOUR

KNEE DEEP IN DISHONOUR

The Scott Report and its Aftermath

**Richard Norton-Taylor, Mark Lloyd
and Stephen Cook**

VICTOR GOLLANCZ

LONDON

First published in Great Britain 1996
by Victor Gollancz
An imprint of the Cassell Group
Wellington House, 125 Strand, London WC2R 0BB

A Gollancz Paperback Original

© Richard Norton-Taylor, Mark Lloyd and
Stephen Cook 1996

The right of Richard Norton-Taylor, Mark Lloyd and
Stephen Cook to be identified as authors of this work
has been asserted by them in accordance with the
Copyright, Designs and Patents Act, 1988.

A catalogue record for this book is
available from the British Library.

ISBN 0 575 06385 8

Typeset by Textype, Cambridge
Printed in Great Britain by
St Edmundsbury Press Ltd, Bury St Edmunds, Suffolk

All rights reserved. No part of this publication may be
reproduced or transmitted in any form or by any means,
electronic or mechanical including photocopying,
recording or any information storage or retrieval system,
without prior permission in writing from the publishers.

This book is sold subject to the condition that it shall not,
by way of trade or otherwise, be lent, resold, hired out, or
otherwise circulated without the publisher's prior consent
in any form of binding or cover other than that in which it
is published and without a similar condition including this
condition being imposed on the subsequent purchaser.

96 97 98 99   10 9 8 7 6 5 4 3 2 1

Contents

'On virtually every page of the report there are details of answers that are untrue, inaccurate, misleading. Is no one going to take responsibility for that? . . . If the Prime Minister cannot answer . . . the Conservative Party and the Conservative Government will remain knee deep in dishonour.'

Tony Blair, leader of the Labour Party, House of
Commons, 20 February 1996

'The answers to Parliamentary Questions, in both Houses of Parliament, failed to inform Parliament of the current state of Government policy on non-lethal arms sales to Iraq. This failure was deliberate and was an inevitable result of the agreement between the three junior Ministers that no publicity would be given to the decision to adopt a more liberal, or relaxed, policy, or interpretation of the Guidelines, originally towards both Iran and Iraq and, later, towards Iraq alone. Having heard various explanations as to why it was necessary or desirable to withhold knowledge from Parliament and the public of the true nature of the Government's approach to the licensing of non-lethal defence sales to Iran and Iraq respectively, I have come to the conclusion that the overriding and determinative reason was a fear of strong public opposition to the loosening of the restrictions on the supply of defence equipment to Iraq and a consequential fear that the pressure of the opposition might be detrimental to British trading interests.'

Sir Richard Scott, *Report of the Inquiry into the Export of
Defence Equipment and Dual-Use Goods to Iraq and
Related Prosecutions*, Section D, Chapter 4, paragraph 42

Preface

The agencies of government knew that British companies were breaking export guidelines to help Saddam Hussein build up his war machine, turned a blind eye, and then prosecuted them: since the late 1980s, these essential facts of the arms-to-Iraq scandal have floated just beneath the surface of British political life, threatening to blow a hole in the ship of state. First there were embarrassing revelations in newspapers, then the humiliating collapse of the Matrix Churchill trial and a public examination of dirty linen at the hearings of the Scott Inquiry. Surely, it seemed, the publication of the Scott Report would finally sink a couple of ministers, if not the Government itself.

As the long-awaited day arrived, however, it quickly became clear that nothing would be quite so simple. Ministers and Whitehall mandarins had mounted an insidious campaign of denigration and intimidation against Sir Richard Scott. The judge, they said, knew nothing about government and could not be taken seriously. Scott, torn between outrage at what he had discovered and determination to be seen to be fair, gave the world a report rivalling the length of *War and Peace* and laced with frustrating ambiguities. The Government, by a combination of luck and low politics, managed to survive a crucial vote in the House of Commons.

Those who had hoped to see John Major's limping administration fatally damaged by the Report turned on Scott, saying that he had 'bottled out' – backed away at the last minute from handing them the ammunition for a *coup de grâce*. Others say he was working, as in a criminal trial, to a standard of proof beyond reasonable doubt, that his task was to avoid any hint of party politics and present the evidence to Parliament and the public. 'The final Report – and the final Report alone – contains my concluded views,' declared Sir Richard.

Parliament has delivered its initial verdict, but what about the public? The flaw in Scott's approach is that he presents no summary or set of clear conclusions. The public, unlike a courtroom jury, was not compelled to listen to all the evidence, and few people are likely to plough through 1,800 pages of labyrinthine prose, despite its occasional dry aside, *bon mot* or demotic phrase. By the end of June 1996 the Scott Report, price £45, weight more than a stone, had sold just 4,700 copies, 2,500 of which went, at a cost to the taxpayer of nearly £120,000, to MPs, civil servants and the media. The Denning Report on the Profumo sex scandal of the 1960s sold 124,000 copies, the Scarman Report on the first Brixton riots 14,000, and the Franks Report on the Falklands War 17,000.

Those who have summoned the dedication to read Scott's Report tend to find themselves caught between admiration and frustration. The admiration is for a man with a fierce and persistent commitment to effective Parliamentary scrutiny of the executive and the independence of the judiciary – in other words, to restore a system of proper checks and balances – coupled with the intellectual rigour and persistence to dissect complex events in painstaking detail. The frustration stems from his failure to present the kernel of his work in a more straightforward and manageable form, and place it more effectively into the political and bureaucratic processes of Whitehall. It is heightened by the presence of a rattling good detective story lurking in the Report: dirty business is uncovered, and the investigator is drawn into a tangle of intrigue, wrongdoing and dissimulation by individuals who, unused to being called to account, try to put him off the scent and blacken his character. Scott is faced with all sorts of hostility, obstruction, double-dealing and dirty tricks; but he sticks to his guns, tracks down the suspects, squeezes the evidence out of them, and drags them before a public tribunal.

This book is both a tribute to Scott's work and an attempt to make up for one of its perceived shortcomings. It charts the Government's ruthless attempts to neutralize the Report, offers a concise summary of its prolix contents, and analyses how the Government escaped apparently unscathed. A final section looks at the hidden impact of Scott on the culture of Whitehall and argues that Scott's revelations have strengthened the case for governments to be less secretive and more accountable to Parliament and the electorate.

Our thanks go to David Price, spokesman for the Scott Inquiry, and Christopher Muttukumaru, the Inquiry's secretary, for helping us to fight through some of the more impenetrable thickets. We would also like to thank Sean Magee, senior commissioning editor at Victor Gollancz, for appreciating the significance of the Scott Report and the implications of the arms-to-Iraq affair, Katrina Whone, managing editor at Gollancz, for arranging a speedy publication, and Hazel Orme for copy-editing our text with such skill and patience.

Introduction

'I doubt if there is any future market of such a scale anywhere where the UK is potentially so well placed – if we play our diplomatic hand correctly – nor can I think of any major market where the importance of diplomacy is so great on our commercial position. We must not allow it to go to the French, German, Japanese, Koreans etc. . . . The priority of Iraq in our policy should be very high: in commercial terms, comparable to South Africa in my view . . . A few more Bazofts or another bout of internal repression would make this more difficult.'

William Waldegrave, Foreign Office minister, in October 1989, a month after Farzad Bazoft, the *Observer* journalist, was arrested in Iraq

The events covered by the Scott Inquiry had their origin in the eight-year war between Iran and Iraq, which began in 1980 when a dispute erupted over control of the Shatt-al-Arab waterway which forms the southern boundary between the two countries. The conflict between Arabs and Persians, rivals in the Middle East for centuries, brought a return to trench warfare on a scale not seen since the First World War. In the brutal 'war of the cities', each side rained long-distance Scud missiles on the other's main towns. By the time of the 1988 ceasefire, a million people had been killed.

Warfare on such a scale brought a huge demand for armaments in the two countries. Their capacity to produce their own weapons was limited, but their huge oil revenues had allowed them to buy formidable armouries from Britain, France and the two superpowers. Britain had traditionally supplied Iran under the Shah, but after the Islamic revolution what remained of this trade went underground. Whitehall was soon eyeing the alternative market in Iraq, hitherto supplied mainly by the Soviet Union and France: in 1981, minutes of the Cabinet's

Oversea and Defence Committee (OD), chaired by Margaret (now Baroness) Thatcher, recorded discussion about how to exploit Iraq's 'promising market' for arms. Whitehall was unwilling to let Saddam Hussein's abuse of human rights, including the gassing of Kurdish villagers in the north of his country, prevent British industry from seizing the big prize.

At first, ammunition and spares flowed freely from Western suppliers, but as the war deepened some democratic governments began to have second thoughts, with the consequence that arms dealers began to use circuitous routes and dubious documentation to make sure the goods got through.

As mass Iranian attacks took their toll on the smaller Iraqi forces, Saddam Hussein started to use chemical weapons and missiles and initiated his search for an exotic weapon, the Supergun, with a proposed range of up to 1,000 miles. His ultimate aim was to acquire a nuclear warhead. He also decided to end his dependence on unreliable foreign suppliers by developing an indigenous arms industry. Iraqi businessmen approved by the Baghdad regime set out to try to buy the technical expertise and equipment needed for the new factories. In London, they set up TDG, which in 1987 bought Matrix Churchill, the Coventry machine tool company, whose computer-controlled lathes were suitable for making shell and missile cases and parts for Iraq's nuclear programme. Shortly after the ceasefire in the Iran–Iraq war was declared in August 1988, British ministers secretly relaxed the guidelines on exports to the combatants. The scene was set for the Matrix Churchill débâcle.

At one level, the arms-to-Iraq affair was an example of the conflict between moral considerations and the demands of a privileged armaments industry that makes Britain one of the world's largest weapons exporters. According to the Ministry of Defence (MoD), nearly 400,000 jobs are dependent directly or indirectly on the arms industry, although an estimated 1,000 jobs have been lost every month since 1989. Britain sells about £2 billion worth of weapons abroad each year, and the arms industry is one of the few large high-technology manufacturing sectors still under British control. 'No other sector of UK industry is as successful in the international market place,' Roger Freeman, the public service minister, said when he was Minister for Defence Procurement in 1994.

William Waldegrave, one of the two ministers most criticized in the Scott Report, pointed out the tension during a hearing of the Inquiry: 'There is in this country a certain ambivalence . . . People want the jobs but they do not always want to think about them. Whenever Mrs Thatcher (*sic*) or Mr Major comes back, having batted for Britain and won a great deal, everyone says, "Hooray!" They are heroes on the front page.' Labour MPs are also aware that it is easy to shout about the immorality of arms deals, but not so easy to stand by while the jobs of their constituents are threatened.

Under the governments of Margaret Thatcher and John Major, however, selling arms abroad seems to have become an obsession. Asylum laws and human rights principles have been distorted in the drive to sell arms to lucrative Middle Eastern and Asian markets; official criteria on overseas aid have been manipulated to persuade foreign governments to buy British weapons; and MI6 and the Government Communications Headquarters (GCHQ) have been asked to watch out for promising arms deals before they go to Britain's competitors. Secret intelligence has even been provided to other countries, including Saudi Arabia, in the hope of rewards in the shape of weapons deals.

The unprecedented Al-Yamamah arms deal between Britain and Saudi Arabia, worth an estimated £20 billion and signed by Thatcher in 1985, provides an illustration of the lengths to which the Government has been prepared to go to support the British arms industry. A National Audit Office report on the deal, including references to alleged 'kickbacks' paid by British companies, has been suppressed by the Commons Public Accounts Committee on the grounds that its publication would upset the Saudis and thus put British jobs at risk. That same year Thatcher signed a £270 million Jordan Defence Package, even though the Government knew that Jordan was a conduit for British arms sales to Iraq.

The Al-Yamamah deal was also behind a more recent episode that illustrates the uniquely privileged relationship arms companies have with the intelligence agencies, the MoD and the Foreign Office (FCO). Correspondence leaked in September 1995 showed how Sir Colin Chandler, chief executive of Vickers, and Dick Evans, chief executive of British Aerospace

(BAe), hatched a plan to placate the Saudi royal family over the activities of Mohammed al-Mas'ari, a leading Saudi dissident seeking asylum in Britain. Al-Mas'ari had been flooding Saudi Arabia with faxes criticizing the regime, and Vickers and BAe were concerned about the effect of this on Prince Sultan, King Fahd's brother, who had played a key role in the multi-million pound Al-Yamamah deal which had been the saviour of BAe.

Chandler suggested that the Government 'might try to offset some of the Saudi criticism of us' by inviting Saddam Hussein's son-in-law, who had fled Iraq and sought asylum in Jordan, to visit the UK for a debriefing by the intelligence services: some of the information gleaned from him could then be fed back to Riyadh. 'Dick [Evans] said he would join in supporting it with the Foreign Office,' Chandler wrote to a colleague. The letter made clear that the arms companies had access at will to senior FCO officials.

An example of how aid policy is distorted by the prospect of lucrative arms deals occurred in 1989 when the Government earmarked £234 million from the overseas aid budget for Malaysia's Pergau dam project. The origins of the decision, which was subsequently ruled unlawful by the High Court, lay in Thatcher's promise to provide money for the economically questionable project when she was negotiating a £1.3 billion arms deal with Malaysia. *Per capita* aid to Indonesia has more than quadrupled over the past fifteen years in spite of that country's relative wealth and its continuing occupation of East Timor. The aid offer came after Indonesia agreed to buy BAe Hawk aircraft, with the prospect of further deals.

The Government spends more than ten times as much taxpayers' money promoting arms sales as it does civil exports. The World Development Movement, a leading Third World campaigning group, has unearthed a huge undeclared bill paid by British taxpayers for British weapons exports. In each of the five years up to 1995, the Export Credits Guarantee Department (ECGD) had to pay out some £250 million to cover arms sales bills left unpaid by foreign governments. Over half of ECGD guarantees devoted to arms sales are accounted for by the Middle East, notably Kuwait, Oman and Saudi Arabia, and the region takes more than half of Britain's total arms exports. Yet, despite the MoD's rhetoric, arms over the past decade have been worth only 1.7 per cent of total British average annual exports.

The ceasefire in the Iran–Iraq war was followed by a push from Britain – articulated by William Waldegrave in the quotation at the head of this chapter – to sell weapons to Iraq. No sooner had the fighting stopped in the 1990–91 Gulf War than Britain, the US and France were hurrying to sell sophisticated weapons systems to oil-rich, undemocratic, Gulf states. Against this background, the prospect of greater openness on arms sales, one of the key proposals of the Scott Report, is not encouraging. The UN Arms Register, which covers exports of seven types of conventional arms, including combat aircraft, battle tanks, and missiles, is a voluntary scheme. The British Government, concerned about its competitors and the sensitivities of prospective customers, is likely to continue to argue that 'commercial confidentiality' should prevent the disclosure of more information about arms deals.

Chronology

The following chronology gives the key dates in the arms-to-Iraq story, some of which only came to light because of inquiries by Parliamentary committees, journalists or Sir Richard Scott. The events in bold type are the ones which were initially kept secret.

1980   Iran–Iraq war begins.

1981   **Cabinet Oversea and Defence Committee, chaired by Margaret (now Baroness) Thatcher, then Prime Minister, discusses how to exploit Iraq's 'promising market' for arms.**

1983   Reginald Dunk, chief executive of Atlantic Commercial Ltd, and Alexander Schlesinger, a consultant, charged with illegally exporting 200 Sterling sub-machine guns to Iraq via Jordan.

1984   **December: Sir Geoffrey (now Lord) Howe, then Foreign Secretary, draws up secret guidelines for arms exports to the warring countries.**

1985   October: guidelines finally announced in a written answer to Liberal Democrat MP David Steel. They say Britain would refuse to supply 'lethal equipment' to Iraq or Iran, 'should not, in future, approve orders for any defence equipment which, in our view, would significantly enhance the capability of either side to prolong or exacerbate the conflict . . . and should continue to scrutinize rigorously all applications for export licences for the supply of defence equipment to Iran and Iraq'.

1985   Start of 'War of the Cities' between Iraq and Iran, with each side firing missiles at the other's capital city.

1985   Dunk and Schlesinger convicted of selling guns to Iraq through Jordan. Dunk fined £12,500, Schlesinger £3,000 and Atlantic Commercial £7,500.

1985   **Joint Intelligence Committee tasked to monitor all future trade with Jordan.**

1986   UN confirms Iraq has used chemical weapons against Iran.

1987   TDG, an Iraqi-controlled company, buys Matrix Churchill, a machine-tool company in Coventry.

1987   November: first MI6 report, based on information from a
        British businessman, confirms British machine-tool com-
        panies, including Matrix Churchill, are selling equipment to
        Iraqi arms factories. Report circulated to ministers and
        senior Whitehall officials. The MoD and MI6 get the first
        hints of the Supergun project.

1988   January: Alan Clark, junior trade minister, meets machine tool
        exporters. They emerge thinking he is happy for them to declare
        in licence applications that exports to Iraq are for general
        engineering even though they could have military applications.

1988   February: approval is sought from three ministers (William
        Waldegrave, Alan Clark and Lord Trefgarne) for a batch of
        exports to Iraq, including Matrix Churchill machine tools,
        despite intelligence reports revealing their true end use in the
        munitions industry. They say 'yes' to protect the intelligence
        source.

1988   March: Saddam Hussein's forces attack Kurdish town of
        Halabja with chemical weapons, killing 5,000 civilians.
        International outcry, but no change in arms exports policy
        by Britain.

1988   June: Tory MP Sir Hal Miller, alerted by a director of Walter
        Somers, tells Alan Clark that the Midlands firm is preparing
        to export pipes to Iraq, which might be used for Saddam
        Hussein's Supergun. No decisive action in Whitehall.

1988   August: Iraq's big final push against Iran fails and the two
        exhausted countries declare a ceasefire.

1988   August: Howe proposes more liberal approach on arms
        sales to Iraq but says secrecy is vital as 'it could look very
        cynical if, soon after expressing outrage about the treatment
        of the Kurds [at Halabja], we adopt a more flexible
        approach to arms sales'.

1988   September: Paul Henderson, boss of Matrix Churchill, is
        reactivated by MI6.

1988   December: ministers agree to secret policy shift relaxing
        controls on exports to Iraq and Iran. It reads: 'We should
        not in future approve orders for any defence equipment
        which, in our view, would be of direct and significant
        assistance to either country in the conduct of offensive
        operations in breach of the ceasefire.' Change is not
        announced in Parliament.

1989   February: Iran announces *fatwa* against Salman Rushdie
        after publication of *The Satanic Verses*. Ministers reapply
        older, stricter arms export guidelines to Iran, while keeping
        new relaxed policy for Iraq. William Waldegrave, Alan
        Clark and Lord Trefgarne approve another batch of Matrix

Churchill exports to Iraq. They include computer-controlled lathes, which can make shell casings or centrifuges for enriching uranium. Waldegrave notes: 'Screwdrivers are also required to make H-bombs.'

1989   Spring: Paul Grecian, boss of the Reading military engineering firm Ordtec, warns Government about Iraqi 'Supergun' project.

1989   September: *Financial Times* says Matrix Churchill and other British companies are selling Iraq machine tools for missile and munitions manufacture. DTI official Anthony Steadman tells ministers that intelligence reports showed the factories involved had general engineering as well as weapons functions and there was no evidence that the British machines were for weapons.
         Observer journalist Farzad Bazoft arrested in Baghdad and accused of spying.

1989   November: ministers agree third batch of Matrix Churchill exports to Iraq – more lathes. An MI6 officer circulates in Whitehall a conclusive report about British firms exporting for the Supergun project; he compares the experience to dropping a brick into treacle.

1990   January: Eagle Trust takes over Walter Somers, and David James, the chairman, tells an MI6 officer that he is suspicious about some pipes the firm is making for Iraq.

1990   March: Gerald Bull, the French-Canadian scientist developing the Supergun for Iraq, is killed by five bullets from a silenced gun as he returns to his apartment in Brussels. Suspicion falls on the Israeli secret service, Mossad.
         Bazoft executed.

1990   April: prompted by an MI6 officer, Customs at Teesport seize the pipes from Walter Somers, which turn out to be barrel parts for the Supergun. Two men are charged. The late Nicholas Ridley, then Secretary of State for Trade and Industry, tells MPs the Government only 'recently became aware in general terms' of the Supergun project.
         May: MI6 station in Jordan tells London: 'Have we not turned a blind eye to Jordanian involvement [in Iraqi arms procurement] in the past?'

1990   June: Customs, acting on a tip-off from Germany, make fact-finding visit to Matrix Churchill. Senior Department of Trade and Industry (DTI) official warns that Whitehall's 'dirty washing' could come out if Customs prosecute.

1990   19 July: Cabinet committee approves significantly more liberal export policy towards Iraq, on grounds that Saddam

Hussein is pro-West and exporters need the business.

1990   27 July: DTI approves final batch of Matrix Churchill exports to Iraq, knowing they are to be used to make shells and missiles.

1990   2 August: Iraq invades Kuwait. UN and UK sanctions imposed, banning all exports to Iraq.

1990   October: Customs defy objections by Nicholas Ridley, and raid Matrix Churchill. Find evidence of false export documentation, arrest Paul Henderson and two fellow-directors.

1990   November: Customs arrest five people connected to the Reading-based firm Ordtec, including Paul Grecian, for exporting an assembly line for military fuses to Iraq via Jordan.

1990   November: charges against two men relating to the Supergun affair dropped on the advice of the Attorney-General. **Counsel had warned that the defence would point out that the firm had told Whitehall of its doubts about the Iraqi order and nothing was done. Customs officials furious at the decision.**

1990   2 December: *Sunday Times* says Alan Clark advised companies to disguise the military potential of their machine-tool exports in their export-licence applications.

1991   February: British land forces engage in Gulf War. Paul Henderson and two fellow Matrix Churchill directors charged.

1991   June: Ali Daghir and Jeanine Speckman, directors of a firm called Euromac (wholly owned by Iraqis), convicted and imprisoned for exporting to Iraq electrical capacitors, allegedly for use in nuclear warheads. **Two ministers, Kenneth Baker and Peter Lilley, sign Public Interest Immunity (PII) certificates in the Matrix Churchill committal proceedings.**

1991   November: the Matrix Churchill Three, including Henderson, committed to trial at the Old Bailey.

1991–92 **DTI at first warns Customs off the Matrix Churchill prosecution, then backs off and allows Whitehall lawyers to vet the witness statements of its officials to ensure they are taking the approved line.**

1992   **PII certificates signed by Baker and Lilley before the Ordtec trial.**

1992   February: at the trial Paul Grecian, Stuart Blackledge, Colin Phillips and Bryan Mason plead guilty and are given suspended prison sentences and fined.

1992   **June–September: four ministers – Malcolm Rifkind,**

Kenneth Clarke, Tristan Garel-Jones, and Michael Heseltine – sign PII certificates for documents relating to the Matrix Churchill trial.

1992   August: *Sunday Telegraph* repeats the story of Clark telling exporters to cloud the truth on the purpose of exports, saying he regarded the guidelines as 'tiresome and intrusive'.

1992   **5 October: Customs telephone Clark, no longer a minister or an MP, about the *Telegraph* story, reporting to counsel that he stands by a witness statement which says he dealt clearly with the exporters.**

1992   12 October: Matrix Churchill trial opens at the Old Bailey.

1992   9 November: trial comes to a sudden halt after Alan Clark admits under cross-examination that he had been 'economical . . . with the *actualité*'.

        10 November: John Major sets up an Inquiry under Lord Justice Scott.

1993   May–July 1994: public hearings of Scott Inquiry, revealing the scale of arms-related exports to Iraq, the secret shifts in Government policy, the misleading of Parliament by ministers, and mistakes, inefficiency and cynicism among Whitehall officials.

1994   **Whispering campaign begins in Whitehall to discredit the Inquiry and Scott's conduct of it. Lord Howe begins bitter correspondence accusing Scott of unfair inquiry procedures.**

1994   May: conviction quashed on appeal against two Euromac directors sentenced in the Iraqi 'nuclear triggers' case.

1994   July: conviction quashed on appeal against Dunk and Schlesinger, sentenced for selling guns to Iraq via Jordan.

1994   October: Lord Justice Scott appointed Vice-Chancellor, head of the Chancery Division of the High Court. His title changes to Sir Richard Scott.

1995   November: conviction quashed on appeal against Ordtec Four because relevant official documents had not been disclosed to the defence.

1996   January: former ministers Lord Howe and Douglas Hurd give interviews criticizing the Inquiry as flawed and unfair. Rows begin over who gets advance copies of the Scott Report.

1996   15 February: 1,800-page Scott Report published.

1996   26 February: Government wins Commons vote on the Report by 320 to 319.

Cast of Characters

The events examined in the Scott Report involved scores of people, ranging from two Prime Ministers, two Foreign Secretaries and various Whitehall mandarins to a collection of secret policemen, intelligence agents, risk-taking businessmen and small-time arms dealers. This guide begins with the businessmen, whose export licence applications (ELAs) sparked off the controversial events, and continues with the ministers and civil servants at the Department of Trade and Industry (DTI), which had to vet and decide whether or not to approve their applications.

Next come the inhabitants of the FCO and the MoD, who had to be consulted on the applications, and those of 10 Downing Street, who were meant to be kept informed of important defence-related ELAs. Two former Home Secretaries are mentioned, and an MP who alerted Whitehall about the Supergun.

Finally there are the main players at Customs and Excise, whose prosecution of Matrix Churchill led to the disastrous trial and the Scott Inquiry, and the Attorney-General and government lawyers who were responsible for supervising and conducting the Customs prosecution.

THE BUSINESSMEN

Paul Henderson Managing director (1987–90) of Matrix Churchill, the Coventry machine-tools company. Henderson was prosecuted by Customs for exporting machine tools to Iraqi munitions factories. An MI6 agent described him at the trial as 'a very brave man', for being an MI6 informant at a time when Iraq was executing spies.

Paul Grecian Managing director of Ordtec, a Reading firm making military production equipment. He also gave information to MI6, was prosecuted by Customs for exporting a fuse assembly line to Iraq, and acquitted on appeal.

THE DEPARTMENT OF TRADE AND INDUSTRY

Alan Clark   Minister for Trade, 1986–89, when he changed places with Lord Trefgarne to become Minister for Defence Procurement at the MoD, remaining there until April 1992 when he stood down as an MP.

Michael Heseltine   President of the Board of Trade, 1992–95. He objected to signing PII certificates designed to withhold official documents from the Matrix Churchill defence.

Eric Beston   DTI official in charge of export controls during the Matrix Churchill affair. He is criticized by Scott for giving misleading evidence at the Matrix Churchill trial.

Anthony Steadman   Worked under Beston. Scott says he chose to play down the significance of intelligence reports about Iraqi arms and signed 'inaccurate and misleading' witness statements for the trial.

THE FOREIGN AND COMMONWEALTH OFFICE

Sir Geoffrey (now Lord) Howe   Foreign Secretary 1983–89. Author of the 1984 guidelines on military sales to Iraq and Iran and the most strident critic of the Inquiry.

Douglas Hurd   Foreign Secretary, 1989–95. He was critical of the Inquiry and said: 'In forty years, I have lived through a lot of cock-ups, but very few conspiracies.'

William Waldegrave   Minister of State at the FCO, 1988–90. He agreed to let arms-related sales to Iraq continue, and signed letters to MPs that Scott condemns as 'designedly' misleading. Now in the Cabinet (1996) as Chief Secretary to the Treasury.

David Gore-Booth   Responsible for the Middle East Department of the FCO, 1989–93. Gave policy advice to ministers in the Matrix Churchill case. Defended giving incomplete answers to MPs, declaring: 'Of course half a picture can be accurate.' Now (1996) High Commissioner to India.

Rob Young   Head of the Middle East Department, 1987–90. Criticized by Scott for recommending incomplete Parliamentary answers to avoid controversy. He is now Chief Clerk, one of the FCO's three most senior posts.

MINISTRY OF DEFENCE

Lord Trefgarne   Minister for Defence Procurement, 1986–89. With Alan Clark, he persuaded Waldegrave to agree to Matrix Churchill exports, and all three decided not to announce the 1988 change in the Howe guidelines. Only gave evidence to the Inquiry after being assured that he would be treated with 'courtesy and consideration'.

Ian McDonald   A minor TV star after his intonations on the 1982

Falklands War as MoD spokesman, McDonald was head of the Defence Export Services Secretariat (DESS) at the MoD during the Matrix Churchill affair. Criticized by Scott for failing to check important documents and writing 'puzzling' memos that conflicted with intelligence reports. Uttered the seminal Whitehall remark: 'I do not have to tell you that truth is a very difficult concept.'

Alan Barrett   Worked with McDonald at the DESS, 1987–90. Played a part in shelving a crucial report on arms exports by his colleague Glazebrook (*q.v.*). On the change in the Howe guidelines, wrote: 'Oh dear! We can expect trouble before long, as there is a chance of this leaking.'

Lieutenant-Colonel Richard Glazebrook   Wrote a paper in 1989 pointing out that 'UK Ltd' was helping Iraq to set up a major arms industry, which was ignored by his colleagues and – says Scott – 'fell into limbo'. A star witness at the Inquiry.

10 DOWNING STREET

Margaret (now Baroness) Thatcher   Prime Minister, 1979–90. Spread the message that arms sales were good for Britain, but was unaware of the detail of the Matrix Churchill affair and the guidelines: 'If I had seen every copy of every minute that I was sent in Government,' she said, 'I would have been in a snowstorm . . . I was concerned with the big issues.'

John Major   Chief Secretary to the Treasury, 1987–89, Foreign Secretary and Chancellor in 1989, Prime Minister from 1990. Like Thatcher, pleaded ignorance: 'One of the charges at the time, of course, was, in some way, I must have known, because I had been the Chancellor, because I had been Foreign Secretary, because I had been Prime Minister – that, therefore, I must have known what was going on.'

Sir Robin Butler   Cabinet Secretary and head of the Civil Service since 1988. Set the tone for Whitehall's response to the Inquiry and locked horns with Scott over ministerial accountability, access to documents and the truthfulness of Parliamentary answers.

THE HOME OFFICE

Kenneth Baker   Home Secretary in 1991. Signed PII certificates intended to block evidence from the security services at the Matrix Churchill and Ordtec trials but was not given vital information, such as that relating to Henderson's work for MI6. Scott criticizes the briefings and legal advice he received.

Kenneth Clarke   Home Secretary, 1992–93. Also signed PII certificates for the Matrix Churchill case, believing lives of agents would be at risk if documents were made public.

MEMBERS OF PARLIAMENT

Sir Hal Miller   Conservative MP for Bromsgrove, near Birmingham, until 1992. Warned Whitehall that pipes machined by a local firm could be parts for the Iraqi Supergun and consistently challenged the inactivity of Government and Whitehall.

CUSTOMS AND EXCISE

Sir Brian Unwin   Chairman of the board of HM Customs and Excise, 1987–93. Furious when obliged to drop the Supergun prosecution; disregarded warning signals on the Matrix Churchill prosecution. Complained about changing Government policies and the difficulty of access to Whitehall documents.

Peter Wiltshire   Senior Investigation Officer. Failed to pass on intelligence reports about Matrix Churchill lathes going to arms factories – the investigation started only after a tip-off was received from Germany.

THE GOVERNMENT LAWYERS

Sir Nicholas Lyell QC   Attorney-General since 1992. Advised ministers that they had a legal duty to sign claims for PII for official documents. Scott reprimanded him for his role in the Matrix Churchill affair and his interpretation of the law. With Waldegrave, he was most at risk from the Scott Report.

Andrew Leithead   Assistant Treasury Solicitor. Went through civil servants' witness statements for the Matrix Churchill trial, advising them what to delete. Said it was part of his job to stop defence lawyers getting hold of Government documents.

Alan Moses QC   Chief prosecution counsel in the Matrix Churchill trial. Hindered by Whitehall's reluctance to disclose documents, but himself criticized by Scott for limiting disclosure of documents to the defence. Appointed a High Court judge, June 1996.

1 • A Padded Cell

'This is a story in which there are no villains.'
Lord Howe of Aberavon, former Foreign Secretary

The arrangements for opposition party representatives to get an early look at the long-awaited Scott Report read like something out of Kafka. Three and a half hours before publication, Government cars would arrive at the House of Commons to take them to the DTI, a few hundred yards away. They would be met by an official:

> This official will escort you throughout your visit [read the instructions]. This is for your own convenience and security. You will be escorted to a room. Your escort will be just outside your door . . . If messages need to be got to you while you are reading the report, they should be routed via the Office of the Manager of DTI Conference Suite . . . I am afraid it will not be possible for you to send messages out . . . When you have finished reading, please contact the escort outside your door, who will arrange for the report to be taken into secure keeping. They will then take you back to the car which will return you to the House.

The Government had received the Report eight days earlier, and these arrangements, hovering between the sinister and the farcical, were what it regarded as reasonable advance access for the other parties. Lord Jenkins and Lord Richard, the Liberal Democrat and Labour leaders in the House of Lords, refused the invitation to what they called 'a padded cell or sealed capsule'. The office of Tony Blair, the Labour leader, also declined the offer, calling the conditions 'extraordinary and insulting'. Robin Cook, shadow foreign secretary, Menzies Campbell, the Liberal Democrat foreign affairs spokesman, and David Trimble, leader of the Ulster Unionist Party, accepted – under protest. To get through the report in the time allotted, they would have to read a page of complex argument every eight seconds.

This bizarre arrangement was the culmination of weeks of wrangling and arm-twisting between Sir Richard Scott and the Government over the publication arrangements. A hint of the bitterness of some of the exchanges came in the covering letter Scott wrote for the formal handover of the Report to Ian Lang, President of the Board of Trade. The letter pays tribute to the Scott Inquiry secretary, Christopher Muttukumaru, who handled relations between the judge and Whitehall, often confronting the most senior officials. Muttukumaru had been a 'tower of strength' who had often had to deal with officials of a rank senior to his own as well as ministers and ex-ministers: 'Those who have dealt with him, and I myself, have come to understand that he cannot be intimidated.'

Asked to elucidate when he gave evidence in May 1996 to the Commons Public Service Committee, Scott said it had been suggested that Muttukumaru's 'career might suffer from the assistance he was giving me'. He added that those concerned knew to whom he was referring – he was not prepared to discuss it in public. It is known, however, that Muttukumaru had been engaged in angry exchanges with senior Whitehall figures over the Inquiry's procedures and the publication arrangements. Scott told the committee that his concerns were eventually laid to rest, and Muttukumaru, who had been seconded from the Treasury Solicitor's Department during the Inquiry, was later offered a job as a senior legal adviser to the MoD.

The Government wanted to get its hands on the Report as soon as possible, take its time to prepare a response, and spring it on the nation at a moment of its own choosing. The Bingham Report into the BCCI banking scandal was delivered to the Government two and a half months before it was published, and Lord Donaldson's findings on the *Braer* tanker disaster were with ministers a month before publication. In both cases it had been the Government, not the authors of the reports, that decided the timing and manner of publication.

Scott, however, had ensured at the beginning that he himself would be in control of publication. When it was first announced to the House of Commons in November 1992 that he would conduct the Inquiry, the Attorney-General, Sir Nicholas Lyell, said only that 'his report and evidence will be published . . .' A week later, though, John Major told MPs: 'Lord Justice Scott will be entirely free to decide on the publication of his report and on the evidence he takes.' Scott says in his Report:

> I believe the plenary nature of the discretion conferred on me regarding publication to be unique. It is my understanding that in any other comparable Inquiry, the ultimate decisions regarding publication have been taken by the government of the day. The reason for this unique discretion was, no doubt, the nature of the 'cover-up' allegations deriving from the use of the Public Interest Immunity certificates, the investigation of which was one of the main functions of the Inquiry.

In 1992 the Government might have felt that handing over the publication arrangements to Scott would not cause any difficulty. Four years later, the mood had changed. A lot of blood had been spilt in furious, behind-the-scenes exchanges between Whitehall and Scott, who had widened the scope of his Inquiry and had publicly hauled officials and ministers over the coals. As they awaited Scott's judgment, senior civil servants, used to being in control, were in a state of extreme nervousness brought on by fear of the unknown. When Scott opened the bidding over publication by saying that everyone should receive the Report at the same time – Government, Opposition, Parliament, press and public, all on equal terms – Whitehall reacted with astonishment and ill-disguised fury.

In heated negotiations with the Cabinet Office – Muttukumaru acting as go-between – Scott accepted that it was reasonable for certain ministers and senior officials to see the Report before the official publication date so that they could have time to prepare a response. He agreed that they could have it eight days before a publication date of Tuesday 13 or Wednesday 14 February. The Government wanted longer, but was also terrified of leaks, and was eventually persuaded that the shorter the period, the less the risk. As for the date, Tuesday was not convenient and Wednesday was the anniversary of the St Valentine's Day Massacre. The two sides settled on Thursday 15 February. After more skirmishes, it was agreed that six ministers and eighteen officials could see it in advance. Whitehall insisted that their names should not be disclosed: if they were published, argued

John Alty, principal private secretary to Ian Lang, President of the Board of Trade, the recipients might be the victims of 'electronic and personal surveillance'. The notion that ministerial offices would be bugged and long lenses trained on the study windows of permanent secretaries was regarded by Scott and his Inquiry team as just one more example of excessive secrecy and paranoia in Whitehall.

Two days before publication the horse-trading reached a new intensity. The Government suddenly insisted that some of those criticized in the Report should also be given advance access – in a less controlled environment than Robin Cook's 'padded cell'. Those for whom it demanded special treatment included Lord Trefgarne and Lord Howe. Howe had been hostile to Scott, while Trefgarne had made clear that he resented having to give evidence to the Inquiry at all. Muttukumaru's response to their demands could scarcely have been more blunt. 'Sir Richard is not prepared to countenance it,' he told Alty. Next day the Government climbed down.

There was a particular irony in the Government's insistence on secrecy and its concern about pre-publication leaks. For more than a year, it had manoeuvred to pierce the secrecy that Scott had imposed on draft extracts of his Report, which had been sent out to people he was planning to criticize to give them the opportunity to respond before he sent the final version to the printers. Scott demanded from everyone to whom the extracts had been sent a strict undertaking to keep them confidential. He had learned enough about Whitehall to suspect that it might engineer self-serving leaks, and co-ordinate a joint attack on his proposed criticisms.

Any expectation that Whitehall might be observing Scott's request collapsed before the completion of the final Report when a fax from MI5 arrived by accident at the Inquiry offices. Headed 'Piecing together the Scott Report' it made clear that agents officially tasked with countering terrorism and espionage had been spending their time in assembling snippets about a judge's independent report into Government misdeeds. The fax should have been sent to the Cabinet Office, but someone in MI5 had dialled the wrong number.

The tone of this protracted running battle with Whitehall had been set three years earlier in March 1993, when the terms of reference and the procedures of the Inquiry had been established. Scott held a press conference – the first and last he gave before his Report was published – to describe how he intended to proceed. A key question was what evidence would be heard in secret, and Scott released correspondence on the issue he had exchanged with Sir Robin Butler.

Butler had told Scott: 'Our proposal is that you should direct that hearings should go into closed session when in your view disclosure in public would be damaging to the public interest and that in other cases Government witnesses should be instructed to request a closed session on occasions when, in their view, the disclosure of information might be damaging.' Whitehall's definition of 'damaging' would almost certainly have been so broad as to include evidence that was merely embarrassing. Scott replied that he would go into closed session only when, in his view and his view alone, an open hearing would 'cause serious injury to the interests of the nation'. Had Butler persisted in his demands, Scott would have been able to point to the Commons debate during the uproar that followed the collapse of the Matrix Churchill trial the previous November when Michael Heseltine, then President of the Board of Trade, told MPs: 'Lord Justice Scott will have unfettered discretion as to what to publish and whether, or what parts of, his Inquiry will be in public.'

However, Scott did agree that GCHQ – the Government's electronic eavesdropping centre – must not be named as the source of intelligence, notably relating to Matrix Churchill's relations with Iraq. Unlike those from MI5 or MI6, GCHQ reports are identified only as 'Intelligence Reports' or 'IR'.

As the Inquiry got into its stride, Whitehall became increasingly alarmed. It had been assumed that Scott would limit his investigations to specific issues – Government policy towards exports to Iraq, the use of PII certificates in the Matrix Churchill trial, and the handling of other arms-to-Iraq prosecutions. But it soon became clear that he intended to tackle wider issues. He and his team began by reading thousands of Whitehall documents which had never been intended for public consumption, and then held a series of high-profile public hearings where ministers, former ministers and senior officials were questioned intensively on all the ramifications of the 'arms-to-Iraq' affair. The country was treated to a unique insight in the way politicians and civil servants made mistakes, dissembled, and manoeuvred to bend the rules and deceive Parliament and public about what was going on in Whitehall. The objects of this exposure did not like it, and decided to fight back.

It started as a whispering campaign, with smears discreetly dropped into the ears of chosen journalists, mainly from the Parliamentary lobby. Articles began to appear in the press hinting that Scott was hopelessly naïve and that he lacked understanding of the real world of government decision-making. Stories were printed about his tolerance of the conversion to Islam of two of his grown-up children; his enjoyment of fox-hunting; and his riding a bicycle to work, featuring pictures of him pedalling through London traffic with a self-conscious smile. Sir Bernard Ingham, Thatcher's blunt, Yorkshire-bred former press secretary, came straight out with it: Scott was 'the wettest, most liberal judge they could find'.

One of the most combative and resentful witnesses at the Inquiry hearings was Lord Howe, the former Foreign Secretary who had authorized the formulation and eventual publication of the original guidelines on defence exports to Iraq and Iran. When he arrived to give evidence, he sprang a prepared statement on Scott, which accused him of being 'detective, inquisitor, advocate and judge'. He had borrowed the phrase from Lord Denning, who had used it to describe his own role when conducting his Inquiry into the Profumo affair in 1963. Howe was frosty in his exchanges with Scott and the Inquiry's QC, Presiley Baxendale, and made his reluctance to give evidence abundantly clear.

Howe intensified his efforts at the end of 1994, when drafts of Scott's Report began to circulate. An acrimonious correspondence opened between the two men, which was to cover nearly a hundred pages of typescript and continue until July 1995. Words such as 'erroneous', 'misconceived', 'disproportionate' and 'distorted' flew back and forth.

The essential argument between them concerned the so-called Salmon Principles, which had been drawn up by a Royal Commission on Tribunals of Inquiry chaired by Lord Justice Salmon in 1966. This body had been set up to try to improve tribunal procedures after the Denning Report on Profumo. Howe said that Scott should have followed the Salmon Principles exactly; Scott reserved the right to interpret them flexibly. Indeed, he eventually drew up his own set of principles and put them in his recommendations. Salmon had said that injustice could be avoided if 'six cardinal principles' were followed in inquiries: no one should give evidence unless the circumstances concerned them; witnesses should be told of allegations and evidence against them and should have legal help at public expense; they should be allowed to state their case to the tribunal; any relevant witness should be heard; and they should be able to cross-examine other witnesses on evidence affecting them.

Scott believed that the Salmon Principles carried strong overtones of the adversarial litigation of the courts and were not necessarily suitable for an inquisitorial inquiry of which the aim was not to prove a case but to establish the truth. He believed that the first five principles were largely upheld in his Inquiry, but to have complied with the sixth would, in the words of the Report, have turned the oral hearings into 'a procedural morass'. The principles of telling people of adverse evidence about them, allowing them to reply, and of submitting draft criticism to them for comment safeguarded fairness, he said.

Howe would not accept this and complained that Scott's way of doing things was unfair to witnesses:

> The whole process comes to resemble a game of blind man's bluff, with the important difference that everyone is blindfolded except for the presiding judge. The mutual ignorance of every other player means that the sole sighted participant (himself unassisted by any advocates or lay assessors and colleagues, who might offer insights based upon practical experience) is seriously deprived of guidance. This may go some way to explaining the seemingly lonely petulance of some of the comments proffered in the present draft.

The case for assessors had also been pressed at the Inquiry hearings by Douglas Hurd, Howe's successor at the FCO, and Sir Richard Luce, the former FCO minister. Scott dismissed it, pointing out that such assessors would inevitably have been drawn from the ranks of those whose behaviour was under scrutiny.

In the summer of 1995, when Howe received Scott's draft of the section of the Report dealing with his role in the export guidelines, he hired, at taxpayers' expense, the City solicitors Allen and Overy, who were also employed by William Waldegrave, and demanded a new oral hearing with counsel to represent him. The draft Report contained material which could seriously damage reputations, he said; witnesses had a real and legitimate sense of grievance, and he wanted a chance to give 'an overall view of material events'. Scott replied that if Howe had a new hearing, everyone else could demand one; if he wanted to submit further observations, he could do so in writing. 'A repetition, no matter how frequent, of allegations of unfairness (which we reject) does not advance the case,' Scott wrote.

Howe gave up and went on holiday. But as publication loomed in early 1996, he turned to the press, declaring in the *Spectator* that Scott and Baxendale had acted like 'a double-barrelled inquisition'. The Inquiry, he went on, 'is not a tribunal upon whose judgement the reputation of anyone should be allowed to depend'. He added: 'This a story in which there are no villains.'

Others joined in. Lord Rawlinson, a former Tory Attorney-General, told *Daily Telegraph* readers that the Report could not lay down the law. 'If it expresses any judgement which reflects on the honour and reputation of any individual, it will not be worth the alleged five volumes of paper which it is said to have been written on,' he trumpeted. Sir Richard Luce, whose anxieties had led to the original Howe guidelines, wrote in the *Sunday Telegraph* that Scott and Baxendale 'appeared to me to act as prosecuting advocates rather than as independent seekers of the truth'. The Inquiry should have been carried out by Privy Counsellors, he said, with Whitehall assessors.

Scott counter-attacked on Channel 4: 'I do not see how you can have an inquisitorial inquiry without it being inquisitorial,' he said. If everyone had had a lawyer cross-examining every other witness, 'it would have been a circus both in the Roman sense and the Bertram Mills sense'. He added that Howe and Hurd 'weren't on my Christmas card list anyway' and retaliated by publishing in volume 5 of the Report most of the correspondence with Howe, which leaves the impression of a self-important individual, a former Cabinet minister, piqued at having to defer to Scott. For some observers, the bitter exchanges between the two men were reminiscent of Cabinet Room arguments between Howe and Thatcher.

On publication day, Scott flew off with his wife to hunt in Ireland, leaving MPs and the media to make of his Report what they would.

2 • An Outsider in the Establishment

'Precedent shouldn't lead you by the nose.'
Sir Richard Scott

Why John Major appointed Scott, a judge with a reputation for rigorous independence, to conduct the Inquiry is a question that was asked repeatedly by the growing number of ministers, ex-ministers and civil servants who resented the decision. One view is that Lord Mackay, the Lord Chancellor, a man of utmost integrity with a strict Scottish Presbyterian background, was so concerned about the charges levelled against Government lawyers during the Matrix Churchill arms-to-Iraq trial that he was determined to recommend a judge who would go fearlessly to the heart of the matter.

Asked why he was chosen for the task, Scott says only that it had to be a judge, since a former senior civil servant or Cabinet minister would not be seen to be independent. And since matters of 'high policy' were involved, it had to be a senior judge. It might come as a surprise to those who followed the Inquiry that Scott did not relish the prospect when he was first asked to take on the job.

He had already demonstrated liberal credentials, certainly when it came to official secrecy. In 1987, he roundly dismissed the Government's attempts to prevent the press from publishing the contents of *Spycatcher*, the memoirs of the former MI5 agent Peter Wright. 'The ability of the press freely to report allegations of scandals in government is one of the bulwarks of our democratic society,' he said. 'The importance to the public of this country of the allegation that members of MI5 endeavoured to undermine and destroy public confidence in an elected government makes the public the proper recipient of the information.' Scott infuriated the Government in another judgment, in March 1996 – barely a month after the publication of his Report – when he dismissed its attempt to seize £90,000 owed to George Blake, the Soviet agent, for his memoirs. In a tightly argued judgment, he ruled that the Government's claim that Blake – and, by implication, any other former Crown servant – could not gain financially from writing about his work, whether or not the information was confidential, amounted to 'an interference with his rights of free expression'.

Scott is a questioner of established practice, whether it is Whitehall's traditional obsession with secrecy, or previous judgments handed down by the courts. 'Precedent,' he says, 'shouldn't lead you by the nose.' He is wary of labels: when asked if he would describe himself as liberal or libertarian, he said, 'Self-analysis is not a very profitable experience. . . . I start from the principle that everybody should be allowed to do what they like unless there is a reason why not.' In 1985, citing 'unreasonable harassment', he granted a group of South Wales working miners an injunction which stopped mass-picketing by NUM officials. 'It seemed to me if those people wanted to go to work they should be allowed to work without being subjected to a barrage of insults and so forth,' he said.

But he is no iconoclast. In 1984, he found for the Government against the *Guardian* and ruled that documents about the stationing of US cruise missiles in Britain which had been leaked to the newspaper by Sarah Tisdall, an FCO clerk, had to be returned – not on grounds of national security but because the documents were Government property.

Richard Rashleigh Folliott Scott was born in 1934 in Dehra Dun, in the foothills of the Himalaya where his father, an accomplished horseman, was a colonel in the 2/9th Gurkha Rifles. He spent his early years on the North-west Frontier in the twilight of the Raj before his father was invalided out of the Indian Army in 1942 and his parents moved to South Africa, to a 500-acre farm on the Mooi river in Natal. Scott was educated at Michaelhouse in Natal, which had been modelled on an English public school. There he excelled both academically and at sport, including boxing, sprinting and rugby. He went on to read law at Cape Town University.

Scott says he was never involved in politics in South Africa. It is likely, however, that during his formative years there he was struck by the dangers of excessive state power. What is not in doubt is that his initial legal training was in Roman Dutch law, which attaches greater importance to identifying principles than English law, which is based largely on precedent. In 1955 he was awarded a Commonwealth scholarship to Cambridge, where he was awarded first-class honours – and a rugby blue as a wing forward in the 1957 Varsity match against Oxford. Then he was awarded a fellowship at Chicago University, where he met his wife, Rima Ripoli, a New York-born Panamian studying at a nearby university and an accomplished flamenco dancer. 'My wife wishes me to correct the fallacy that she was a flamenco dancer, as if I picked her up in some Cuban bar,' he once told an interviewer.

Scott spent the last of his $5,000-dollar stipend on a honeymoon trip back to Europe via the Caribbean on a German banana-boat captained by a former U-boat commander. He settled down to life as a barrister, and he and his wife had four children. 'There was no great life plan,' he says. 'I had to earn my living.' In 1982 he was elected chairman of the Bar where he took steps to monitor the lack of advancement of black barristers. The following year he was appointed a Chancery judge, and was admired – especially on the northern circuit – for his straight-talking, a quality he admires in others.

It was the dissembling and circumlocution of witnesses at the Inquiry as much as anything that prompted some of Sir Richard's sharp interventions. He once rebuked Whitehall lawyers for giving 'junk' advice, a comment that prompted the response from Gerald Hosker, then the Treasury Solicitor, that 'as a basic principle, it is not necessarily total junk'. On another occasion, Scott told a hapless MoD official that 'they don't make lavatory seats in a munitions factory'.

His rise up the judicial ladder led to his appointment first to the Court of Appeal, and in 1994 to the post of Vice-Chancellor, head of the High Court Chancery division. Shortly before his Report was published, Lord Mackay appointed him to oversee radical changes in the civil justice system, proposed by Lord Woolf, that were designed to make it quicker and cheaper.

Naïvety, especially about politics, is the criticism most frequently levelled at Scott, principally from people who also acknowledge his tenacity and incisiveness as a lawyer. He spent a long period of his legal life cutting through the complexities of cases in the Chancery division, and before the Inquiry he had had little contact with the deviousness of politicians. Those who worked with him say that he was genuinely shocked by the Machiavellian habits uncovered during the Inquiry, and by the leaks of draft extracts of his Report. The day his Report was published, he fell headlong into a trap: asked by a journalist whether it was a fair summary to say that there had been 'no conspiracy and no cover-up', he agreed. By the time he qualified his answer, it was too late. Ministers seized on and repeated his initial answer.

The two lawyers chosen by Scott to help him with his Inquiry were Presiley Baxendale, QC, and Christopher Muttukumaru, neither of them a typical member of the British Establishment. Baxendale, educated at a convent school and Oxford, is the daughter of an accountant who became chairman of one of the country's biggest manufacturers of Turkish Delight. One long-standing friend has described her as 'an unconventional product of boarding school'. Scott valued her experience of long and difficult inquiries – she had been on the teams investigating the Jasmine Beckford and Kimberley Carlisle child abuse scandals in the 1980s. She had also represented Government departments in civil cases, developing an apparently insatiable appetite for official documents. When Lady Thatcher told the Scott Inquiry she had never seen so much paper, Baxendale replied cheerfully: 'That is only part of it. There is much more.' She unnerved some self-regarding witnesses at the oral hearings with one of her idiosyncrasies: a disarming giggle produced before delivery of a particularly searching question.

Baxendale is a member of the legal chambers of Lord Lester, the Liberal Democrat peer and human rights lawyer who, ironically, advised Lord Howe in his criticisms of the Inquiry's procedures. She is also a governor of the London School of Economics and vice-chairman of the executive committee of Justice, the British section of the International Commission of Jurists, and was on the Independent Committee for the Supervision of Standards of Telephone Information Services – where she rejected the idea of banning the 'Dial Mr Dark' black chatline. 'I find it extremely boring,' she said. 'It makes no reference to chopping up one's mother.'

Muttukumaru was Baxendale's contemporary studying law at Oxford. His father was an aide-de-camp to the Queen and at one time Sri Lanka's ambassador simultaneously to Iraq and Iran. He was a member of the chambers of Sir Dingle Foot, a former Labour Solicitor-General, before he joined the legal secretariat of the Attorney-General's chambers and then the Treasury Solicitor's department. At the secretariat he worked closely with Sir Nicholas Lyell, a key witness at the Scott Inquiry who was severely criticized in the Report, as were members of the Treasury Solicitor's department.

He became a specialist in European Union (EU) law, and was closely involved in the Spanish trawler – *Factortame* – case, which established the precedence of EU law over British domestic law. Scott chose him mainly for his knowledge of the Whitehall machine, and his function during the Inquiry was to obtain and co-ordinate the supply of documents it needed. This led to constant correspondence, some acrimonious, with senior figures including Sir Robin Butler and Lord Howe. He was also involved in writing the questionnaires to witnesses, one of which, to the prosecuting counsel in the Matrix Churchill trial, Alan Moses, ran to 172 pages.

3 • The Grail of Administrative Convenience

'It appears to me ... that the powers, now permanent, conferred on Government by the 1939 Act are totalitarian in concept and in effect.'
 Sir Richard Scott, in a discussion document during his Inquiry, 1993

Before Scott could find out what happened in the arms-to-Iraq affair, he needed to establish *how* it could happen: what was the system of export controls which gave legal sanction to such secrecy and subterfuge? It was a system which, as Scott reveals in the first section of his Report, was outdated and anti-democratic.

For nearly half a century, successive governments in Britain have enforced export controls with the Import, Export and Customs Powers (Defence) Act 1939, which had been rushed through Parliament as an emergency measure shortly before the outbreak of the Second World War and had never been repealed. Despite misgivings over the years, politicians and civil servants have found the legislation so convenient that they have resisted replacing it with a new Act designed for peacetime. The only change came in 1990 when the reference to its provisional nature was dropped and it became permanent.

Scott condemns the present position as an abuse of Parliamentary democracy. The Act is notable, he says, for the breadth of the powers it confers on government and for the absence of any requirement for Parliament to scrutinize the export control orders it allows ministers to make. As well as allowing the Government total control over imports and exports, the Act stated that it shall stay in force 'until such date as His Majesty may by Order in Council declare to be the date on which the emergency that was the occasion of the passing of this Act came to an end'. The need for such broad measures in wartime was evident, Scott says, 'But the absence of any provision for Parliamentary control . . . serves to confirm, if it needs confirming, that it was never contemplated by Parliament in enacting the 1939 Act that the powers would be exercised in peacetime.' Executive power to create offences and prescribe penalties without Parliamentary control is, except in a great emergency, 'a violation of the democratic constitutional principle that it is generally for Parliament to legislate and for the executive to administer'.

Between 1939 and 1945 most exports were controlled, but as the war ended trade was gradually released from restriction. The Act remained in force, however, to be used for a variety of post-war policy purposes, such as the protection of national security, animal welfare and the national heritage. Scott's opinion that none of these purposes had been authorized by Parliament was challenged in a Government paper sent to his Inquiry, which referred to several occasions when the Act had been raised or debated in the Commons. He sticks to his view, though, and notes in his Report that Douglas Hurd, then Minister of State at the FCO, had said in the Commons in 1980 that the Act was 'a block-buster within the field that it covers'.

The debate of the late 1940s over whether or not the emergency was over culminated in 1950 when a Mr Willcock was prosecuted for failing to produce his national registration identity card, which people were still required to carry under the National Registration Act 1939, another piece of emergency legislation.

Willcock appealed against conviction and the case was put before seven judges, including the Lord Chief Justice and the Master of the Rolls, who decided that the statute was still in force and refused the appeal. But Lord Goddard said: 'To use Acts of Parliament passed for particular purposes in wartime when the war is a thing of the past . . . tends to turn law-abiding subjects into law breakers, which is a most undesirable state of affairs.'

This case allowed the then Government to believe that it was still lawful to use the 1939 Act on import-export controls. Doubts about whether or not it was right to do so sparked a debate in Whitehall which lasted through the 1950s, but a Bill put forward in 1958 to repeal several emergency laws did not include the import-export Act. In 1958 the Solicitor-General, Sir Harry Hylton-Foster, told the Commons: 'I think the whole House would agree that we need these powers, at least for the moment, for the purpose of strategic control.' Powers such as those conferred by the Act, he added, 'have a persistent and powerful way of living on on their own because of their administrative convenience'. Scott calls this remark 'highly pertinent'. Fresh doubt arose in 1982, when Sir Michael Havers was Attorney-General. A DTI lawyer wrote to his officials to say that repealing the 1939 Act 'would almost certainly give rise to contentious debate on the philosophical aspects of trade policy and that the Department would almost certainly be tied with Parliamentary procedures which are now not necessary . . . The conclusion is therefore that from an administrative point of view new legislation should not be recommended.'

The Act was challenged in court the following year by Chris International Foods, which asked for judicial review of the DTI's refusal, as part of a policy of protecting Commonwealth countries in the Caribbean, to allow the company to import bananas from dollar area states. Mr Justice Woolf ruled that no Order in Council had ended the provisions of the Act, it was therefore still in force, and the company could not succeed. This case caused further anxiety in government, and ministers wanted emergency legislation prepared in case an appeal succeeded.

When Chris International's final appeal was withdrawn, there were sighs of relief: 'I can confirm,' a DTI solicitor told Customs, 'we are letting a sleeping dog lie by leaving the Act alone until some other person raises the question of whether it is still valid.'

Scott calls the continued use of the Act

> a matter of legitimate criticism. The omission by successive Governments to bring into effect the requisite Order in Council was deliberate . . . It was prompted by considerations of administrative convenience and political expediency. It could not sensibly have been argued that the emergency which had occasioned the passing of the 1939 Act had not come to an end . . . from 1950 until December 1990 there was, in my opinion, a reprehensible abuse of executive power by successive administrations.

In 1990 the Government finally took action: it repealed the section of the 1939 Act which said that its provisions would end when an order was made declaring the emergency to be over. In other words, it simply made the emergency powers permanent. 'The impropriety in the continuing failure to cause the requisite Order in Council to be made was cured,' writes Scott. 'The impropriety in using in peacetime wartime powers of subordinate legislation without Parliamentary control became entrenched *de jure*.'

The move had been prompted by fears that the imminent reunification of Germany would make more likely a successful challenge in the courts to the 1939 Act. But the late Nicholas Ridley, then Secretary of State for Trade and Industry, said he was against 'full blown legislation' and asked his civil servants to prepare a short emergency Bill to make the 1939 powers permanent.

John Meadway, a senior DTI official, wrote that 'the prospective four-power settlement with Germany will make it difficult or even impossible to sustain the convenient fiction that the 1939 emergency continues'. Meadway's paper proposed a single-clause Bill to make the 1939 powers permanent, possibly subject to negative resolution, which would mean that import and export control orders, once made, could be challenged and voted on in Parliament. But it could well be argued, Meadway went on, that 'a blanket power to control imports and exports only subject to negative resolution is excessive in peacetime'. Scott seizes on this last observation: 'Since 1945, Government had been exercising that same blanket power in peacetime without negative resolution procedure and without even any requirement that orders be laid before Parliament.'

Peter Lilley, Ridley's successor as Trade and Industry Secretary, asked for a short Bill with an optional clause allowing for negative resolution. In the meantime, however, Iraq's invasion of Kuwait had produced a crisis in the Persian Gulf, giving new urgency to the question of the Government's powers of export control. Christopher Kerse, a senior DTI lawyer, wrote that it was 'somewhat of a surprise to legal practitioners' that the 1939 powers were still in use. Scott remarks drily: 'The surprised legal practitioners could hardly have included those who had been involved in the "bananas" case.'

Meadway now produced a paper about the tactics for getting the Bill painlessly through Parliament. His advice was that ministers should present the Bill privately to the opposition 'in its boldest form', keeping negative resolution up their sleeves as the preferred concession.

Meetings were held first with Gordon Brown, then opposition spokesman on trade and industry, and later with Joyce Quin, his deputy, at which notes made by civil servants suggest that it was the opposition MPs, not Government ministers, who were arguing that negative resolution should be omitted from the Bill. Brown and Quin wrote to the Scott Inquiry saying that this had certainly not been the case. But Lilley wrote too, insisting that it was the Government's 'instinctive preference' to include negative resolution; it had been left out only because of opposition concerns, shared by the Government, about delivering a longer Bill speedily: 'So we agreed to the preference of Gordon Brown and Joyce Quin for a Bill without a negative resolution procedure.'

Scott says that he cannot understand how the need to get opposition co-operation could be put forward as a reason for omitting negative resolution: 'I can understand that there may be an issue of fact as to whether Mr Brown and Ms Quin gave positive support for the omission, but the suggestion that the omission was extracted as a price to be paid for "opposition co-operation for fast track passage of the Bill" seems to me to be contrary to probability.' He does not try to resolve the conflict of evidence and determine whether the opposition should share blame for the omission of negative resolution. 'The main responsibility . . . must rest with those putting forward the Bill, the Government.'

The Bill went smoothly through Parliament and received Royal Assent on 6 December 1990. Scott delivers a broadside on the now-familiar constitutional theme that powers to create offences and impose penalties, such as the 1939 powers made permanent by the 1990 Act, should be a matter for Parliamentary legislation rather than executive diktat:

> The wider the ambit of the powers, the more necessary is the maintenance of Parliamentary scrutiny and control. The neglect of these principles is to give substance to the charge, usually attributed to Lord Hailsham, that the constitution has become an

'elective dictatorship'. . . . nothing can, in my opinion, excuse the continued reliance by Government on the emergency powers after the emergency had long since passed other than, if it be an excuse, the pursuit of the Grail of administrative convenience.

A final salvo is directed at Sir Nicholas Lyell QC, the Attorney-General, for his submission to the Inquiry in December 1994 that to complain about the lack of Parliamentary scrutiny of the 1939 Act betrayed 'a lack of understanding of how Parliament really works . . . The real safeguards are the freedom to question, probe, debate and ultimately to vote on an issue.' Scott responds that this contradicts comments made over many years by ministers, MPs and officials and lists no fewer than nineteen examples. 'These comments are consistent in their recognition of the absence of provision for adequate Parliamentary scrutiny of or control over orders made under the 1939 Act,' says Scott. He dismisses the notion that backbenchers' ability to question ministers and the activities of the obscure Committee on Statutory Instruments constituted proper Parliamentary control.

4 · The Howe Guidelines

'The closer you approach the more does their similarity to the Cheshire Cat become apparent. They were an ideal Whitehall formula; imprecise, open to argument in almost every instance, guaranteed to generate debate, if not dispute between different departments (thus generating much paper, sub-committees and general bureaucratic self-justification). They were high-sounding, combining, it seemed, both moral and practical considerations, and yet imprecise enough to allow real policy considerations an override in exceptional circumstances.'
Alan Clark

The outbreak of war between Iraq and Iran in 1980 presented Western policy-makers with a dilemma. Pre-revolutionary Iran had been seen as a pro-Western bulwark in an unstable region; ranged against it was Iraq, an Arab state that was a client of the old Soviet Union. However, with the Iranian revolution, the 1979–81 American embassy siege in Tehran, and a move away from Soviet influence by Iraq, a change occurred in the region which required a new diplomatic approach. Suddenly, as far as the West was concerned, Saddam Hussein's regime was the only regional power that had any chance of keeping in check the overweening expansionist ambitions of what were perceived as the 'mad mullahs' in Tehran.

But the Iran–Iraq conflict posed its own problem. As Scott says starkly: 'The war produced casualties on a massive scale, the use by Iraq of horrifying chemical weapons, and the use by Iran of children as infantry soldiers. It produced for the United Kingdom serious problems of policy regarding sales of arms and defence-related equipment to the combatants.' In spite of popular belief to the contrary, there was no United Nations arms embargo, and it was left to individual countries to formulate their own approach to the two sides. Early on in the fighting,

Britain adopted neutrality and banned the sale of 'lethal items' to both Iran and Iraq.

At the same time, the British Government was dazzled by the sheer scale of the potential market in Iraq, which was made clear on 29 January 1981 at a meeting of the Oversea and Defence Committee of the Cabinet (OD). It was agreed that, in spite of the ban on lethal equipment to either side, 'every opportunity should be taken to exploit Iraq's potential as a promising market for the sale of defence equipment; and to this end "lethal items" should be interpreted in the narrowest possible sense, and the obligations of neutrality as flexibly as possible'. There were two other difficulties with the policy as it then stood: the near impossibility of satisfactorily defining 'nonlethal' defence goods; and the outstanding contracts with Iran, entered into in the time of the Shah, which involved the supply of naval vessels and spares for tanks. The main contractor was International Military Services (IMS), a wholly owned MoD subsidiary. It was calculated that reneging on these contracts could lead to compensation claims of over £200 million. Yet for Britain to be seen to supply Iran would provoke outrage, particularly from the US which was still smarting from the embassy siege, during which most of the American community in Iran had been held hostage for 444 days, between November 1979 and January 1981.

In early 1984 the issue came to a head in the FCO when it was decided to draw up a set of guidelines to govern arms-related exports to Iran and Iraq. By November a draft was ready for discussion with the MoD and the DTI. After minor modifications, the final wording was sent by Sir Geoffrey Howe to Margaret Thatcher on 4 December. She approved it eight days later and the new policy was born.

The guidelines said:

(i) we should maintain our consistent refusal to supply any lethal equipment to either side;
(ii) subject to that overriding consideration, we should attempt to fulfil existing contracts and obligations;
(iii) we should not in future approve orders for any defence equipment which, in our view, would significantly enhance the capability of either side to prolong or exacerbate the conflict;
(iv) in line with this policy we should continue to scrutinise

rigorously all applications for export licences for the supply of defence equipment to Iran and Iraq.

Guideline (iii) addressed the problem of defining 'non-lethal' defence equipment and guideline (ii), with its reference to 'existing contracts', provided a fig leaf to cover the Iranian orders. To police the stricture in guideline (iii) that defence equipment should not 'significantly enhance the capability of either side to prolong or exacerbate the conflict' a new body was formed: the Ministry of Defence Working Group – Iran/Iraq (MODWG). It would assess export licence applications (ELAs) and pass on its recommendations to the Interdepartmental Committee on licensing of exports to Iran and Iraq (IDC). This had representatives from the MoD, DTI and FCO, who put their views as to whether or not an export should be allowed to their junior ministers; if the ministers disagreed or failed to reach a decision, the next step was to approach their Secretaries of State and, ultimately, the Cabinet.

The system looked seamless, but there were strains. Alan Clark, Minister for Trade 1986–9, regularly complained that British industry was being penalized by the guidelines and tried twice to have them either watered down or dropped. In his written evidence to the Inquiry, he produced his scathing comparison between the guidelines and the Cheshire Cat:

> 'an ideal Whitehall formula; imprecise, open to argument in almost every instance, guaranteed to generate debate, if not dispute between different departments . . . '

The arrangements made to extend credit to Iraq increased the strain. In 1983 and 1984 two financial protocols had been signed with Baghdad making available £250 million of medium-term credit, backed by the ECGD. At that time it was made clear that this would be for civil goods and did not extend to defence-related equipment, but by the end of September 1984 the MoD was already demanding that some should go towards non-lethal defence equipment, such as radar and tank spares. By April 1985 it had been allocated £17 million for radio equipment for the Iraqi Ministry of Defence, and continued to fight for more. Soon it had £25 million, a figure it regarded as 'woefully inadequate'. No public disclosure was made of the defence-related allocation, even though opportunities had arisen in Parliamentary answers from 1986 onwards to make the position plain.

Ian Lang, President of the Board of Trade, later defended the secrecy surrounding the ECGD defence allocation to Iraq. It was introduced, he told Scott in a letter dated 2 October 1995, 'not as a means of opening up cover for eligible defence-related products, but to limit the amount of cover available for them . . . ' Lang's explanation, says Scott, 'is inconsistent with the facts and I reject it'.

Scott points out that the defence allocation was known to seven ministers, including John Major (then Chief Secretary to the Treasury) and the Prime Minister: 'It was not the defence allocation policy itself, but, rather, the concealing of that policy from Parliament and the public, while at the same time repeatedly professing a defence sales policy that was impartial and even-handed as between Iran and Iraq, that was, in my opinion, reprehensible.'

In March 1990, shortly after the execution in Baghdad of the *Observer* journalist Farzad Bazoft, Norman Lamont, Chief Secretary to the Treasury, said that 'we should cut our losses now and close down the credit line [to Iraq]'. Scott notes that Douglas Hurd, the Foreign Secretary, strongly disagreed. Hurd told Lamont: 'Iraq would see any action against credit as a further political response to Bazoft and would hit back hard. That would be bad for our wider commercial interests, where our competitors would happily step in to take up our share of the market.'

Scott finds that before the 1988 ceasefire in the Iran–Iraq war, the system for implementing the guidelines worked reasonably well when it came to exports of items such as radar equipment or spare parts. The possible impact of such exports on the two sides' war effort could be relatively easily assessed. Where the procedure came to grief was in its approach to machine tools. Previously they had been subject to export control by the Co-ordinating Committee for Multilateral Strategic Controls (COCOM), an international group set up to control the export of sensitive technology. The FCO (but not usually the MoD) would advise the DTI on technology transfer risks. As far as the

DTI was concerned machine tools were not, in spite of their dual-use (i.e. military/civil) capability, 'defence-related equipment'.

It must therefore have come as a shock when an MI6 intelligence report dated 30 November 1987 landed on Whitehall desks. The report, based on information from Mark Gutteridge, a Matrix Churchill executive, revealed that five British companies, including Matrix Churchill and BSA Tools Ltd, were supplying Iraq with equipment to manufacture a range of munitions at two factories, the Hutteen General Establishment in Iskandariyah and the Nassr General Establishment in Taji. The projected annual production target for Nassr alone was 10,000 122mm missiles, 150,000 130mm shells, 100,000 mortar shells (60, 80 and 120mm) and 300,000 fin-stabilized 155mm shells.

The Defence Intelligence Staff (DIS), a unit within the MoD responsible for assessing arms trade intelligence, had known for some time that Hutteen was an armaments factory and suspected the same of Nassr, but this was the first time that information relating to the true nature of the two establishments had been passed to the DTI's export licensing departments. A number of exports to which the report referred, however, had already been given the go-ahead. All the ELAs submitted to the DTI had described the end-use of the products in vague terms such as 'general mechanical engineering', which the DTI took to mean civilian use, and those applications which had found their way to the MODWG had been considered on the basis of the risk of technology transfer to the Soviet bloc, rather than possible military use.

BSA's application, which had been processed the month before the intelligence report came in, by chance was the only one which led to suspicion within the DTI that the machine tools had the potential for military production. Anthony Steadman, director of the Export Licensing Branch (ELB), suggested, 'It may be possible to get the FCO and MoD to accept, as a general principle, some by-passing of the IDC procedure in cases of this sort where there is no obvious military connection . . . no applications for CNC [computer numerically controlled] machines have been refused where a non-military end-use has been stated.' The application was later deleted from the IDC list and was granted without any ministerial approval.

Muddles in the MoD and delays by FCO officials (who later admitted that the report was 'lost' in a cupboard) meant that nothing was done about the intelligence report of 30 November 1987 until an emergency interdepartmental meeting was summoned on 8 January 1988 to discuss the report. There it was agreed that the options open to government were either to do nothing about the licences already granted while refusing all future applications to Iraq, or to revoke the licences. Steadman phoned the companies to discover how much of the equipment had already been shipped and to warn them that the licences were at risk. He then wrote to the FCO and MoD on 13 January recommending that the companies should be allowed to complete their contracts. Among the reasons he gave were the 'catastrophic' commercial consequences for the companies and – a familiar DTI argument – that machine tools were not, strictly speaking, defence equipment and were therefore not caught by the guidelines.

Twelve days later, Alan Barrett, of the MoD, recommended to his minister, Lord Trefgarne, that the licences should not be revoked and deployed the same arguments as Steadman. (Their views were not shared elsewhere in the MoD and Scott finds Barrett's failure to check his position with other officials in his own ministry 'unacceptable'.) But there was one crucial extra point in Barrett's submission: Trefgarne was told that 'the intelligence community recommends against revoking the licences as they fear for the safety of their source and they also believe that far more important information could cease to become available as a result.' This could be understood to refer either to a fear for the life of the individual involved, or to a fear that, if identified, that individual would no longer be able to provide useful information. Those concerned within the MoD assumed it was a question of personal risk and, accordingly, Trefgarne concurred, with the agreement of the FCO, that the licences should stand. At this stage all ministers assumed that the individual was inside Iraq. In fact the intelligence source then was Mark Gutteridge, a director of Matrix Churchill in England.

Only three days before Barrett's submission to Lord Trefgarne, however, the FCO had received a letter to Sir Geoffrey Howe from an anonymous employee of Matrix Churchill, which stated that the company was involved in a £30 million project to supply munitions-making equipment to Iraq. Hamish Cowell, an official in the Middle East Department of the FCO, told Barrett the gist of the letter on 28 January. Barrett passed the information neither to DIS, as he should have done, nor to his minister, Lord Trefgarne. In Scott's view, this was a lamentable omission, because the letter meant that the Government need no longer rely exclusively on the 30 November intelligence report, that 'source protection' was not at issue and that ministers could reconsider the Matrix Churchill exports.

Just over a month later Cowell wrote to the MoD again to say that he had been telephoned by a businessman who described Hutteen as a well-known armaments centre. In early April Mr J of DIS asked the defence attaché in Baghdad what he knew of Hutteen and Nassr. The reply confirmed the former as 'one of the main ammunition production factories in Iraq' and expressed concern over the latter. The attaché concluded that he could 'not see any reason for granting export licences for anything connected with these two areas unless you are devious enough to wish to gain unique entrée!'

Despite these clear warnings, the Matrix Churchill ELAs of 1987 were not revoked. Others that came up later were put into the pending tray. The excuse for approving them was not long in coming.

5 • Flexible Interpretations

'The continuing ceasefire has necessitated reconsideration of
the operation of the ministerial guidelines and weakened to
the point of extinction any case for prohibiting exports of
general purpose industrial equipment for fear that it might be
put to military use.'
Lord Trefgarne

On 20 August 1988 a ceasefire in the Iran–Iraq conflict was
announced, a move that put a new question mark over the 1984
guidelines. The immediate impact was to render guideline (iii)
null and void as it referred to prolonging or exacerbating 'the
conflict', which had now ceased to exist. Moreover, the very
existence of the guidelines as a self-denying ordinance was at
risk. With peace in the offing, both Iran and Iraq presented huge
potential for British business as both countries sought to recover
from the war and rebuild their shattered economies. Events, by
Whitehall standards, began to move fast.

Eleven days later, a paper from Sir Geoffrey Howe, entitled
'The Economic Consequences of an End to the Iran/Iraq
Conflict', was put on the Prime Minister's desk by her private
secretary, Sir Charles Powell. Howe emphasized British
commercial interests and said: 'Our defence sales policy will
need to be reviewed.' Powell's covering note referred, too, to the
prospects of increased business and the need for an amendment
to the existing guidelines, but also spoke of the detention of
British hostages in Beirut, which was controlled by Iran and was
preventing normal relations with Tehran. His reply to Howe
said that Thatcher was content with Howe's strategy and added:
'The Prime Minister will wish to be kept very closely in touch at
every stage and consulted on all relevant decisions.'

On 9 September Hamish Cowell, of the FCO, put forward a
submission to William Waldegrave arguing for a 'phased

relaxation' that could lead to the 'revision or removal of the guidelines', but he also pointed out problems with public opinion and the danger of alienating the Gulf states, who would not take kindly to more favourable treatment for Iran, their traditional enemy. Scott notes that, unlike Powell, neither Howe nor Cowell mentioned the hostages or Iraq's atrocities against the Kurds: in March that year, Saddam Hussein's forces had used chemical weapons on the town of Halabja, killing 5,000 Kurdish civilians. It was this, says Scott, which lay behind the 'problems' with public and Parliamentary opinion referred to by Cowell.

Howe told Waldegrave he was 'reluctant to put this paper forward and thereby to initiate a process whereby it will become known that our line on arms sales to Iraq has relaxed, while the Kurds/CW [chemical warfare] question is still hanging over us . . . it could look very cynical if so soon after expressing outrage over the Iraqi treatment of the Kurds we were to adopt a more flexible approach on arms sales.' On 28 October Howe was still refusing to budge, judging it 'premature to circulate the paper to Ministers'. The domestic and US reactions to the gassing of the Kurds were still uppermost in his mind.

Further down the Whitehall ladder Alan Clark was chafing at the bit, telling Waldegrave, Trefgarne and the Prime Minister that '. . . the case for continuing to apply a wide-ranging unilateral UK embargo on defence sales is now well-nigh impossible to justify to British firms'. A special meeting of the IDC on 21 November decided to approve seven ELAs relating to spares for Iranian helicopters and other aircraft.

On 30 November Clark fired off another letter to Waldegrave, again with copies to Trefgarne and the Prime Minister, arguing that it was 'not only illogical but unnecessarily restrictive to continue to allow ourselves to be constrained by "guidelines" whose original raison d'être has now been removed'. Clark, Waldegrave and Trefgarne agreed to meet on 21 December, and the FCO came up with a possible rewording of guideline (iii) that would deny exports 'which, in our view, would be of direct and significant assistance to either country in the conduct of offensive operations in breach of the ceasefire'. The DTI wanted 'to secure a significant change in the guidelines so that only lethal military equipment is automatically embargoed'.

The MoD was more cautious and wanted to defer any decision until March 1989, by when it was anticipated that the Armilla patrol – a British naval force protecting tankers – would no longer be in the Gulf, vulnerable to attack from Iraq.

The junior ministers met, discussed the FCO's revision of guideline (iii) and decided that embassies in Washington and the Gulf would be consulted before the matter was referred upwards. The worry was not so much the effect of sales to Iraq as that of sales to Iran; the US and the Arab states were implacably opposed to Khomeini's regime.

The embassies in Riyadh and Washington expressed concern, pointing out that since the Bush administration would be taking office on 21 January 1989 any public announcement should be delayed until then. The three ministers agreed to this and Waldegrave's private secretary wrote to his opposite number in Clark's office on 7 February to say ' . . . DTI, MoD and FCO officials have agreed that the form of words tabled on 21 December appears after all to meet our joint requirements, and should continue to be used on a trial basis for the time being . . . Mr Waldegrave is content for us to implement a more liberal policy on defence sales, without any public announcement on the subject.' Five years after this letter was written, and eight months after he had given oral evidence to the Inquiry, Waldegrave wrote to Scott, trying to distance himself from his private secretary's use of the words 'a more liberal policy'. In his view 'far too much weight has been put on those words' and what had really taken place was nothing more than 'a pretty fine modulation in the application of an existing policy'.

In his oral evidence, Trefgarne was of a similar opinion, admonishing the Inquiry, 'if there are words in any of the documents that lead you to think otherwise, I would wish you to disregard them'.

Scott says:

Whatever subsequent events might show to be the result of the changes that were being discussed, the contemporary documents make it impossible, in my opinion, to quarrel with the expression 'a more liberal policy' as being a fair and accurate description of what the players, including Mr Waldegrave, had in mind at the time. Mr Waldegrave did not find the expression jarring at the time. He did not do so for the reason that the words, 'a more liberal policy', describe in ordinary and simple language the reality of what he and his colleagues were discussing.

On 6 February 1989, members of the MODWG were circulated with the new wording of guideline (iii) from the 21 December meeting and were asked to apply it on a trial basis. Two days later that is exactly what they did: they considered an application for export of tactical radar to Iraq, which had initially been refused on the grounds that it could have prolonged or exacerbated the conflict, and granted it. They did the same for an application to export radar to Iran.

The smooth evolution of this change to policy was rudely interrupted on 14 February when Khomeini issued his *fatwa* against Salman Rushdie because, he said, Rushdie's novel *The Satanic Verses* blasphemed against Islam. Howe told the Commons, 'The Government have concluded that . . . it is neither possible nor sensible to conduct a normal relationship with Iran.' In briefings for the Prime Minister, however, he was unenthusiastic about introducing a defence sales embargo on Iran; exports were not running at a high level and a ban could prompt the feared compensation claim of £220 million over unfulfilled IMS contracts.

Discussions continued in the three ministries on how to react to the *fatwa*, and by late March the consensus seemed to be that the way forward was to carry on with the new guideline for Iraq, but revert to the old, stricter one for Iran. Objections from Clark were overruled, and the MODWG was told henceforth to apply the new relaxed formula to Iraq and the old stringent one to Iran.

Scott concludes that by April there had been a policy change and the concept of 'even-handedness' between Iran and Iraq had died. Waldegrave's arguments to the contrary are 'not even remotely tenable', he says. No formal approval was given by the secretaries of state to the changes agreed by the junior ministers, neither was any explanation of what had occurred put forward to the Prime Minister. The first time she would have been aware of it was when she read a Cabinet paper three months later on the proposed sale of Hawk aircraft to Iraq. But Scott accepts that the references that paper contains regarding changes to policy after the ceasefire are oblique and lacking in detail. (The proposed sale of Hawk is described in chapter 8.) Both Waldegrave and Howe offered explanations in their oral evidence to the Inquiry as to why the Prime Minister was left in the dark: Thatcher had seen and approved Lord Howe's 31 August 1988 paper ('Economic Consequences of an End to the Iran/Iraq Conflict') which outlined the general direction of policy following the ceasefire; any changes were only minimal adjustments and the Prime Minister would not have wanted to be bothered with minor and unimportant details.

Scott finds these explanations 'unconvincing'. The changes were designed to allow British industry to take advantage of expanding markets and the intentions of those who formulated the changes were that they would amount to more than 'minor adjustments'. As for the fear of prime ministerial wrath, Scott finds this 'without substance', pointing out that Powell had specifically said that after reading Howe's paper the Prime Minister had said she wanted to be 'kept very closely in touch'.

On the question as to why no public announcement of the changes was made, Howe and Trefgarne both referred to the plight of the hostages held in Iraq – the nurse, Daphne Parrish, and the businessman, Ian Richter – and Beirut. Scott is also unconvinced by this. His reading of the documents suggested to him that the principal reason was fear of an adverse reaction, first, from the British public at any relaxation of the guidelines towards Iraq, and, second, from Washington and the Gulf states if Iran were to benefit. In Scott's view, there had been a 'gradual drift' from the expectation that there would be an announcement, to an application of the new guidelines on a 'trial basis', to the final position of following markedly different policies towards Iran and Iraq.

In June 1995 – some two years after he had first given evidence – Waldegrave was still insisting to the Inquiry that the revised guideline (iii) was only used by the MODWG and IDC as a temporary working tool on a 'trial basis'. After the *fatwa* had been issued, Waldegrave argued, the proposed changes were scrapped and the original guidelines came back into play – albeit with greater 'flexibility'. The rewording of guideline (iii), he said, was only used as 'an interpretative gloss on the original guidelines'. Scott comments:

> The viewpoint expressed . . . is one that does not seem to me to correspond with reality . . . To describe this revised formulation as no more than an interpretation of the old, is, in my opinion, notwithstanding the many advocates who espoused the thesis, so plainly inapposite as to be incapable of being sustained by serious argument.
>
> I accept that Mr Waldegrave and the other adherents of the 'interpretation' thesis did not, in putting forward the thesis, have any duplicitous intention and, at the time, regarded the relaxed interpretation, or implementation, of guideline (iii) as being a justifiable use of the flexibility believed to be inherent in the guidelines. But that that was so underlines, to my mind, the duplicitous nature of the flexibility claimed for the guidelines.

Behind this tortuous legalese is the simple point that even though the witness sincerely believes that wrong is right, he is still in the wrong.

Waldegrave argued at the Inquiry that the export guidelines could not be changed without the approval of senior ministers, including the Prime Minister. This did not happen, so the guidelines were not changed.

Scott dismisses the argument: 'I regard the explanation that this could not be so because the approval of the senior Ministers and the Prime Minister had not been obtained as sophistry.'

In July 1989 the chemistry between the MoD, the DTI and the FCO underwent a subtle and profound change. In a ministerial reshuffle Thatcher moved Alan Clark and Lord Trefgarne into each other's jobs. While Clark had been at the DTI he had consistently argued the case for UK exports to both Iran and Iraq and chafed at the restrictions imposed by the guidelines. It was natural that he would carry these opinions with him as he crossed Whitehall to become the new Minister for Defence Procurement. Until this changeover the DTI's interests had been in the minority: whenever Clark had flexed his muscles he had found himself ranged against the combined weight of the other two departments. When Trefgarne arrived at the DTI he inevitably inherited the job of promoting Britain's trading interests, but with Clark ensconced in the MoD, ready to challenge export bans recommended by officials, the balance tilted: it was now the FCO that found itself in the minority. Under this changed balance of power the tug-of-war continued over the nature of the guidelines and the reasons for their existence.

At a meeting on 1 November 1989, Waldegrave managed to stave off Clark's proposal to make the guidelines on Iraq even more flexible, but on 8 February 1990 a Cabinet meeting to discuss commercial relations with the Middle East resolved that policy on defence sales to Iran and Iraq should be reviewed. In March, however, the Government faced a crisis over the *Observer* journalist, Farzad Bazoft, who had been arrested by the Iraqis and condemned to death as a spy. The Cabinet met to discuss how to react if Baghdad went ahead with the execution and considered restricting credit, defence sales and military training. When the execution took place, relations with Iraq took a downward turn, which was exacerbated by the events that followed.

On 20 March components described as 'nuclear triggers' arrived from the US at Heathrow airport *en route* to Baghdad. Eight days later an Iraqi-born British citizen, Ali Daghir, was arrested and charged with attempting to export them without a licence. On 10 April Customs raided the docks at Teesport, impounded the giant barrels for the Supergun, and by June were also closing in on Matrix Churchill. (The tale of the ensuing prosecutions is told in chapters 9 and 10.) In spite of the international opprobrium over these highly publicized incidents that clearly indicated Saddam Hussein was bent on acquiring more than a conventional military capability, Baghdad threatened to withhold payment on credits with the UK for interfering with its trade. An estimated £1 billion was at stake, and an alarmed Secretary of State for Trade and Industry, Nicholas Ridley, wrote to the Prime Minister calling for a thorough policy review. Thatcher responded by asking Douglas Hurd to chair a meeting to plot the way ahead.

The meeting, which took place on 19 July 1990, was preceded by an interdepartmental drafting of a paper that became known as the 'Iraq Note' and which was distributed to ministers on 13 July. Scott gives it detailed attention, not only because it affords a definitive insight into Government thinking, but also because the members of the 'there was no change' school rely on it as a justification for their argument. The fourth paragraph refers to the 1984 guidelines and says ' . . . despite the 1988 ceasefire the guidelines have remained in force'. Scott's verdict is that 'The paragraph does not, in my opinion, come close to providing an accurate summary of what the junior Ministers had agreed between December [1988] and May 1989.'

Paragraph eight of the Iraq Note, which says, 'Ministers have allowed the supply of some Matrix Churchill machine tools, for ad hoc reasons of an intelligence nature', had produced a striking response from MI6 the moment it found its way to the service's then headquarters at Century House, a grim concrete tower on London's Westminster Bridge Road. A Mr T2 told the Cabinet Office that his understanding of the situation was somewhat different: 'At an early stage of our coverage of Iraqi procurement activities in the UK, we did indeed express some reservations about a proposal to take action against Matrix Churchill in the context of its exports of machine tools to Iraq, on grounds that it might compromise our operational interest in the matter. However, we later withdrew our reservations . . . '

At the 19 July meeting, the FCO was against abandoning the guidelines, while the DTI and the MoD argued for much greater leeway. In the end, however, the meeting decided that the 1984 guidelines 'had served their purpose', that there would in future be much greater latitude for exports of defence related equipment to both countries, and that this decision was to be made public. The Prime Minister gave her blessing.

But the public announcement was delayed because of tensions on the border between Iraq and Kuwait, and the subsequent Iraqi invasion rendered the changes irrelevant. The guidelines had, indeed, finally run their course. The initial difficulty in defining 'non-lethal' had brought constant pressure to extend the range of exports to Iraq, and the ceasefire had increased the clash between a free market government culture and moral concerns.

The question of whether the guidelines had been changed or merely interpreted differently did not become a vital public issue until the collapse of the Matrix Churchill trial and the institution of the Scott Inquiry towards the end of 1992; so no immediate interest had been aroused in January that year when John Goulden, a senior FCO official, addressed it during the Inquiry into the Supergun by the Commons Trade and Industry

Select Committee (TISC). He said: 'The guidelines announced by Sir Geoffrey Howe in 1985 (and agreed in 1984) applied until December 1988 when the third guideline was amended . . . It was updated to take account of the fact that there was a ceasefire.' Once the Scott Inquiry was under way, the Government realized that if it conceded that the guidelines had been 'changed' or 'amended', it would be admitting that a crucial policy change towards Saddam Hussein's regime had been kept secret from Parliament and public, and that the Government had lied about its true position.

The task of defining the line that the Government would take was choreographed in the Cabinet Office by Nicolas Bevan, now Secretary to the Speaker of the House of Commons. From an examination of two FCO files (Scott emphasizes that it was *only* two), Bevan concluded that ministers had indeed wished to change policy and make it public: 'In the end, however, owing to the difficulties inherent in an announcement, they decided to secure the same objective by a more flexible interpretation of existing policy . . . ' The implication of this approach was that Goulden's evidence to TISC had been simply a mistake.

As late as June 1995 Waldegrave passed to the Scott Inquiry correspondence between himself and the Cabinet Secretary, Sir Robin Butler, about the variance between what Goulden had said and the 'no change' posture that the Government had since adopted. Butler said that the Government had noticed the contradiction in November 1992 and concluded that they should await the outcome of the Inquiry before deciding what action to take.

Scott had already circulated his draft Report and refused to change it to accommodate this late challenge to Goulden's form of words. He says: 'The Inquiry was not instituted until mid-November. I would have expected the Government, following the publication of the TISC Report [in March 1992], to have challenged an important statement of fact based on evidence it believed to be wrong. The Government had eight months in which it could have done so. It did not do so.' To rub salt into the wound Scott also latches on to a minute of 18 November 1992, which was after the Inquiry had been set up, written by Sir Timothy Daunt, Deputy Under-Secretary of State at the FCO. Under the heading 'altering the guidelines' he wrote:

It is now much clearer that in late 1988/early 1989 the three Ministers of State concerned . . . spent a lot of time discussing changes to policy on exports to Iraq. They agreed to change the guidelines to take account of the ceasefire . . . They also made a conscious decision . . . not to make any announcement . . . Arguably this was not misleading Parliament but it may be represented as culpably failing to inform Parliament of a significant change to the guidelines announced in October 1985.

Of the July 1990 meeting about the Iraq Note, chaired by Douglas Hurd, which agreed that further changes were to be made public, Daunt says, 'The fact that this revision was to have been announced is obviously helpful. But much of the revision had already been implemented for the past eighteen months and not announced.'

6 · Half the Picture

'I think the way in which questions are answered in Parliament tends to be something of an art form rather than a means of communication.'
Eric Beston, DTI official

In concluding that the guidelines had been changed it was inevitable that Scott would notice that various Parliamentary answers on the subject asserted the opposite. What he uncovered was not so much the occasional drafting mistake as a pervasive culture of secrecy on the part of the Government and a deep-seated unwillingness to reveal what it knew to either the public or Parliament.

Shortly before the Prime Minister had given her approval to the introduction of the guidelines in December 1984, Sir Geoffrey Howe had been advised that their publication would best be achieved by answers to Parliamentary questions and media inquiries. The first opportunity to follow this advice came on 16 April 1985 when the Labour MP Arthur Latham asked Howe for a statement of policy about the arms embargo to Iran and Iraq. The answer, signed by the FCO minister, Sir Richard Luce, was: 'The United Kingdom is impartial in the Gulf conflict and supplies no items of defence equipment to either side which might significantly prolong or exacerbate the conflict.' The actual wording of the four guidelines was not included. Scott observes that the answer 'revealed a part of Government policy on defence sales but not the whole'. In particular, he points out that the omission of any mention of guideline (ii), which said that existing contracts should, as far as possible, be honoured, meant that Luce's reply to Latham was 'inaccurate and potentially misleading'. A few days later, on 24 April, Merlyn Rees, the former Labour Home Secretary, put a similar question to Howe; he was given exactly the same answer as Latham. Both questions had been written ones, but on 22 May Cyril Townsend, a Conservative, asked an oral question on the recent dispatch to Iran of two ships from the Yarrow shipyard. Luce replied that it was policy not to sell defence equipment 'that can in any way prolong or exacerbate that war', and that the two ships 'cannot be used in the war between Iran and Iraq and are principally for disaster relief'. Scott says: 'A frank answer to Mr Townsend's question would have said that the ships were not "lethal equipment", had potential for use in the war but were the subject of a long-standing contractual commitment and that in accordance with guideline (ii) the supply had been approved.' Scott also mentions an FCO note of 13 February which says that the ships 'appear to be intended solely for the use of the Armed Services, and it sounds as though they are designed to land troops, tanks and other military equipment on a beach head, or to take them off again'.

Finally, on 29 October 1995, Howe set out the guidelines in full in an answer to Sir David Steel, the former leader of the Liberal Party. Scott views the delay in giving a full answer as neither acceptable nor logical, and examines why it had not been provided in either April or May. Howe argued that if guideline (ii) had been announced before the Yarrow ships were delivered, there could have been pressure from the Middle East to ban all exports to Iran. But Scott points out that the export of the ships was completed by 5 April, before the first misleading answers. He concludes that the reason behind this was not only fear of Middle Eastern reaction to continued supply of equipment to Iran, but also anxiety over public reaction to the news that Iraq, known to be using chemical weapons against the boy soldiers of the Iranian army, was still receiving British equipment.

A government document called *Questions of Procedure for Ministers* describes the duties and responsibilities of ministers. Paragraph 27 of the code says that the process of explaining Government policy includes 'the duty to give Parliament, including its Select Committees, and the public as full information as possible about the policies, decisions and actions of the Government, and not to deceive or mislead Parliament and the public'. (A recent amendment to the final phrase is discussed in later chapters.) Scott says that the answers given to Latham,

Rees and Townsend did not comply with these principles:

> The obligation of ministers to be forthcoming with information in answer to PQs [Parliamentary Questions] about their department's activities lies, in my opinion, at the heart of the important constitutional principle of Ministerial accountability . . . Throughout the period that the Inquiry has had to examine [1984 to August 1990], there is to be found, in my opinion, a consistent undervaluing by Government of the public interest that full information should be made available to Parliament.

After the 1988 ceasefire and the change to guideline (iii) the Government's record of truthfully answering inquiries from the public and Parliament deteriorated. Between February and July 1989, forty-one letters were sent from the Foreign Office, signed by either Waldegrave or Howe, to MPs who had passed on constituents' concerns about, for example, military exports to Iraq, atrocities against the Kurds and Baghdad's appalling record on human rights. Thirty of the replies included the phrasing (or its gist), 'British arms supplies to both Iran and Iraq continue to be governed by the strict application of guidelines which prevent the supply of lethal equipment which would significantly enhance the capability of either side to resume hostilities. These guidelines are applied on a case by case basis.' This was preceded by the statement: 'The Government have not changed their policy on defence sales to Iraq or Iran.' This statement, says Scott, was untrue, regardless of Waldegrave's sincere understanding to the contrary, and the assertion of a common export policy to both countries was misleading; the new, more relaxed guideline (iii), of which Waldegrave had been one of the midwives, was in force for Iraq alone. As for Howe, Scott recognizes that he had been unaware of the change by the three junior ministers in guideline (iii) when he signed some of his letters. But Howe persisted at the Inquiry hearings in asserting that none of the answers was misleading, and argued that he had to perform an important balancing act between the desirability of disclosure and protection of Britain's foreign policy interests.

In August and September further letters were sent out, including the phrasing either that applications were 'rigorously scrutinised to ensure that they fall within these [1984] guidelines' or 'the Government have pursued a policy of impartiality' between Iraq and Iran. Even if Waldegrave believed there had been no intrinsic change to policy these letters could not have been accurate following the clampdown on Iran after the Rushdie affair and the greater flexibility shown towards Iraq.

Scott also considers a letter signed by Margaret Thatcher and two by John Major, as Foreign Secretary. Thatcher had read the OD report on Hawk which referred to a change in policy, and Major, in his first briefing as Foreign Secretary, had also been told of the policy relaxation towards Iraq. Both, however, are given the benefit of the doubt; as the emphasis of the information they received was on Hawk, neither properly digested the implication that the policy had changed. Over the same period some twenty letters sent out by the MoD were also misleading. The letters, mainly drafted for and signed by Lord Trefgarne, were in response to letters from MPs on behalf of constituents concerned about the presence of British firms at an international military exhibition in Baghdad. They did not refer to the new guidelines and claimed that the Government maintained a 'strict' export licensing policy to Iraq. Scott describes the letters as 'not, in my opinion, accurate'.

Several answers to Parliamentary questions were similarly inaccurate, and Scott alights on the answer to a question from the Labour MP Mo Mowlem in November 1989. She had asked what investigations the DTI were making into allegations that Matrix Churchill were supplying parts for Iraq's development of ballistic missiles. The DTI's then junior minister, John Redwood, assured her, 'I have no reason to believe that the company has contravened UK export controls.' The reply was based on a draft prepared by Eric Beston, which he had cleared with the MoD and FCO. But Beston had chaired a meeting of the Working Group on Iraqi Procurement (WGIP) on 23 June that year which had been told that the end-use of a batch of Matrix Churchill lathes was 'known to be the Iraqi missile programme'. Beston later explained to the Inquiry that this had slipped his mind.

On this shabby episode of Parliamentary democracy in action Scott doesn't mince his words: 'This failure was deliberate and was an inevitable result of the agreement between the three junior Ministers that no publicity would be given to the decision to adopt a more liberal, or relaxed policy, or interpretation of the Guidelines, originally towards both Iran and Iraq and, later, towards Iraq alone.'

During the Inquiry both Sir Robin Butler and David Gore-Booth, one of the most senior FCO officials, gained some notoriety by saying that the lack of candour in Parliamentary answers was acceptable because 'half a picture' could be accurate. Howe's version was more frank: he admitted that the truth had been concealed because he believed that 'Government knows best.' Scott comments: 'Without the provision of full information it is not possible for Parliament, or for that matter the public, to hold the executive fully to account . . . In the circumstances, the Government statements made in 1989 and 1990 about policy on defence exports to Iraq consistently failed . . . to discharge the obligations imposed by the constitutional principle of Ministerial accountability.'

7 • Introducing Dr Habobi

'UK Ltd is helping Iraq, often unwillingly but sometimes not,
to set up a major indigenous arms industry.'
Lieutenant-Colonel Richard Glazebrook, MoD official

The much-disputed guidelines, drawn up by Sir Geoffrey Howe
and later modified by Lord Trefgarne, William Waldegrave and
Alan Clark, were put to their greatest test from 1987 onwards,
when Iraq set about establishing an international network of
companies for obtaining arms and defence equipment. Saddam
Hussein was tired of paying inflated prices for supplies from the
Soviet Union, and he wanted machinery and other technology
which would allow Iraq to make its own munitions, continue its
missile programme and develop nuclear weapons.

Scott's examination of how the procurement network
operated in Britain draws him into detailed consideration of the
reports produced by the intelligence services, which were meant
to be monitoring Iraq's activities. What he found was another
catalogue of mistakes, crossed wires and, in some cases, wilful
misunderstandings. Much of the time, Saddam's men had run
rings round the obstacles meant to deter them.

The intelligence report of 30 November 1987 (see page 51)
had revealed that five British companies, among them Matrix
Churchill, were supplying Iraq with machinery to make
munitions. The following summer, an application landed on
officials' desk for a visa and work permit for Dr Safa Al Habobi,
the head of Iraq's procurement network in the West and a
director of Matrix Churchill. (TDG, an Iraqi-owned company,
had taken over Matrix Churchill in 1987.)

The FCO raised immediate objections. Correspondence with
the Home Office followed, and on 14 June 1988 it was agreed
that the visa would be turned down 'because of the risk of

compromising our neutral stance over the Iran/Iraq war' and because his admission 'would jeopardise the United Kingdom's international relations, and in particular the policy of refusing to allow the supply of defence equipment to either side in the Gulf conflict which would enhance their ability to prolong that conflict'. The language seemed to echo the Howe guidelines. But, as usual, there was a problem. On 21 June, a report from Mr C3 of MI6, based on information from the informant at Matrix Churchill, Mark Gutteridge, warned that Habobi's exclusion could lead him to pull his business out of the UK. It was sent to the FCO, the MoD, the DTI and the Home Office.

A week later the FCO reversed its position. To refuse Habobi's visa might lead to a loss of trade worth more than £20 million, and the possible collapse of Matrix Churchill. It was agreed that letting him in and monitoring him closely would be the best way to frustrate his procurement network; and 'source protection' suddenly reared its head as another reason for granting the visa.

At the Scott Inquiry hearings, MI6 officers denied to Scott that 'source protection' had been an issue. Mr B said, somewhat cynically, that it had been 'a classic case of Whitehall wishing to have it both ways – preserve Matrix Churchill's trading relationship, and yet deny its military benefits to Iraq'. Mr C3 concurred that Whitehall had 'latched on to source protection to support a decision to preserve the trading relationship'. But the question of why MI6 allowed the FCO to base its decision partly on 'source protection', which MI6 did not endorse, remains unanswered.

In the event Habobi was allowed into the UK to run the procurement machine with such success that a grateful Saddam Hussein promoted him; and the intention to keep a close eye on his activities was frustrated by the general relaxation in vigilance over export control procedures following the ceasefire. The episode was typical of poor and obstructive communications in Whitehall and conflicting priorities in different departments: the hard work in monitoring and assessing Iraq's military intentions and capabilities was squandered through a failure within government to digest and act upon the information.

Shortly after the 1988 ceasefire it was decided that MI6 should place Iraq at the top of its priorities. There followed a stream of intelligence reports – eccentrically described by Lord Howe at the Scott Inquiry hearings as 'cornflakes in the wind' – that painted an alarming picture of Baghdad's strenuous efforts to acquire nuclear, biological and chemical (NBC) technology. The reports, circulated widely in Whitehall, made frequent reference to Habobi, Matrix Churchill and the military factories to which the company was shipping its machine tools. Two reports at the end of March 1989, drawing on information from GCHQ, appeared to alarm the Prime Minister: the response was to set up the Working Group on Iraqi Procurement (WGIP), under the chairmanship of Eric Beston, the senior DTI official. Participants at its meetings included officials from GCHQ, the MoD, the DTI and the FCO, some of whom, such as Beston, Anthony Steadman and Alan Barrett, were closely involved in the process of monitoring ELAs.

At one of the WGIP's meetings, on 23 June 1989, proposed exports by Matrix Churchill were discussed and the minutes recorded that ' . . . the end-user was known to be the Iraqi missile programme'. This was the information that Beston had forgotten when he drafted the Parliamentary answer to Mo Mowlem. The licences were granted in spite of the intelligence reports. (One report that would have been circulated to Thatcher was the Joint Intelligence Committee's (JIC) weekly survey of intelligence for 6–12 July 1990, which said that Matrix Churchill was 'a major supplier to Iraq, probably for military purposes' and was involved in 'making parts for Iraqi project K1000, a possible weapons system'. It was not until 1990, shortly before the outbreak of the Gulf War, that it was established that K1000 was part of Iraq's nuclear programme.) In July and September 1989 MI6 became aware of a 'project 1728' involving the modification of Soviet-supplied Scud missiles. Copies of two of their reports were circulated to the FCO. On 13 October 1989 a report from GCHQ mentioned a project planned by the Chilean arms manufacturer Industrias Cardoen for the construction of a large munitions factory in Iraq. The report, which was widely circulated, said that twenty-four machining centres for various types of fuses would be supplied to this plant by a 'UK firm'. It was not until 24 November that Anthony Steadman of the DTI's export control unit asked the name of the firm. The reply came on 8 December:

Matrix Churchill. Nothing, however, was done.

Throughout 1989 reports continued to thud onto Whitehall desks, several from GCHQ, all full of references to Habobi, Matrix Churchill, the Supergun project, Iraq's NBC warfare ambitions, and its plans to acquire the technology needed to detonate nuclear bombs. On 6 October Waldegrave received a briefing from his officials which said that Iraq was pouring money into military procurement and recommended that everything should be done to frustrate its efforts to become a military nuclear power and to enhance its ballistic capability.

In April that year, Paul Henderson had handed to MI6 a copy of 'the Iraq Fuse Plan contract', worth £24 million, which eventually went to the Reading firm Ordtec (see chapter 12). But Scott points to the evidence Mr T of MI6 had given at the Matrix Churchill trial, in which he said that MI6's interest was not in conventional weaponry such as fuses but in 'nuclear capability, long range missile capability, biological and chemical'. This bias was evident at a meeting in London on 22 September 1989 at which three MI6 officers quizzed Henderson over his knowledge of what the Iraqis were up to. That meeting became the subject of dispute between Henderson and MI6, the former insisting that he gave far more information than the latter allows. (Scott complains that no proper record was made of the meeting, contrary to MI6 practice: an explanation for this could be that one of the MI6 officials was going on honeymoon the next day and another, Mr O, had struggled to the meeting with a bad back and had spent most of it lying on the floor.) In the end, Scott concludes that the dispute came about because much of Henderson's information had not been new, and covered Iraq's conventional weapons programme in which MI6 was losing interest. He accepts that Henderson mentioned at the meeting the contracts which later formed the foundation of the Customs prosecution.

Meanwhile Mark Gutteridge left Matrix Churchill and ceased to supply information to the security services. MI6 reactivated Henderson, who had worked for them earlier in Eastern Europe and was on the board of Matrix Churchill alongside Dr Habobi. MI6, of course, hoped that this connection would lead to information on Iraq's attempts to acquire nuclear weapons.

Several paragraphs on this issue are missing from the

published report, their place taken by the stern phrase 'PARAGRAPHS CLOSED'. But it is clear that, following the execution of Bazoft in March 1990, MI6 was worried that any retaliation against Baghdad might provoke Habobi to take his procurement network elsewhere, where it could not be watched. Several MI6 reports referred to this possibility, mentioning Paris or Switzerland as possible alternative sites: one said 'we may learn more about the network by letting [Dr Habobi] remain to carry on his activities in the UK.'

One person who did not have access to the intelligence information flowing in from GCHQ and MI6 was Lieutenant-Colonel Richard Glazebrook, who vetted ELAs on the MODWG. Yet, even though he was deprived of up-to-date intelligence, he spotted what Iraq was up to. Early in 1989 he had attended a COCOM meeting where, over a cup of coffee, a German colleague had mentioned how Libya circumvented international controls on chemical warfare by placing orders for equipment in small quantities and in several different countries.

The penny dropped. Glazebrook explained later to the Scott Inquiry that ' . . . seeing the [ELAs] passing in front of us month by month, I came to the conclusion that the same thing was happening on arms manufacture for Iraq, that we were getting lots of little orders, and it was only when you aggregated them together into a total that you realised the scale on which the Iraqis are building up an arms manufacturing capability.' He drew up a paper for his colleagues on the MODWG which warned of 'the amount of assistance which "UK Ltd", and in particular our machinery manufacturers, are giving to Iraq towards the setting up of a major arms R&D [research and development] and production industry'. Some of the ELAs Glazebrook had in mind were from Matrix Churchill, and he wanted his paper drawn to the attention of the Minister for Defence Procurement. However, it was agreed that before it went to the minister, the paper needed an annex, to be compiled by Defence Intelligence Staff (DIS), which would draw on intelligence information to which Glazebrook had no access.

In the event the annex was never written and the paper never landed in any ministerial in-tray. As Scott says, 'It simply fell into limbo.' He blames Alan Barrett and his immediate superior,

Ian McDonald, at the Defence Export Services Secretariat
(DESS) for failing to act on Glazebrook's report. Scott's
conclusion is that, as with MI6, the focus of attention in the
MoD had switched from the conventional to the NBC aspects of
Iraq's military build-up. Glazebrook's prescient analysis was
regarded as having no real weight or importance.

It is against this background of growing knowledge of what
was occurring in the various military factories and plants inside
Iraq that Scott turns to the manner in which Matrix Churchill
ELAs were dealt with in 1989 and 1990. Of particular
significance are the events that led to an important meeting
between Clark, Trefgarne and Waldegrave.

At the end of 1988 Matrix Churchill had been complaining of
delays to its ELAs and it was decided that the matter should be
settled by ministers. Before they did so, the Restricted
Enforcement Unit (REU) met to discuss the issue and was
advised by Mr C3 of MI6 that 'the security of our source was
now best guaranteed if reasonable exports of machine tools by
Matrix Churchill were allowed to continue. We also drew
attention to the recent expansion of activities of the procurement
network into the nuclear proliferation field and the importance
this placed on maintaining access, through [Gutteridge], to the
general activities of the network.' (Mr C3 seemed to have been
unaware that in 1988 Gutteridge had left Matrix Churchill.) On
1 February 1989 Stephen Lillie, of the FCO's Middle East
Department (MED), prepared a briefing for Waldegrave on the
outstanding Matrix Churchill ELAs. In it, he said that the
department could no longer argue convincingly that munitions
production was the top priority of the Iraqis: 'We have reason to
believe that the refusal of these export licences could force
Matrix Churchill to close down. If this happened we would lose
our intelligence access to Habobi's procurement network. By
keeping access open, we could obtain more important
information, in particular on the procurement of some item
which is far more incriminating . . .' In fact, MI6 was no longer
concerned about the potential closedown of Matrix Churchill
because it was in the process of establishing another source of
information on the procurement network. They did not,
however, correct Lillie's submission. David Gore-Booth, the
assistant under-secretary with responsibility for the MED, was

doubtful of the wisdom of allowing exports of potentially lethal equipment just to save an intelligence connection and wanted the ELAs refused. But Waldegrave supported them, scrawling on Lillie's recommendation, 'I agree. Screwdrivers are also required to make H-bombs.' A briefing similar to Lillie's went to Trefgarne at the MoD, who agreed to grant the ELAs. As far as the DTI was concerned, Scott notes that their approach relied on the argument that after the ceasefire the Iraqis would be concentrating on civil reconstruction and that, unless evidence could be found which proved the opposite, exports of dual-use equipment should proceed. Throughout 1989 Matrix Churchill received further orders and by the end of September had six outstanding ELAs. Two were for 'project 1728', two for the plant being constructed by Cardoen and two for the 'Central Tool Room' project at Nassr.

On 6 September Waldegrave, despite his earlier point about screwdrivers, wrote to Trefgarne at the DTI, recommending the refusal of four of the applications. Trefgarne and Clark disagreed, and the former wrote back, saying: 'Since August 1988 . . . the continuing ceasefire has necessitated reconsideration of the operation of the Ministerial Guidelines and weakened to the point of extinction any case for prohibiting exports of general purpose industrial equipment for fear that it might be put to military use.' Scott says that Trefgarne's letter indicates a reluctance by the DTI to treat the intention to use machine tools for munitions as a reason to refuse an export licence; but he also acknowledges that before Trefgarne wrote the letter, he had been misinformed at a personal meeting with Henderson about the true end-use of the machine tools. Lord Trefgarne told the Inquiry that after a meeting in September 1989, Henderson deceived him about the real purpose of Matrix Churchill exports to Iraq.

At the MoD, Clark lined up with the DTI against the FCO, and it was accepted that only a meeting between the three ministers could resolve the impasse. Scott is highly critical of the briefing papers prepared within the DTI and MoD for this meeting. The former, drafted by Anthony Steadman, misrepresented the true nature of the intelligence information concerning the destination of previous exports. One version of it asserted that ' . . . intelligence sources reported that the factories in which the machines were to be used had substantial munitions manufacturing programmes as well as general engineering activities. Even so there was no evidence that the British made machine tools would be used other than for the purpose originally stated.'

Scott remarks that the misleading nature of this briefing was 'a step in the process whereby it became, by the time of the Matrix Churchill prosecution, part of the DTI credo that Government had had no knowledge of the intended use of Matrix Churchill machine tools for production of military goods'. He says that the briefing Clark received was 'slanted', in that it failed to make full use of the intelligence information then available, especially the known views of the MODWG and the DIS. But it is the advice that Waldegrave received which causes the greatest puzzle for Scott.

Ranged against Trefgarne and Clark, who used the meeting to propose abandoning the guidelines altogether (see p.60), Waldegrave's only hope lay in convincing his two colleagues that sufficient evidence existed to show that the Matrix Churchill machines were known – not just suspected – to be destined for military purposes. Yet the day before the ministerial meeting Simon Sherrington, who had succeeded Lillie on the Iran/Iraq desk at the FCO, presented a briefing which read: 'Our friends [MI6] have since said that they believe that the lathes may not, at any rate initially, be used for the direct manufacture of munitions or for nuclear applications.' The briefing flew in the face of all the information about the destinations in Iraq for the Matrix Churchill exports.

Scott accepts that part of the problem here lay in Sherrington's having been a relative newcomer to his post: he had been cleared to see intelligence information only the month before. But he is highly critical of the failure by MI6, yet again, to correct the erroneous beliefs attributed to them when a copy of Sherrington's briefing later arrived at Century House. When the three ministers finally met on 1 November 1989, the briefing meant that Waldegrave could not argue with certainty that the machine tools were for military use, and the ELAs were duly granted.

This meeting was something of a watershed: although further ELAs continued to be the subject of debate between the three ministers, it is plain that Waldegrave had lost the argument. His position was further weakened when, on several occasions, the DTI chose to circumvent the normal scrutiny procedures for ELAs by granting Matrix Churchill temporary licences, intended for equipment which was for exhibition only and which would later be returned to the UK. It also issued licences without reference to the MODWG or the IDC, which should have been consulted. The person responsible was Steadman, who pleaded later that he had been struggling with an impossible workload when he approved the ELAs. Nevertheless, Scott says, his actions were reprehensible.

Scott concludes that by November 1989 the evidence pointed so strongly to a military end-use for the machine tools that talk about lack of certainty and possible civil use was 'equivalent to the Nelsonian use of the blind eye'. But he also recognizes the formidable combination of Trefgarne and Clark, who minded less about exports for use in the manufacture of conventional arms than about NBC proliferation. Scott accepts that two arguments could be presented: the moral, which said that nothing that could help the Iraqi military machine should be exported, and the pragmatic, which asserted that preventing the export of dual-use goods – which were freely available from other countries – would merely harm the UK economy. What disturbs him most is the lack of democratic contribution to the discussion: 'The failure of Government to be forthcoming in its public statements about its export policy to Iraq precluded a public debate on this important issue taking place on an informed basis. Parliament and the public were designedly led to believe that a stricter policy towards non-lethal defence exports and dual-use exports to Iraq was being applied than was in fact the case.'

8 • H-Bombs and Screwdrivers

'We are unable to stop the export of screwdrivers on the grounds that they may be useful for bomb making.'
   William Waldegrave's private secretary describing his minister's views

Hawk

Matrix Churchill and certain other companies became well known because their directors were prosecuted, but there were other instances of Britain's readiness to supply defence-related equipment to Saddam Hussein. Some, like the proposal to sell the Hawk aircraft to Iraq, were already known, although Scott uncovered more information about attempts by Whitehall to subvert official policy. Others came to light only because of the meticulousness with which Scott conducted his Inquiry.

The proposed sale to Iraq of the trainer model of the British Aerospace (BAe) Hawk jet aircraft was significant for the part that the Cabinet, including Margaret Thatcher and John Major, played in the ELA and for the curious role of Mr David Hastie.

Hawk has been a highly successful product and has sold worldwide in both its combat and trainer versions. During the Iran–Iraq war, export to Iraq had been ruled out as a possible breach of the pre-ceasefire guidelines. The moment hostilities ended, BAe revived its attempts to conclude a sale. At the meeting on 21 December 1988 when Alan Clark, William Waldegrave and Lord Trefgarne discussed the relaxation of the guidelines, officials had urged that Hawk was 'just the sort of proposal they would want to recommend for approval in applying any new flexibility in the guidelines'. The project was enticing: the first stage, lasting eight years, would involve providing aircraft assembly facilities, the construction of an airfield and the supply of at least forty trainer aircraft in kit form. On 12 June 1989 BAe made a formal ELA, which the MoD approved on the grounds that as the aircraft were for training and not combat they were not caught by the guideline banning 'lethal' equipment. The number of aircraft was not seen as a significant enhancement of Iraq's military capability.

However, warning bells had begun to sound over possible Parliamentary and public reaction: any decision would have to be taken by the Cabinet's Oversea and Defence Committee (OD), and the ministries involved prepared briefing papers for their secretaries of state and the Prime Minister. Waldegrave wrote to Sir Geoffrey Howe: 'It is a horrible situation. Iraq's regime is one of the most vicious in the world . . . The judgment is, are we strong enough as a trading nation to spurn their market on the grounds of morality? If we were, we should. On balance, I judge that we are not . . . ' At the MoD, the Secretary of State, George Younger, expressed reservations, but on 20 July the MoD submitted a paper to the Cabinet Office concluding that BAe should be shown the green light. Shortly after this, Major became Foreign Secretary, and on 25 July, his first day in the job, was given a briefing paper which warned that a sale would inevitably be seen as a cynical breach of Government policy. The Prime Minister, too, was warned off the sale by Sir Charles Powell, her private secretary, who thought the proposition dubious: 'We are being asked to give carte blanche to a distant and hazy sales prospect . . . Iraq is run by a despicable and violent government . . . ' She also received a note from Leonard Appleyard, a Cabinet Office official, which referred to the 'revised guidelines' and the imbalance in the way that Iraq and Iran were now being treated; Major's 25 July briefing contained a similar wording. Scott comments that this reference constitutes 'the high water mark of the case that the Prime Minister was put on notice that the original guidelines had been revised'. He also finds it 'inherently credible' that Thatcher would not have focused on this point, but rather on the 'big issue' of whether or not to approve the Hawk project.

The OD meeting took place on 27 July 1989 and seems to have lasted only a few minutes. The proposal was rejected out of hand, due to distaste for Saddam Hussein's regime and the risk that the trainer could be converted easily into a combat aircraft and used for chemical warfare attacks. In the days that followed, letters sent out from the FCO, including one drafted by them for the Prime Minister to sign, referred to the guidelines as the chief reason for turning down Hawk. Scott notes that a frank response would have been to cite the record of the Iraqi regime and the fear that it would adapt the aircraft for further gas attacks on the Kurds. He calls the letters 'a very good example of the FCO's preference for the presentationally convenient, as opposed to the factually accurate, answer'; but he concedes that complete frankness might have provoked the Iraqis, who were still holding Ian Richter and Daphne Parrish as hostages, into retaliatory action.

While this was going on, extraordinary events were unfolding behind the scenes. The then head of defence sales in the Defence Export Services Organization (DESO) was Sir Colin Chandler, who had previously worked for BAe. While there his responsibilities had covered the marketing of Hawk and he had recruited David Hastie to help him. In April 1988 Hastie was seconded from BAe to act as 'Business Development Adviser' to Chandler at DESO. Hastie had been closely involved with the Hawk project while he was at BAe, and for at least two months before he joined the MoD he had been receiving copies of MoD correspondence about Hawk. Hastie's secondment was to last a year but his salary and allowances would continue to be paid by BAe. The job Chandler had in mind for him was to improve relations between DESO and some of the smaller companies with which it had previously had little contact. Hastie was due to return to BAe in March 1989 but was given an extension of six months; during this period he became involved in the discussions concerning the viability of the Hawk project. Scott makes clear that this included helping to draft a briefing to Younger in support of the Hawk sale.

Hastie also played an extraordinary role in the International Military Production Exhibition staged in Baghdad from 26 April to 2 May 1989. Trefgarne was happy for British equipment, including the Hawk trainer, to be shown but ruled, with support from the FCO, that there should be no DESO stand at the exhibition. On the eve of the exhibition, however, the Iraqis refused an entry visa to BAe's team leader. The company contacted DESO and asked if Hastie could go on their behalf to

Baghdad. Chandler found no difficulty with this, and explained later to the Inquiry: 'In view of the urgency, it seemed to me that the best thing to do was to second him back to BAe. I certainly did not think there was any conflict . . . So far as they [the Iraqis] were concerned, and indeed, for the period of the desecondment [*sic*], he was a BAe man.' In the twinkling of an eye Hastie ceased to be a sober-suited civil servant and metamorphosed into a BAe sales representative. On his return he turned back into a civil servant.

Scott says that Hastie should have been 'ringfenced' from any dealings with Hawk: 'The principle that people should not be placed in a position in which their interests and duty may conflict is not simply an ancient principle of equity (which it is) but ought also, in my opinion, to be regarded as a necessary principle to be applied to all secondments into Government service from industry. In the case of Mr Hastie the principle was evidently lost sight of.' Both Chandler and Hastie disputed this interpretation and wrote to the Inquiry to say so. Scott's response was: 'It is as plain as a pikestaff that, so far as MoD advice to Government on the Hawk project was concerned, Mr Hastie was in a position of potential conflict between duty and interest.'

Going Nuclear

William Waldegrave's views about defence related exports appear to have swung from one extreme to another during the period covered by the Inquiry. At first, and throughout 1988, he was concerned about the export of dual-use machine tools to Iraq on the grounds that they could be used to make conventional weapons. By February 1989, he was rejecting warnings that Matrix Churchill machine tools could be used for Iraq's nuclear programme, making his now well-known manuscript note: 'Screwdrivers are also required to make H-bombs.' In 1990 he went further still and approved the export of equipment to Iraq despite warnings that it could be used in nuclear weapons.

Early in that year, an Iraqi order for integrated circuits had been placed with PMK Electronic Consultants, a company owned by teaching staff at Liverpool Polytechnic. Officials from the MoD, the FCO and the DTI had warned Waldegrave in April that the equipment was capable of being customized for use in nuclear weapons, chemical and biological warheads and delivery systems: 'In the light of our serious concerns at Iraqi activity in all these fields, we have no alternative but to recommend refusal of the package.' The MoD warned MI5 that PMK was being used as an Iraqi procurement agency for research facilities. Their concerns convinced Clark, then Minister for Defence Procurement, that an export licence should be refused. But at the FCO Simon Sherrington, one of Waldegrave's advisers, told Waldegrave: 'There is little possibility that we would be able to prevent other possible supplier countries from providing the Iraqis with what they require.' Waldegrave argued in favour of granting the licence – otherwise it might seem that Britain was 'looking for excuses to irritate Iraq for no reason'. He later told the Inquiry that 'damaging British firms for no perceptible gain in diplomatic or other policy objectives, minor irritants for minor irritants' sake, seemed to me to be stupid then and still does now'.

Scott contrasts the serious concern of officials that the equipment might be used in weapons of mass destruction with Waldegrave's 'presentational' concerns: Farzad Bazoft had only recently been executed, much was already known about Iraqi military procurement activities, and Waldegrave would have had an easily defensible position if there had been any public recrimination over blocking the exports. In the event, the PMK equipment was never exported: the University of Technology in Baghdad, which had placed the order, delayed providing letters of credit.

Three days before Christmas 1988, Consarc Engineering Ltd told the DTI that it wanted to sell nine vacuum furnaces to Iraq. In April 1989, the FCO's Scientific, Energy and Nuclear Department (SEND) objected to the sale of three of the British-manufactured furnaces because of their potential applications in the development of nuclear weapons. Anthony Steadman at the DTI told the FCO that two of the furnaces did not need licences: 'The Iraqis have apparently said that they need the equipment for research into materials for the manufacture of artificial limbs.' The FCO's views were not passed on to other Whitehall departments.

In July 1990, FCO officials told Waldegrave that the US was trying to persuade Britain to prevent the export of the British-manufactured machines, warning that they could 'enhance Iraq's nuclear or missile capabilities'. Waldegrave's private secretary replied: 'Mr Waldegrave thinks . . . we will have to let the furnaces go. We are unable to stop the export of screwdrivers on the grounds that they may be useful for bomb making. The only option would be to invent a whole new category of potentially nuclear-related machinery the export of which we could stop worldwide . . . ' On 15 August, the DTI confirmed that the furnaces did not need an export licence, but by then the issue had become academic. Following the Iraqi invasion of Kuwait on 2 August 1990, the Government imposed a total embargo on exports to Iraq.

The case had serious implications for nuclear proliferation. The Non-Proliferation Treaty (NPT) binds its signatories, which include Britain, 'NOT IN ANY WAY TO ASSIST, encourage or induce any non-nuclear-weapon state to manufacture or otherwise acquire nuclear weapons . . . ' (Scott's emphasis). Scott points out that before 1991 'there was no export prohibition based on the intended use of . . . goods for the production of nuclear weapons'. Roland Smith, then head of the FCO's non-proliferation desk, later conceded to the Inquiry that the lack of controls meant it had been possible that a machine tool that was known to be destined for use in a nuclear facility might not need an export licence. 'I consider much too broad the proposition that the United Kingdom was obliged by the [NPT] to take all possible steps to prohibit the supply to a non-nuclear State not only of goods specially designed for the manufacture of weapons and devices of a nuclear nature but also ANY goods which could . . . in any way assist in the manufacture of such weapons or devices' (Smith's emphasis). Smith added that he understood the word 'assist' to imply an intention, and he did not believe Britain ever intentionally assisted Iraq in its efforts to acquire nuclear weapons. Scott points out that a new export control order, which came into force in 1991, created a regime that was more obviously in compliance with the UK's obligations under the NPT than had previously been the case.

Explosive Bolts

One of the more tantalizing episodes examined by Scott was an Iraqi attempt to acquire explosive bolts, which are needed when a used stage of a rocket is jettisoned. It appears that this is another example of Scott's agreement not to name GCHQ, but the footnotes indicate they were the organization which alerted Whitehall in October 1989 that a Swiss company was placing orders with a UK firm for explosive bolts on behalf of an Iraqi company connected with the missile development programme. The identity of the UK firm is not revealed in the report in line with GCHQ's normal habit. Two months later the Baghdad embassy alerted the MoD and the FCO to local media reports of the successful launch of an Iraqi three-stage rocket capable of launching satellites into space. DIS expressed disbelief that Iraq could have achieved such a launch without foreign assistance, especially in the technical area of stage separation.

On 15 January 1990 the UK company submitted an application to export 300 explosive bolts to the Space Research Corporation (SRC) in Geneva for onward shipment to the Iraqi national oil industry. The GCHQ report does not seem to have come to the attention of anyone involved with the licensing system and a meeting of the MODWG on 7 February raised no objection to the ELA. But at an IDC meeting on 16 February an official from SEND objected to the application, pointing out the bolts could be used for missile separation. The licence was put in the pending tray by the DTI.

On 6 March a Mr Lyster-Binns from SEND noted the bolts' possible application in missile technology but said he was inclined to agree the licence because of the bolts' small size and quantity. Two weeks later, a report from DIS on the application ended with the comment, 'On balance I would not like to be seen selling these to the country concerned.' This attitude suddenly hardened when a DIS official, Mr G, annotated the report, 'Under no circumstances must these be sold. I have first class collateral confirming the real end-use as missiles. SRC is now closed.' The annotation is undated, but it may be relevant that SRC's founder, Gerald Bull, was assassinated on 22 March.

The application was refused, and when Clark objected to this several internal MoD minutes record that if necessary a special briefing for the minister might have to be arranged to acquaint him with the highly classified intelligence indicating the real end-use of the bolts. Clark acquiesced. Scott comments that this episode was a good example of the procedures working well. It is also an example of unusual reticence on the part of Scott to flesh out the evidence on which GCHQ, MI6 and DIS relied.

Tripod

He is a little more open about Tripod Engineering Ltd and its strange relationship with the Royal Airforce Institute of Aviation Medicine (IAM). IAM, part of RAF Strike Command, studies responses to the physiological and psychological stresses of flight and advises manufacturers on its findings.

Between 1975 and October 1987 Air Vice-Marshal Peter Howard was in command. On 4 May 1981, just over six months after the outbreak of the Iran–Iraq war, IAM was asked to help a company bidding for an Iraqi air force contract, which included human-centrifuge and ejector-seat training apparatus. Approval was given and on about a dozen occasions Howard gave advice to the company, although this did not involve any meetings with the customers. In December 1983 the Iraqis appeared to lose interest and the project was suspended.

Three years later Iraqi interest revived and Tripod Engineering approached IAM for help in the design and construction of an 'aeromedical system' in Iraq. Two Tripod staff, a Ms Purcell and a Mr Hindi, arrived at IAM and explained that their client's interests had expanded to include flight simulators, an air crew selection centre and facilities for medical examination of air crew. The specifications, Howard later told the Inquiry, indicated that the client was the Iraqi air force. At the time, however, Howard was unaware of the Howe guidelines, which had been announced a year earlier.

Howard advised Tripod, mainly by telephone, until June 1987 when he was told of an impending visit by three Iraqi air force officers who wanted to discuss the project. Howard thought that although it would be improper for them to visit IAM without permission from the MoD, there could be no objection to a meeting at a London hotel. Howard later told the Inquiry that he had made it clear to the Iraqis at that meeting that his function was solely 'to clarify and attempt to resolve any aeromedical questions that the Iraqis or Tripod might have, and that I was in attendance solely to advise Tripod on such questions, and not as a representative of the British Government'. But the only question the visitors put to him was why Iraqi air force officers had been refused admission to an IAM diploma course, and he left the meeting after ten minutes.

Scott comments that the presence of a senior RAF officer at a meeting of this kind was ill judged: 'The Iran/Iraq war was in progress at the time and the questionable propriety of providing advice, in effect direct to the Iraqi Air Force, should have been apparent to the Air Vice-Marshal and have led him to think twice and to take MoD advice . . . I should make clear, however, that Air Vice-Marshal Howard has expressly denied having received any remuneration from Tripod while Commandant of the IAM and I accept that denial.'

The next stage came in December 1987 when Howard was told that Tripod was close to clinching a deal, but the customer, because of 'internal administrative reasons', was now Iraqi Airways instead of the Iraqi air force. The project remained, however, under the control of an Iraqi air force officer. Scott says this cosmetic change was almost certainly an attempt to divert attention from the patently military nature of any contract entered into by the Iraqi air force.

In February 1988 14 ELAs were submitted with a total value of over £7 million and were considered at a MODWG meeting in March. The officer with expertise on air force matters, Group Captain St Aubyn, was despatched to IAM for further information and, it appears, made Howard aware of the Howe guidelines. The officer reported with astonishment that Howard had been advising both sides in the war for seven years. But his advice was that the ELAs could be granted because the project would take up to three years to get under way and could be regarded as a dual-use enterprise.

The IDC nodded the licences through in March, without drawing them to the attention of FCO ministers. At the MoD Trefgarne agreed to the exports, but made it clear that he wanted the IAM and Howard to withdraw discreetly from further contact with the Iraqis. Two months later Howard retired and immediately became a consultant to Tripod. He did not, as he should have done, clear this appointment with the MoD. The failure to do so, he later told the Inquiry, 'was certainly not deliberate'.

Diversionary Routes

Another issue that Scott chose to examine was whether other countries – in particular Iraq's Arab neighbours, Jordan, Egypt, Kuwait, the United Arab Emirates and Saudi Arabia, but also Austria and Portugal – were used as diversionary routes for getting weaponry to Baghdad. The prohibition on 'lethal' equipment would not have applied to such countries, and there was potential for Iraq to receive supplies that had been barred under even the relaxed interpretation of the guidelines.

Scott shows how Allivane, a Scottish-based firm, exported millions of pounds worth of ammunition for the Iran–Iraq war – contradicting the Government's press briefing pack of February 1996 which said that the Scott Report 'confirms that no lethal weapons were exported' to the two countries. Export licences were approved for the company even after Customs officials began an investigation into Allivane in 1987. Two executives of Allivane, who requested not to be identified in the Report, revealed that twenty-four of twenty-five contracts between 1985 and 1989 were destined for both combatants via Saudi Arabia, Portugal, Jordan, Egypt, and Austria. From the early 1980s, MI6 knew that Saudi Arabia was a diversionary route, and Allivane had come to the attention of MI6 in 1987 when it was named as the supplier of artillery explosives for Iran. A Customs' report concluded: 'There is no doubt that the Allivane explosives were eventually shipped to Iran.'

In the second half of the 1980s, the FCO thought that Jordan was moving dangerously close to Iraq. It occupied a key position in the Middle East: Iraq had no access to the Gulf, because of the war with Iran, and was heavily dependent for its supplies on the long overland route to the Jordanian Red Sea port of Aqaba, part of which was exclusively devoted to Iraqi goods. Scott observes: 'The main highway from Aqaba to Iraq was regularly upgraded and some witnesses spoke of streams of lorries carrying goods from Aqaba to Iraq.' Transit fees for this considerable traffic were a useful boost to Jordan's economy, and the Jordanians did not seem concerned as to what was in those shipments.

In an interview with the BBC in 1993 the Jordanian ambassador in London said, ' . . . we helped to purchase and send some arms and equipment to Iraq. And, in point of fact, those arms and equipments were financed by other Arab countries as well as they were done [*sic*] with the full approval of Western powers and other Arab countries too.' The ambassador declined an opportunity to give evidence to the Scott Inquiry.

Jordan had made its own deal with Britain to buy weapons: in September 1985 a 'Memorandum of Understanding' (MOU) was signed with Jordan that covered a package of military equipment and services worth up to £270 million. But intelligence reports referred to at least three instances of false end-user certificates signed by the Jordanian authorities. In July 1988 the Jordanian Chief of Staff, Field Marshal Bin Shaker, candidly told visiting officials from the MoD that Iraq had asked Jordan to 'front' for them in acquiring military equipment, adding that he would not do anything behind the back of the British Government. In spite of these warnings no licences were ever refused for exports to Jordan and although limited measures were taken by DIS and Glazebrook to monitor the situation, ELAs for Jordan were not referred to the MODWG for closer scrutiny. Scott says this possible solution was not put before ministers for their consideration.

It was clear that Jordan was handled throughout with kid gloves. After Reginald Dunk was convicted for sending machine guns to Iraq via Jordan (see chapter 12), the FCO reproached neither the Jordanian ambassador in London nor the Amman government. When it was discovered that PRB, a Belgian company that had been bought by the British firm Astra, was providing propellant for the Supergun under cover of a fraudulent Jordanian end-user certificate, the FCO's only reaction was to protest to the Belgians. And when the same misuse of a Jordanian certificate occurred in the Ordtec case in May 1990 (see chapter 12) it was similarly reluctant to administer an official rebuke.

At the end of May 1990 during a visit to Jordan the Foreign Secretary, Douglas Hurd, raised the issue of diversion in the mildest of terms with King Hussein. That month, a telegram sent to London from an MI6 official based at the British Embassy in Amman made clear that Britain had been colluding in the trade. 'Are we trying to ensure that the problem does not arise again by putting a stop to further Jordanian involvement in Iraqi procurement?' it said. 'Have we not turned a blind eye to Jordanian involvement in the past? (The ambassador seems to think that this has been the case).'

Hurd undertook to provide the Jordanians with more details about Britain's concerns, but he also made clear Britain's wish to preserve close military links with Jordan. FCO documents also show that the 'further information' was to be supplied not by the FCO or the ambassador but by MI6, who reacted with some disquiet at being given a task they regarded as one for the diplomatic service. And the likely outcome of the MI6 approach, the FCO noted, was that 'the Jordanians will arrange any further assistance to Iraq with greater discretion!' Scott is clearly astonished by the episode.

> When it is borne in mind that the events that gave rise to the conclusion that a démarche would have to be delivered to the Jordanian Government had included incidents in which a false end-user certificate designed to defeat UK export controls had been signed by a very senior Jordanian official, the mild tone of the proposed approach, the decision that the approach should not be made through normal diplomatic channels but by SIS [MI6] and the acceptance of the likelihood that Jordan would continue to allow itself to be used as a diversionary route but with 'greater discretion', are somewhat surprising.

Even after the invasion of Kuwait, Government officials still displayed anxiety at the prospect of upsetting the Jordanians when it was discovered that a ship docked at Hull was about to take on board forty wagon loads of armour-piercing tank rounds and spares destined for Aqaba. With much wringing of hands the shipment was held up for a year.

Scott also refers to what became known as the 'Vereker Gap', after the name of the official who gave evidence on the subject at the Inquiry. At the end of 1991 the Arms Control and Disarmament Department (ACDD) in the FCO, where Peter Vereker worked, proposed to circulate a list of 'countries of concern' in the proliferation of nuclear weapons. The list included Jordan because of its past record as a diversionary route to Iraq. However, another FCO official, Charles Haswell, was alarmed at the potential damage to diplomatic relations if the list was published with Jordan's name included. By the time the list went to Downing Street for John Major's approval Jordan had been deleted, without any clearance from FCO ministers. A scribbled note on the file read: 'Mr Haswell, Jordan has disappeared. Well done.' Scott's conclusions on Jordan's role as a diversionary route through which Iraq illicitly obtained military equipment are unequivocal: from the inception of the guidelines to the invasion of Kuwait, he says, Jordan's role 'represented a continuing threat to the Government's policy on restricting defence related exports to Iraq'. And while he accepts the 'key position' Jordan occupied in the Middle East throughout the period he is critical that officials and not ministers took the initiative in playing down Jordan's role in aiding Iraq.

9 · Much More than Muddle

'The surveyor of Customs said: "It all seems a bit unlikely. It is your decision. Do we make complete fools of ourselves or do we not?" I took a walk around the building . . . I went back in and said: "Okay, we take it." '
   Mr Q, MI6 officer directing the seizure of the Supergun barrels

'Muddle undoubtedly had a part to play. But it went further than mere muddle.'
   Sir Richard Scott

What Scott describes as 'the fantastic story' behind the Iraqi Supergun affair was a dry run for the more extraordinary and, as far as the Government was concerned, much more damaging Matrix Churchill case.

The first hints that Saddam Hussein was planning what became known as Project Babylon emerged in late 1987 when Bill Weir, a metallurgist employed by the MoD, was approached by the DIS who had got wind of an ELA from a subsidiary of Sheffield Forgemasters, a large engineering group. The company had been approached by SRC to supply nickel alloy material for a large gun barrel. Weir knew nothing of SRC at the time but recalled that a former colleague, Mick Bayne, with whom he had worked in the Guns and Rockets Division at the Royal Armaments Research and Development Establishment (RARDE) had since joined the company. Weir put forward Bayne's name to MI6 as a possible lead. 'On the evidence available to Mr Weir by June 1988,' says Scott, 'he must have realized that SRC was probably involved in the design of armaments. He must also have been conscious of the possibility that Sheffield Forgemasters were themselves concerned with armaments manufacture. Moreover, a link between SRC and Sheffield Forgemasters could not be excluded. These fragments were soon to become the first piece in the complex jigsaw of Government knowledge of the Iraqi long range gun project.'

The complexity of who knew what when and who told whom is neatly illustrated by a full-page flow-chart drawn up by the Inquiry, with most of those involved identified only by initials. The text reflects Scott's agreement to protect the anonymity of MI5, MI6 and DIS officers: ' . . . Mr Weir did not himself speak to Mr C5 but spoke to Miss M. The probability is that Miss M spoke to Mr C5 but that in doing so she concentrated on Bayne as a potential contact. Indeed Miss I3's minute to Mr L on 11 November . . . ' But Scott is confident that the broad outlines of the saga are clear. In June 1988, Weir was told about suspicions held by Dr Rex Bayliss, managing director of the Walter Somers steel firm based in Halesowen, West Midlands, about an order placed with the company by SRC for large pipes, ostensibly for a petrochemical plant in Iraq. Bayliss thought they might be for some kind of missile launcher.

He passed on his concerns first to a friend, Sir Hal Miller, then Conservative MP for Bromsgrove. Miller immediately telephoned the private office of the trade minister, Alan Clark. He was given Anthony Steadman's name. Miller says he told Steadman: 'You know, this is serious. Someone must take it seriously.' Steadman passed on Miller's concerns to MI6 and the MoD. Weir was also informed. He contacted Steadman, who gave him Bayliss's telephone number. Miller, too, was given Weir's name. Miller also said he spoke to someone – he called him Anderson, although he could not remember the name – from a 'third agency'. Anderson, according to Miller, said 'this confirms everything we know', although Scott is sceptical about the accuracy of Miller's memory concerning this incident.

Weir told the Scott Inquiry that in 1988 'he had no knowledge of Iraqi arms procurement'. Scott notes that MI6 reports of November 1987, March 1988 and June 1988 about Iraq's world-wide search for new weapons had all been sent to the MoD branch in which Weir worked, but that there was no evidence they had been brought to his attention.

However, Weir privately warned both DIS and Steadman that the pipes could be used for military purposes. DIS suggested the pipes might have nuclear research implications, but failed to pass the warning to Whitehall's Restricted Enforcement Unit (REU) or to the special MoD Working Group on Iraqi Procurement (WGIP). Steadman, meanwhile, maintained that the pipes did not need an export licence.

Later, in evidence to the Scott Inquiry, Weir claimed that Bayliss had misled him. Bayliss's descriptions of the pipes were 'ambiguous', Weir claimed. But Whitehall documents shown to the Inquiry showed that Weir had plenty of evidence – indeed, he had drawn detailed diagrams of the pipes following a telephone conversation with Bayliss. 'I do not accept Mr Weir's suggestion that Dr Bayliss attempted to deceive him,' says Scott, who makes plain that, in his view, Weir failed to alert the relevant parts of Whitehall about his own suspicions that he himself admitted in contemporary documents.

'In the event,' says Scott, 'the warning signs were missed and two possible clues, one at the DTI, and one at the MoD, which could have led to the identification of one of the corner-pieces of the long-range gun jigsaw, simply fell into a chasm.' MI5 said it had 'no interest in Mr Weir's information' or talk of a 'fancy gun' since it did not 'bear on terrorist-related arms-trafficking'. According to Scott, Mr Q of MI6 became 'the principal hound in the hunt to uncover the details of the Iraqi long-range project'. Q told his MI6 colleagues that the agency 'ought to take the story seriously however bizarre it sounded'. His main task, says Scott, was to find the 'monster' barrels, which 'were in fact on the shop floor at Walter Somers'.

At about the same time an Astra executive, Stephan Kock – the company's non-executive director who had a mysterious long-standing relationship with the intelligence services – told MI6 about a suspiciously powerful propellant being produced by PRB, the Belgian company Astra had just acquired. Other Astra executives passed on their suspicions about PRB's sale of explosives – ostensibly for Jordan, but almost certainly destined for Iraq – to two MoD arms salesmen, Robert Primrose and Roger Harding. Primrose had a meeting with Mr Q from MI6, and the two men agreed that the suspicions 'should be reported to Ministers as a matter of urgency'. 'In fact', says Scott, 'MoD Ministers were never told.'

Meanwhile, Paul Grecian, a director of Ordtec, a military engineering company involved with SRC, met his long-time police Special Branch contact, Steven Wilkinson. Wilkinson noted: 'The Iraqi government has recently undertaken a top secret project known as Operation Babylon. In essence the plan is to build an artillery piece with a range of 600 miles, thus surpassing all other standard artillery weapons currently available.' He sent his report to MI5 who passed it to MI6.

Scott reveals that in late 1989 MI6 privately acknowledged that the Government had known since at least June 1988 of the possibility that Iraq was planning to build a Supergun, that Walter Somers and SRC were involved, and that the 'petro-chemical' pipes were 'probably intended for use as artillery gun barrels'. Yet there was no reference to any of this in a report on the 'Iraqi Gun Project' sent to Peter Lilley, the trade and industry secretary, by Sir Robin Butler more than two years later, in December 1990. Butler was responding to a request from Lilley after the dropping of charges against two men in connection with the Supergun affair. Instead, Butler trotted out what by now had become the Government's official line – that is, referring only to its state of knowledge after September 1989. That line, described by Scott as 'misleading', was repeated by Whitehall witnesses to the Commons Trade and Industry Select Committee's Inquiry into the Supergun in 1992.

Lilley's request for information led to another bout of panic in Whitehall. Sir Colin McColl, the then Chief of MI6, tried to absolve his agency from blame over the failure to act sooner on intelligence reports. He wrote to Sir Percy Cradock, Margaret Thatcher's foreign policy adviser and chairman of the Joint Intelligence Committee (JIC), saying: 'I believe that ministers were on safe ground in continuing to state that in June 1988, HMG had no knowledge of the existence of an Iraqi supergun project.' He suggested that the MI6 briefing note of October 1989, which said that it had been known since June 1988 that Walter Somers was probably involved in supplying Supergun barrels, was simply a mix-up by a 'very junior' officer.

In an unprecedented dressing-down, Scott describes McColl's note as 'incorrect': 'On such an important issue such as this, I would have expected Sir Colin to take a personal interest in checking some at least of the underlying material. In the event, on one reading of the purpose of his letter to Sir Percy Cradock, it was a defensive operation to seek to distance [MI6] from responsibility for the failure to act . . . ' The letter, Scott concludes, was 'apt to mislead'.

In November 1989, Mr Q produced a lengthy report on Project Babylon, which he called a plan 'to develop the technology for a hypervelocity gun with extreme range capability'. Mr Q eloquently described to Scott Whitehall's reaction to his report: it had been 'rather like throwing a brick into a puddle of treacle, a loud plop and nobody took any interest, so the barrel became an issue to me because I was suffering a credibility problem with the people to whom I was addressing my reports'.

A month later, Mr Q drew up another, even more detailed, report about Babylon. Scott discloses that an MI6 intelligence digest based on their report, dated 5 December 1989, was sent to 10 Downing Street and was seen by Margaret Thatcher. It stated: 'Iraq is in the early stages of developing an ultra long-range gun, similar in concept to the German V3 of World War II. The weapon is suited to a strategic bombardment role, as an alternative to ballistic missiles, using cluster munitions or Chemical Warfare payloads.'

Sir Hal Miller re-entered the fray. He told Thatcher later that he 'went through the same procedure again in respect of a second order [by the Iraqis for pipes from Walter Somers], which was again subsequently cleared'. He acted after Peter Mitchell, who had taken over from Bayliss as managing director of the company, telephoned him about 'a repeat order' from Iraq for six more pipes.

In January 1990, David James, chairman of Eagle Trust, which had taken over Walter Somers, visited the company's factory. There he saw what he described as a 'thumping great muzzle' akin to a medieval 'siege gun'. He decided to 'begin an internal investigation by covert means'.

On 22 March 1990 Dr Gerald Bull, the Canadian-born founder of SRC and designer of the Supergun, was assassinated in Brussels. The killers were widely assumed to be the Israeli secret service, Mossad, although British intelligence pointed the finger at the Iranians.

Shortly afterwards, an MI6 officer telephoned Mr Q, who was out of London. According to Mr Q's evidence to the Inquiry, the MI6 officer had had a call from 'a senior gentleman in the City who had reportedly taken over finance control of Walter Somers, and he was getting increasingly alarmed about what they were up to, and had this rather wild story about some monstrous sort of gun'. Mr Q's MI6 colleague commented: 'It is quite unbelievable. Has the guy finally taken leave of his senses, or is there anything in it?' Scott comments: 'The gentleman was Mr David James. He had not taken leave of his senses.'

On 27 March, James met Mr Q. More details emerged about letters of credit, the dimensions of the pipes ordered by Iraq and the involvement of Sheffield Forgemasters. James had discovered that one barrel had been shipped the previous January on an Iraqi military plane from Manchester airport. Mr Q greeted James's new information with 'whoops of joy'. On 30 March 1990 – nearly two years after Miller had first raised the issue with Whitehall – the REU was finally told by MI6 that Walter Somers was involved in Project Babylon.

A week later, David James and Charles Whyte, a business colleague and metallurgical engineer, took away nine hundred pages of Walter Somers' documents, on the pretext that the group's bankers needed an immediate forecast of the company's trading prospects. With Mr Q's help, they photocopied them in a nearby hotel room.

Meanwhile, a foreign intelligence organization (which Scott does not name but which is understood to have been Mossad) warned MI6 that parts of the Supergun were likely to be shipped from Teesport on the north-east coast within the next twenty-four or forty-eight hours. On 10 April, Mr Q rushed to the docks. The gun parts made by Forgemasters had been loaded on board the MV *Gur Mariner* for export to Umm Qasr in Iraq. Anxious to keep in the background, Q briefed Customs officers to look for 350 mm gun barrels. This was based on the best information he had. He later told the Inquiry he had been 'mortified' to be told by Customs that nothing like barrels answering to his description had been found. He asked Customs officers to look at the pipes again and report back. According to Scott: 'They did so, and reported that the key dimension was 1000 mm.'

Mr Q was in a quandary. He told the Inquiry: 'The surveyor of Customs said, "It all seems a bit unlikely. It is your decision. Do we make complete fools of ourselves or do we not?" I took a walk round the building. I thought, the evidence is all there, but it is pretty tenuous. Do you believe your own assessment or not? I went back in and said: "Okay, we take it."' Mr Q continued: 'They detained them . . . I then got out of the scene as fast as possible and an expert from the Royal Armaments Research and Development Establishment, John Coleman, was brought in to give an attributable expert view on the guns, which he confirmed were part of a gunnery system, and they were "seized" on 12 April. Thereafter it all went rather public.' Back in Whitehall, officials from the DTI, the FCO, and the MoD met to ensure that all departments were aware of the full details. However, documents passed to Scott made it clear that, despite these assurances, key points were not passed on.

On 17 April, Sir Hal Miller telephoned Alan Clark's private office at the MoD to ask whether his earlier warnings had been recorded. He also informally approached Tom King, the defence secretary, in the Commons lobby. The following day, Nicholas Ridley, the trade and industry secretary, delivered a carefully prepared statement to the Commons about the seizure of the pipes. He told MPs that although the DTI had been approached by Walter Somers in 1988, 'until a few days ago, my department had no knowledge that the goods were designed to form part of a gun'. He added: 'The Government recently became aware in general terms of an Iraqi project to develop a long-range gun based on designs developed by the late Dr Gerald Bull.'

Scott comments: 'The statement that Government had "recently" become aware of an Iraqi project to develop a long-range gun was a far more elastic use of the word "recently" than was warranted by the known facts.' He notes that two years later, in 1992, Alan Clark and Nicolas Bevan were questioned by the Commons Trade and Industry Committee (TISC) about the use of the word 'recently'. Bevan said he thought the Government had been first made aware in the autumn of 1989. Later, he told the Inquiry: 'I had not anticipated the question and therefore had not prepared for it: I had to think quickly. As a witness appearing on behalf of ministers I could not accept the premise of the question that ministers had deceived Parliament. It seemed to me that the lesser evil was the course which I adopted, that is, to opine that an event which took place four months previously fell within a reasonable definition of "recently".'

Martin Stanley, Ridley's private secretary, rallied to his fellow civil servant's defence. He told the Inquiry that he did not think the use of the word 'recently' was misleading. 'After all,' he said, 'it is a word whose interpretation depends very much upon its context.' He added in parenthesis: ' "Recent history" suggests a different timescale to "recent weather" . . . ' MoD, DTI and MI6 officials all knew that Ridley's April 1990 statement had been inaccurate. Alan Clark conceded in his evidence to TISC that it was an 'exaggeration'. Scott concludes: 'It is, in my opinion, clear that the word "recently" was deliberately chosen and that its use was apt to be misleading.' Furthermore, says Scott, Ridley's statement did not mention that Miller had been involved in discussions with the Government in June 1988 or that he and Bayliss had alerted the DTI and the MoD about their concerns.

No fewer than eight drafts of Ridley's statement were drawn up. In the course of redrafting, the phrase 'last year' had been substituted for 'recently'. Scott comments: 'The change in the text is consistent with an attempt to avoid criticism of the Government for not having acted sooner than it did.' Another phrase – 'enquiries were made [in 1988] but there was no evidence that the tubes were designed for military use' – was also deleted.

Scott also notes that TISC was prevented from calling Bob Primrose and Roger Harding, the two MoD arms salesmen with first-hand knowledge of the events: their appearance was blocked by Sir Michael Quinlan, MoD Permanent Secretary, Sir Robin Butler and Nicolas Bevan on the grounds that they had left the MoD and were no longer serving civil servants. Officials, TISC was told, gave evidence 'on behalf of ministers and are responsible to ministers for their evidence'. Retired civil servants were no longer beholden to ministerial whim and therefore could not appear at TISC. Scott concludes: 'The refusal to facilitate the giving of evidence to TISC by Mr Harding and Mr Primrose may be regarded as a failure to comply fully with the obligations of accountability owed to Parliament.'

In May 1990, the Labour MP Tam Dalyell asked a Parliamentary question about attempts by SRC to obtain grants from the Northern Ireland Industrial Development Board to buy Learfan, a high-tech engineering firm. William Waldegrave replied that 'in the light of the charges laid against individuals [over the Supergun], and of the continuing investigations by Customs and Excise, it would be wrong . . . to comment'. Scott points out that, contrary to Waldegrave's suggestion, Learfan was not being investigated. Waldegrave subsequently said that Scott was wrong to criticize him for the answer and for legal advice which he received from officials. Scott brushed this aside: Waldegrave's response, he says, 'represented an inadequate response to Mr Dalyell's request for information'.

In December 1990, the Labour MP Richard Caborn asked Peter Lilley, now social security secretary, what action the DTI took 'when it was first made aware of the pipeline equipment built in the United Kingdom for Iraq having possible military implications'. Lilley said that 'when military implications of the equipment became clear the department responsible for taking action was HM Customs and Excise. That department acted with commendable swiftness to prevent the export of the equipment.' As Scott points out, that was not an answer to the question. Moreover, it made no reference to the Government's state of knowledge in 1988. He states: 'The failure to respond adequately to the question constituted, in my opinion, a further example of failure to discharge the obligations of accountability.'

'What went wrong?' Scott asks. In a post mortem, written in November 1990, Mr Q put it all down to 'a typical Whitehall muddle'. And Scott agrees, up to a point: 'Muddle undoubtedly had a part to play. But it went further than mere muddle. No contemporaneous written record was made by the DTI of the information provided by Sir Hal Miller and Dr Bayliss.' Scott continues:

> DTI and MoD officials failed to make a sufficient record of the exchanges between them in June/July 1988. Nor did the DTI make any record of the advice given by them to Walter Somers in June/July 1988. As a consequence, officials in the DTI/ELB [Export Licensing Branch] were not in a position to identify the connection between the Forgemasters and Walter Somers orders. MoD, DTI and Security Service [MI5] officials failed in June/July 1988 to use the system for the exchange of information available to them at the time, namely the REU.

Scott adds that if MI6 did reach the opinion – as Mr C2 of MI6 insists – that in June 1988, SRC had been involved in an attempt to acquire Walter Somers pipes 'probably intended for use as gun-barrels', it had then been a 'serious omission' not to have told the REU. But in any event, Scott says,

> there is clear evidence that some time before October 1989 Government officials had had information which raised the suspicion that Walter Somers' tubes were probably intended for use as artillery gun-barrels . . . The evidence indicates suspicion that an Iraqi long-range artillery project with unusual features was in contemplation. Parliament could, and should, have been told this. TISC could, and should, have been told this . . . senior officials who were directly involved were left unaware of the true facts, and were not in a position to brief ministers adequately.

TISC, whose Inquiry into the Supergun was obstructed by Whitehall and provided with far less information and documents than the Scott Inquiry, had concluded in March 1992: 'Only one gun was assembled and it was fired only in tests. We cannot tell whether the action taken across Europe in April 1990 merely delayed or actually prevented the completion of the project. Only the Gulf War and the subsequent access by UN inspectors to the sites ensured that these tubes did not become strategically significant. There should be no complacency about how narrowly this prospect was avoided.'

The Supergun Prosecutions

> 'In the final analysis the jury might well conclude that the DTI were either highly incompetent or possibly turning a blind eye to the obvious.'
>   Julian Bevan, prosecution QC

Dr Christopher Cowley, a metallurgist and SRC employee at the time that the orders for the gun barrels were being negotiated, was arrested by Customs officers on 24 April 1990. A week later Peter Mitchell, the managing director of Walter Somers, and sixteen others were arrested. Counsel were first briefed on the case by Customs lawyers in late July. They used – as they must – the test laid down in the Code for Crown Prosecutors that a prosecution should be pursued only when there is a 'realistic prospect of a conviction'. Julian Bevan, leading counsel for Customs, advised as regards Mitchell: 'It

would be fundamentally wrong to continue with the prosecution
... especially bearing in mind the fact that he contacted Sir Hal
Miller in the summer of 1989 and revealed his suspicions to
him.' Cowley, Bevan added, would also have a defence.

Bevan and his junior, Peter Finnigan, added: 'We are very
concerned about the fact that the MoD and DTI were told of the
suspicions of the companies at a very early stage. Once the
approach had been made, the companies were effectively
inviting the MoD and DTI to investigate the matter as and when
they wished. In short, they were opening their cupboard for
inspection at any time.' A jury, they concluded, would be
reluctant to convict.

Alexander Russell, Customs director of policy, was not
convinced. He argued that neither Mitchell nor anyone else
associated with the companies had sent any material about the
later contracts with Iraq, and that Mitchell's contacts with
Miller were merely 'an insurance policy if things should go
wrong'. Unhappy with Bevan's advice, Customs commissioners
sought guidance from the then Attorney-General, Sir Patrick
Mayhew.

Douglas Tweddle, head of the Customs Investigation
Department ('an administrator', Scott notes earlier, 'who was
appointed to the post without any prior experience of
investigative work'), pressed for the appointment of a QC with
'a strong commitment to success in the case'. He added: 'As the
trial is likely to have a very high media profile we need somebody
with excellent presentational skills.' Tweddle's comments were
'quite inappropriate', says Scott: such skills were irrelevant. As
Mayhew put it, in oral evidence, 'Prosecuting counsel have a duty
to the Court, and to justice primarily, and not to secure a
conviction.'

Meanwhile, Bevan noted that Anthony Steadman at the
DTI had not responded to the original warnings about the
pipes, that the DTI had never asked for drawings from
Walter Somers and had said that no export licences were
needed for the pipes. 'In the final analysis,' he said, 'the
jury might well conclude that the DTI were either
highly incompetent or possibly turning a blind eye to the
obvious.'

But Customs remained determined. Failure to proceed with

the prosecution, it said, 'would deal a heavy blow to the credibility of enforcement in the area of export controls'. It noted that Bevan had admitted that there was some evidence, at least, that the companies knowingly intended to evade export restrictions. In November 1990, Customs lawyers held a meeting with Mayhew and Sir Nicholas Lyell, then the Solicitor-General. Bevan and Finnigan again advised that an acquittal was the likely outcome of a trial.

Sir Brian Unwin, then chairman of Customs, now intervened. He told the Inquiry that he felt 'frustration and great concern and [his] very crude view was that if [Customs] did not take the prosecution through, it would not be because there was no evidence of knowledge, complicity, and intention to mislead . . . but because certain exchanges had taken place with one or more Government departments back in 1988 which would induce a jury to reject the case'.

In a prophetic comment, in the light of the forthcoming Matrix Churchill case, Unwin added that a decision to abandon the trial would 'hamper efforts to enforce sanctions where Customs and Excise frequently met substantial commercial pressures'. Other difficult cases were being prepared and Customs was worried that its role in enforcing export controls would be threatened.

But counsel stood firm that a conviction was unlikely. Charges against Cowley and Mitchell were dropped at Sheffield Magistrates' Court on 15 November 1990. On 5 December, Unwin wrote to Michael Saunders, a Customs solicitor, about the forthcoming Matrix Churchill prosecution. The note, which must have come back to haunt Unwin, referred to reports that Alan Clark, the former trade minister, had given a 'nod and a wink' in 1988 to machine tool exporters selling equipment to Iraq known to be used to make weapons. 'To put it crudely,' Unwin said, 'I do not want to have a repetition of the gun affair in which the results of our investigations are negated for prosecution purposes by exchanges, or allegations of exchanges, of this kind. Apart from the damaging effects on morale here, and indeed on the credibility of our sanctions effort more generally, we do not have resources to waste on complex and labour intensive investigations that are unlikely to lead to a successful prosecution.'

If Sir Brian and senior Customs officials felt frustrated by the dropping of the Supergun charges, the Customs investigators who had been amassing the evidence were bitterly angry. They expressed their feelings in a 1990 Christmas card: under a picture of an officer stabbed in the back by a knife were the words: 'To all Operation Bertha staff, from: HMG, the DTI, the MoD, the Attorney-General . . .'

10 · A Prosecution too Far

'The dirty washing liable to emerge from the action proposed by Customs and Excise will add to the problems posed by the gun.'

Michael Coolican, senior DTI official, in a warning to his Secretary of State, Nicholas Ridley

In October 1990, a month before the Supergun case collapsed, three directors of Matrix Churchill – Paul Henderson, Peter Allen and Trevor Abraham – were arrested and charged with evading export controls on arms-related equipment to Iraq. 'It may be taken as self-evident,' says Scott bluntly, 'that a trial which collapses before the conclusion of the prosecution case is, with the benefit of hindsight, a trial that ought never to have commenced. The questions to be asked, therefore, are why the Matrix Churchill prosecution was commenced and whether the wisdom of hindsight was in fact available at an earlier stage.' His answer, developed over a 400-page, at times picaresque, chronicle of an astonishing series of cock-ups and desperate attempts at cover-up, is clear.

The investigation of Matrix Churchill by Customs officers began in March 1990, following a tip-off from their German counterparts. UK Customs could have acted much sooner without any help from the Germans: by the end of 1989, if not earlier, intelligence had been received that would have made a Customs investigation, as Scott puts it, 'unsurprising and well justified'. In particular, he had in mind the 13 October 1989 GCHQ report which disclosed that a 'UK firm' – acknowledged two months later by GCHQ to be Matrix Churchill – had done a deal with Cardoen, the Chilean arms manufacturer, to export machine tools to Nassr, an Iraqi weapons plant. Customs had received a copy of the GCHQ report, and Peter Wiltshire, the senior Customs investigator on the case, had been present at the Restricted Enforcement Unit (REU) meeting where Matrix Churchill was named.

The prosecution augured ill from the start. Wiltshire was head of Customs' B team, responsible not for dubious exports to Iraq – this was handled by the A team – but for exports to the then Communist bloc in eastern Europe. Wiltshire was given charge of the Matrix Churchill case because, unlike members of the A team, he was cleared to read intelligence reports classified Top Secret. The Scott Inquiry demonstrated, time and time again, that officials who needed to see intelligence reports were prevented from doing so because they had not been cleared by Whitehall's cumbersome vetting procedures.

However, in the Matrix Churchill case, as Scott remarks, 'the copy of the 13 October 1989 Report distributed to Customs would have been available to be read, and should have been read, by Mr Wiltshire . . . but could not have been read by the A team . . . notwithstanding that the report dealt with matters that were the A team's, and not the B team's, responsibility'. As it was, Wiltshire could not remember the GCHQ report 'or what, if anything, he did about it'. The vital report played no part in the Customs investigation of Matrix Churchill's machine-tool exports to Iraq, and its existence was never disclosed to the defence at the subsequent trial. 'If the 13 October 1989 report, taken with other relevant intelligence, had been shown to and taken into account by counsel,' says Scott pointedly, 'the prosecution would not have been instituted.'

There was panic in the upper reaches of the DTI when Customs decided to pursue the company. On 14 June 1990, Michael Coolican, a senior DTI official, wrote to Ridley asking: 'Are Ministers willing to have the 1987 and subsequent decisions exposed and made the subject of court-room argument? The dirty washing liable to emerge from the action proposed by Customs & Excise will add to the problems posed by the gun [the Iraqi Supergun]. For DTI the timing is extraordinarily embarrassing given recent correspondence between ourselves, MoD and FCO.'

In his evidence to the Inquiry, Coolican explained that: 'The "dirty washing" was the fact that intelligence had been available in 1987 . . . and that clearly this might come out in court – as, indeed, it did. The embarrassment as I perceived it was that we had been engaging in correspondence with FCO and MoD on the basis that there was no substantive evidence and such evidence had now become forthcoming.'

Six days later, Ridley's private secretary wrote in equally panic-stricken terms to his opposite number in the office of Customs chairman Sir Brian Unwin. 'You assured me the visit [by Customs to Matrix Churchill] would be used for fact-finding only, and no action would be taken as a result without consulting Ministers,' he said. 'I also told you that my Secretary of State would shortly be writing to the Prime Minister asking that Ministers should collectively and urgently discuss the issues connected with the case.'

Two days later, on 22 June 1990, Unwin wrote back, saying that Customs would maintain 'appropriate contacts' with the DTI. He also made it clear that decisions rested with the Customs Commissioners, in accordance with their statutory responsibilities. Scott remarks: 'It is important, in my opinion, to notice the tension between the DTI and Customs at the commencement of the investigation.' He notes that it surfaced again at a meeting in the Cabinet Office on 29 June 1990. Alexander Russell, from Customs, reported 'a fairly astonishing introduction by the DTI spokesman who said fairly explicitly that perhaps the answer lay not in changing policies or guidelines but in Customs & Excise being less assiduous in enforcement . . . I spoke out strongly against any such notion, making absolutely clear that it would be entirely improper interference with the independent powers of the [Customs] Commissioners.' Scott picks up Russell's assertion that Customs, as a prosecuting authority, should enforce 'the [Government's] policy of the day'. He says: 'It would, I think, generally be thought that the function of a prosecuting authority is to enforce the criminal law rather than Government policy.' He adds: 'But one of the consequences of the nature of export control law, as established under the 1939 Act, is that the distinction between what is the "criminal law" and what is Government "policy" becomes blurred . . . the Government can, at a stroke of the pen, change the export control law at will . . . ' Customs believed – they certainly argued the point – that the machine tools Matrix Churchill supplied to Iraq were in effect 'specially designed' to make weapons. Yet the DTI had always classified them as 'dual-use', able to be used for both civil and military purposes. The trouble with the Customs argument, as Scott repeatedly points out, was that the 'special design' or 'package' concept had never before been tested at a trial and did not fit easily into the official classification of products used by the DTI. These were separated into civil or industrial on the one hand, military on the other. The advantage for Customs of the 'special design' concept was that it made the case against Matrix Churchill much stronger. There was less room for doubt that Matrix Churchill directors had deceived the Government. It would also allow the prosecution to argue that the Whitehall documents requested by the defence were not relevant to the case since they pointed only to Government 'suspicions' about 'dual-use' exports.

Scott says:

> The 'specially designed' package theory was . . . not the basis on which the DTI had previously approached the licensability of standard machine tools and their accessories and software. It was not a theory on which any prosecution had ever previously been based. It was untested in Court . . . Given the novelty of the 'package' theory, it was to be expected that it would be subjected to a careful and rigorous analysis by Customs lawyers before a prosecution were based upon it. There is no evidence that this ever happened. A further problem in relation to the 'package' theory was that, given its novelty, no manufacturer or exporter could reasonably be expected to have had it in mind when applying for export licences.

Scott points to another failure in the Customs investigation: in October 1989, Henderson had given his MI6 contact – identified as 'John Balsom' at the Matrix Churchill trial but only as Mr T in the Scott Report – drawings of what was known as Iraq's ABA missile project, which was cited in one of the charges against the Matrix Churchill directors. Customs, Scott notes, knew nothing of this.

Although MI6 told Wiltshire in 1990 at an early stage in the investigations that it had a source in Matrix Churchill, they did not tell him that the source was Henderson. Scott then notes that in October 1990, two years before the start of the trial, Anthony Steadman of the DTI told Customs that the defence would argue that the DTI knew, or should have known, that Matrix

Churchill machine tools were being used by Iraq to make weapons. 'It all makes for a bloody battle,' he warned, 'and some difficult questions of knowledge and the effectiveness of the licensing process which could seriously weaken HMG's case.'

The following month, on 6 November, senior Whitehall officials, including Sir Robin Butler, the Cabinet Secretary, and Sir Peter Gregson, permanent secretary at the DTI, were alerted to the potential pitfalls. An official note of a meeting between the two mandarins recorded: 'The officials [are put] in some difficulty because they had known of intelligence in advance . . . that the machine tools already licensed for export by Matrix Churchill were for the purpose of manufacturing munitions . . . ' The note contained the first hints of a cover-up. It said: 'Sir Peter Gregson would take the advice of his departmental lawyers about whether it was in order for his officials in the meantime to make the factual statements which Customs had requested without volunteering the further information which they had about the intelligence information available at the time.'

Whitehall was also becoming nervous about the potentially damaging allegation that at a meeting with the Machine Tools Technologies Association (MTTA) on 20 January 1988, Alan Clark, the then trade minister, had encouraged the companies to concentrate on the potential civilian uses of their products when completing ELAs for Iraq – the 'nod and wink' episode. But Customs explained away Clark's remarks by saying that he had been referring only to dual-use and not to 'specially designed' equipment.

What Clark had or had not said at this crucial MTTA meeting – the issue that led to the final collapse of the Matrix Churchill trial two years later – was to preoccupy Whitehall in the closing weeks of 1990. The official DTI minute reads:

> Choosing his words carefully and noting that the Iraqis would be using the current orders for general engineering purposes, Mr Clark stressed that it was important for the UK companies to agree a specification with the customer in advance which highlighted the peaceful (ie non-military) use to which the machine tools would be put.

The MTTA version reads:

> [Clark advised that] the intended use of the machines should be couched in such a manner as to emphasise the peaceful aspect to which they will be put.

On 2 December 1990, the *Sunday Times* splashed a story on its front page claiming that Clark had encouraged the companies to export to Iraq even though he knew the machine tools were being used to make weapons. It provoked further panic in Whitehall.

The next morning, John Major, who had just replaced Margaret Thatcher as Prime Minister, summoned Clark to see him. Sir Robin Butler drafted a minute of the meeting. He recorded that Clark told Major that 'he was in effect advising them [the MTTA companies] to downgrade the specification of the machine tools . . . so that they could not be used for military purposes. It was totally false to suggest that he was advising the companies on how to prepare licence applications in such a way as to conceal the military use.'

Clark was unhappy with Sir Robin's minute and changed it. In place of the words, 'so that they could not be used for military purposes', he substituted 'so that they would not be seen as suitable for military purposes'. It was a subtle but important difference, more consistent both with the impression the MTTA was given and with Clark's subsequent testimony at the trial. But the note was not seen by Customs. And Scott did not see it until well after his Inquiry was under way.

A second meeting, this time of an impressive clutch of mandarins, was held at the Cabinet Office later that day, 3 December 1990. Present were Sir Robin Butler, Sir Brian Unwin, Sir Peter Gregson, Sir Michael Quinlan (permanent secretary at the MoD), David Gore-Booth of the FCO, John Meadway of the DTI, Len Appleyard of the Cabinet Office, and Gerald Hosker, the DTI lawyer (who was later promoted to the post of Treasury Solicitor). They had been brought together to discuss the implications of the *Sunday Times* story and what to do about Clark. Contemporary notes of the meeting by Sonia Phippard, Sir Robin's private secretary, included an intriguing passage attributed to Gregson. It said: 'Wld need to brazen beyond that.' Gregson later told the Scott Inquiry that he did not think he had used that precise expression. Butler, however, acknowledged that he thought Clark's remarks were at the very least 'ambiguous'. Clearly, Scott says, senior officials in December 1990 had 'serious misgivings about the prosecution'. These misgivings – reflected in the language used by Butler and Gregson about Alan Clark – were not passed on to Customs investigators or Customs lawyers, the very people responsible for preparing the prosecution.

Meanwhile, Customs instructed a barrister, David Calvert-Smith, to prepare their case for trial. He was not told that the 'specially designed' theory, which was at the heart of the rosecution case, was a totally alien concept as far as the DTI was concerned. Yet DTI officials were becoming increasingly anxious. On 30 January 1991, Steadman told Beston: 'It would be extremely embarrassing for HMG for it to appear to have permitted licences for arms manufacture at the height of the Iran/Iraq war and of course we would not be in a position to comment.' (As far back as October 1989, Beston had told Lord Trefgarne, in a note sent to Waldegrave at the FCO, that: 'Even if the lathes had been intended for the manufacture of munitions . . . there was no longer sufficient reason under the [new] Guidelines to prevent export.') MoD officials, however, assured Customs that 'there was nothing nasty in the woodwork' in their files. And Customs lawyers continued to convince themselves that documents showing Government suspicions – and even knowledge – of the military end-use of the machine tools were irrelevant, since their case was based on the 'specially designed' argument, and Matrix Churchill directors' intent to deceive.

However, as Scott puts it: 'It is difficult to see what significant difference there could have been between Government knowledge that the machine tools and accessories were intended for the manufacture of munitions and Government knowledge that the machine tools and accessories were specially designed to manufacture munitions. Customs' fixation with the special design point seems to have led to a blind spot so far as Government knowledge of intended use was concerned.'

On 29 January 1991, Beston sent his DTI colleague, John Meadway, a minute about what Customs wanted him to say at the Matrix Churchill committal hearing:

> The main problem . . . would be how to draw the line if pressed by [the] defence on whether at any time we knew or had reason to believe that equipment – although not specially designed for military production – was destined for a military establishment and the production of military goods. In light of our knowledge in 1987/8 (and the decision to allow contracts to proceed for source protection among other things) I could not claim that HMG knew nothing, but equally at the moment I am not sure how this question could be answered honestly without causing some embarrassment at the very least. If the decision is made to proceed with prosecution I think we shall need to prepare ourselves for such questions rather carefully.

Scott comments acidly: 'Mr Beston's approach to the question of what he should say, or refrain from saying, might have been appropriate to some audiences and some venues but was not, in my opinion, appropriate to the giving of evidence for the purposes of a criminal prosecution.' Beston's draft witness statement, Scott notes, said the ELAs in question were considered under the original 1984 guidelines, whereas they had in fact been considered under the relaxed 1989 version of guideline (iii). Inaccurate statements at a criminal trial, Scott makes clear, constituted a worse misdemeanour even than misleading Parliament. Beston's statement, which also incorrectly implied that a decision to grant export licences was a matter for the DTI irrespective of the views of FCO or MoD ministers, 'either expressly or by implication, did not accord with and served to conceal the true position,' says Scott.

Alan Moses, QC, was instructed in June 1991 by Customs to lead the prosecution. His initial brief, Scott recalls, 'concentrated on deception regarding the use to which the machine tools were to be put. If the case had continued to be thus focused, there would have been no need to treat the allegedly "special design" of the machine tools as a central feature of the case.' The brief for Moses also claimed that 'Customs first became aware of [Matrix Churchill] dealings with Iraq in June 1990'. This statement, Scott notes, ignored numerous references to Matrix Churchill's dealings with Iraq that were to be found in minutes of earlier meetings of the REU. It also ignored the fact that the WGIP had been concerned in June and July 1989 that the company had pressed for temporary ELAs to be made permanent so that they could be sold to a factory known by the Government to be responsible for the Iraqi missile programme; and the fact that GCHQ's 13 October 1989 intelligence report had been sent to Customs, as had an MI6 report of that month which linked Matrix Churchill with the Iraqi arms procurement network.

The trouble was that neither Annabelle Bolt nor Andrew Biker, the Customs solicitors who prepared the brief for Moses, had seen the GCHQ intelligence report. Nor would they have known about REU or WGIP minutes.

Around the same time, in July 1991, Alan Clark signed a witness statement prepared for Customs by Cedric Andrew. It was intended to be a rebuttal of the defence argument that Clark had encouraged the machine-tool exporters to be less than truthful in their ELAs. It stated that at the now notorious MTTA meeting of 20 January 1988, Clark 'was advised by the MTTA delegation that the machine tools were intended for general engineering purposes'. But as Scott points out, the MTTA had not advised Clark that the machine tools were intended for 'general engineering purposes'. Moreover, Clark knew, from the original 30 November 1987 intelligence report, that they were intended for the production of munitions and missiles. Clark later told the Inquiry that he regarded the expression 'general engineering purposes' when applied to dual-use goods as covering both civil and military production. Given what Clark knew from the intelligence report, the wording of his witness statement was, says Scott, 'singularly meaningless'. There was no doubt that Cedric Andrew, who drafted the sentence, intended 'general engineering purposes' to mean 'civil production'.

To an ordinary reader, Scott says, Clark's witness statement would have given a misleading impression. Scott adds: Clark 'is a highly articulate and literate man but did not, I conclude, give to the wording of his statement the serious and careful attention that was required'. The reason for that could have been Clark's belief that there was no question of a prosecution and that Customs were questioning him so that they could close the file on the case. In any event, Scott places the responsibility for the deficiencies in Clark's statement squarely on Andrew's shoulders. 'Mr Clark was, both at the Matrix Churchill trial and before the Inquiry, an entirely frank and forthcoming witness,' says Scott. If Andrew had asked Clark some of the probing questions Clark had been asked at the trial, then he would have given the same – honest – answers.

A conscious attempt at cover-up was made when Anthony Steadman had to sign a witness statement, drafted for him by Customs investigators. It referred to his initial involvement with Matrix Churchill in 1987 and 1988 and his concern then that the machine tools might be used by the Iraqis to make weapons. The statement added: 'There was however no evidence as far as I am aware to support these suspicions.'

That, says Scott, was 'not true'. The 30 November 1987 intelligence report amounted to 'firm evidence' of military use. Steadman later told the Inquiry that Wiltshire had told him intelligence information could not be regarded as evidence and should not, therefore, be specified in the statement. He admitted he had been 'unhappy' with the sentence since he 'felt that the knowledge was greater than was being indicated'.

The unhappy Steadman made some handwritten amendments to his witness statement for the Matrix Churchill committal. He added the adjective 'hard' in front of the word 'evidence' so that the text read 'There was however no hard evidence . . .' He returned the amended draft to Customs. Customs retyped the statement, ignoring Steadman's additions and deleting the original final sentence referring to 'suspicions', at the suggestion of Andrew Leithead, a lawyer in the Treasury Solicitor's Department, which is responsible for giving legal advice throughout Whitehall.

Steadman finally signed the statement with the deletions recommended by Leithead, and consequential amendments proposed by Gerald Hosker, then Treasury Solicitor. 'The effect,' says Scott, 'was to turn a fair statement of the position . . . into a misleading one.' Steadman was asked at the Inquiry whether he was concerned that his statement did not refer 'to the knowledge or the information that the Government had received'. He replied: 'I assumed there was good reason why that had to come out.'

Scott: Were you concerned that it did not accurately reflect what had occurred?

Steadman: I did not think I was concerned because I had been advised that it should be deleted. So there must have been good reason for that.

Asked whether his amended statement represented the truth, Steadman agreed it was 'not an accurate reflection'. Asked whether an added phrase stating that he accepted assurances from Matrix Churchill that the machine tools were for civil use was 'more than not accurate. It is just not true?', Steadman replied; 'Yes.' Asked why he let the statement stand, he responded: 'I had legal advice and I assumed that the legal advice was correct.'

Scott makes abundantly clear what he thinks of this episode:

> The statement which Mr Steadman made was a formal witness statement capable of being placed before the Court for the purpose of committal proceedings or of trial in a Crown Court. Its status is evidenced by the standard opening caption in the state-ment to the effect that the statement is true to the best of the witness's knowledge and belief and that he makes it knowing that, if it is tendered in evidence, he is liable to prosecution if he has wilfully stated in it anything he knows to be false or does not believe to be true. The interference by experienced lawyers with Mr Steadman's witness statement was, in all the circumstances to which I have referred, unsatisfactory. I must therefore refer to the explanations given respectively by Mr Hosker and Mr Leithead.

Scott asked Leithead why he had suggested the deletion of the sentence stating 'There was no evidence as far as I am aware to support these suspicions.' Leithead replied: 'It did not seem a sensible thing for a witness to say. As it was, of course, there must have been some evidence, if there were some suspicions.'

Scott: This is a statement of fact, is it not, by Mr Steadman?

Leithead: It is a quite inadequate statement of fact and probably not a true statement of fact . . . I pointed it out and he could then raise it with Customs who are taking a statement from him. Either the statement ought to have been expanded to make it true, or it should not have been made at all. It is precisely the sort of misleading thing one should not say in a witness statement.

Leithead justified the deletions on the grounds that they related to advice to ministers 'and therefore fell squarely within the Public Interest Immunity class'.

Scott concludes that Leithead had no knowledge of the facts

with which Steadman's witness statement was dealing. He says he does not doubt Leithead's good intentions: 'but it was, in the circumstances, dangerous for him to take it upon himself to suggest alterations to the statement'. He adds: 'The practice under which witness statements of fact are drafted or amended by officials without having before them a proof of evidence from the proposed witness and with no personal knowledge of the facts is a practice to be deprecated. This is particularly so where the witness statement (or affidavit) is to be signed (or sworn) by a junior official who might be loath to amend or reject the drafting of his seniors.'

Scott goes on to say that Steadman, as the signatory of the witness statement – which was not the first he had signed – 'cannot escape responsibility for the misleading character of part of its contents'. But he expresses some sympathy for him: 'It is a matter of regret that Mr Hosker, aware that he was advising a non-lawyer . . . did not impress on Mr Steadman the basic duty of a witness . . . to give evidence that is accurate.'

Hosker claimed later that he suggested the deletions to protect an intelligence source. In what had by now become a familiar conclusion, and, indeed, going out of his way to be fair, Scott adds: 'It was certainly not Mr Hosker's intention that this [drafting an inaccurate statement] should happen but he did not give Mr Steadman the advice that might have ensured that it did not happen.'

Steadman's witness statement also said he had 'no reason to believe' that Matrix Churchill's Cardoen and ABA contracts 'were for military projects in Iraq', which lay uncomfortably against what he had himself admitted in DTI documents only six months earlier, when he acknowledged that the contracts could indeed be for military purposes. 'Mr Steadman,' says Scott, 'had every reason to believe that the Cardoen project was a military project in Iraq.' Beston and Steadman were then asked to sign second witness statements. Steadman's said that there was 'no firm evidence' that Matrix Churchill machine tools were being used for military purposes in Iraq. Scott comments that Steadman's hesitation was well justified. Steadman, he says, 'had seen intelligence reports which left little doubt but that Matrix Churchill's machine tools were being used for military production'. He adds: 'The purpose of the new statements was to bring Mr Beston's and Mr Steadman's evidence of the extent of Government knowledge of an intended military use for the Matrix Churchill machine tools into line with the facts. The witness statements failed to do so.' They made no mention that the 30 November 1987 intelligence report had provided firm evidence; or of the letter from the Matrix Churchill employee, or of evidence that Matrix Churchill exports were intended for the Iraqi missile programme, project 1728; and they ignored the GCHQ report of 13 October 1989.

With the trial only weeks away, Alan Clark's unpredictable honesty returned to haunt the prosecution. On 2 August 1992, the *Sunday Telegraph* published an interview with him. When he was asked if it was true that he had tipped off British machine-tool manufacturers as to how they should frame their export applications to get round the guidelines for trade with Iraq, Clark replied: 'Yes, and I did it for two reasons. First, I was Minister for Trade, so it was my job to maximise exports despite guidelines which I regarded as tiresome and intrusive. Second, Iran was the enemy – it still is – and it was clear to me that the interests of the West were well served by Iran and Iraq fighting each other, the longer the better . . . '

Customs lawyers sought urgent advice. Douglas Tweddle wrote to Sir Brian Unwin saying that 'if Mr Clark confirms [the article] we will not be able to proceed with the prosecution against Matrix Churchill'. Alan Moses, the Customs QC, agreed, saying that Clark should be interviewed 'face to face'.

The task fell to Cedric Andrew. After failing to contact Clark at Saltwood Castle, his home in Kent, Andrew realized he must be at his Scottish estate.

Scott refers drily to this incident: Andrew 'had some difficulty in ascertaining Mr Clark's whereabouts'. Instead of the face-to-face interview Moses had demanded, an irritable telephone conversation took place in which Clark told Andrew that while it was difficult to recall precisely what he had said to the *Sunday Telegraph* journalist 'he could not have helped people to fill in licence application forms and it would have been quite improper to have given that advice'. Clark added: 'It is balls I would have said that.' But, according to Andrew's handwritten note of the telephone conversation, Clark did say he had told the MTTA companies 'to stress civil application' of the machine tools.

There, for the moment, the matter rested.

During the weeks leading up to the trial, Moses, accompanied by Customs officials and lawyers, visited the FCO, the MoD, the DTI, MI6 and MI5 to examine files with a bearing on the Matrix Churchill case. The extent varied to which departments were prepared to help. The Cabinet Office did not make their files available until October 1992, just days before the trial was due to start. He was not shown the stream of crucial intelligence reports that indicated Government knowledge of what the machine-tool manufacturers were up to. Neither he, nor Customs officials, saw the key GCHQ report of 13 October 1989 or the subsequent identification of Matrix Churchill in a GCHQ report of December 1989. Moses commented later: 'Since this has been identified as referring to the machines, the subject matter of the Cardoen contract, if that connection was known at the time, I do not see how the prosecution could have continued. It seems to me to show not just suspicion but knowledge of the intended use. I do not understand why this information was not brought to my attention.' He told the Inquiry that if he had known about the GCHQ report he 'would not have gone on with the prosecution'.

Neither was Moses shown the notes of Alan Clark's meeting with John Major on 3 December 1990. The intelligence report of 30 November 1987, which, says Scott, 'started the whole Matrix Churchill saga', was not disclosed at the trial until after the cross-examination of 'John Balsom', Henderson's MI6 handler.

Scott cites fifteen further documents that Whitehall did not consider relevant to the trial. They included minutes and reports relating to suspicions that Matrix Churchill was involved in Iraqi nuclear research, and a series of intelligence reports linking Matrix Churchill to Iraqi arms factories and to Iraq's arms procurement network in Britain.

Moses told the Inquiry: 'The cumulative effect of all this material now casts a wholly different light on the case . . . Quite apart from the fact that I was not shown documents which I should have been shown, I believe it should have been made clear to the prosecution and to me that there was, within either Government departments or [intelligence] agencies knowledge as to the use to which the exported equipment was to be be put.' Scott says: 'The firm conclusion is, in my opinion, justified that if all the relevant documents in the possession of Government departments and agencies had been made available, [Moses] would have advised against a prosecution of the Matrix Churchill defendants.'

Why were the documents overlooked? Scott describes how Whitehall departments blamed Customs for not specifying what documents they wanted, while Customs did not know which files contained relevant papers. He places the blame mainly on Customs. 'In the Matrix Churchill case,' says Scott, 'there was, in my opinion, a failure at all levels to ensure that the requests for documents that had been made to the departments and agencies had been in terms suitable to encompass not simply the prosecution case but also the lines of the expected defence.' Yet there was no deliberate attempt in Whitehall, he says, to withhold documents that had been identified as relevant.

However, Whitehall and the prosecution lawyers made certain that as many documents as possible of those identified as relevant to the case should be covered by Public Interest Immunity (PII) certificates – claims made by ministers to a trial judge that the information contained in the documents should not be disclosed. Later, when he was forced to defend the use of PII certificates, Sir Nicholas Lyell, the Attorney-General, repeatedly cited a 1992 case, *Makanjuola* v. *Commissioner of Police*. There Lord Justice Bingham (now Lord Chief Justice) had stated: 'Public interest immunity is not a trump card vouchsafed to certain privileged players to play when and as they wish. It is an exclusionary rule, imposed on parties in certain circumstances, even where it is to their disadvantage in the litigation.' But he added: 'This does not mean that in any case where a party holds a document in a class prima facie immune he is bound to persist in an assertion of immunity even where it is held that, on any weighing of the public interest, in withholding the document against the public interest in disclosure for the purpose of furthering the administration of justice, there is a clear balance in favour of the latter.' Nevertheless, Bingham continued, 'it does, I think, mean: (1) that public interest immunity cannot in any ordinary sense be waived, since, although one can waive rights, one cannot waive duties; (2) that, where a litigant holds documents in a class prima facie immune, he should (save perhaps in a very exceptional case) assert that the documents are

immune and decline to disclose them, since the ultimate judge of
where the balance of public interest lies is not him but the court.'
He added: 'This is not to say that circumstances may not arise in
the course of a trial which may lead a judge properly to rule that
a document previously immune in the public interest should in the
public interest be disclosed. Even the name of an informer may be
revealed if it is necessary to establish a prisoner's innocence . . . But
such occasions will be exceptional . . .'

Classes of documents regarded in the past as being covered by
PII have included not only information obtained by the security
and intelligence agencies, but also such broad areas as
communications between Government departments, and civil
servants' advice to ministers. Bingham, as Lyell was constantly
to remind both the Inquiry and Parliament, dwelt on the duty to
claim PII. Though Bingham did mention exceptional cases, Lyell
insisted that Matrix Churchill was not such a case. Scott notes
that *Makanjuola* was a civil case, and comments: 'Until the
Matrix Churchill case and the Ordtec case [see chapter 12],
there had been virtually no criminal cases in which PII class
claims [i.e. claims covering whole categories of documents
regardless of the actual information they contained], as opposed
to contents claims, had been made.'

First, though, an argument erupted in Whitehall over DTI
documents which had been passed to MI5. Government
lawyers, including Hosker and Leithead, insisted that they
should be sent back to the DTI since, in Leithead's words, 'it is
likely to be easier to prevent the disclosure of these documents if
they are in the hands of the DTI [than] it would be if the
documents are in the hands of the Customs & Excise as
prosecutors who have to obey the Attorney-General's guidelines'.
Asked at the Inquiry, 'Was not in fact the aim here that you and
Mr Hosker were trying . . . to make it harder for the defendants
to obtain the documents?', Leithead replied: 'Yes.' It was an
attitude, says Scott, 'that is very difficult to justify'. (Leithead
subsequently told the Inquiry that he should have replied, 'No'
to the question.) Scott also quotes from a telling exchange with
Leithead during the public hearing of the Inquiry where Leithead
asserted: 'In practice, when one is dealing with PII claims, one
tends to take a rather sort of generous view . . . generous to the
Government departments. Anything that involves advice to

ministers or documents preparatory to such advice is considered
to be within the class.' He added: 'It is regarded as damaging to
the public interest that any of this process [i.e. the process of
advice to ministers and decision-making] should be exposed . . .'

Scott: Is this approach bred of a desire for convenient
administration? You said it would be very difficult to work it on
any other basis.

Leithead: I think so, yes.

Scott: Is that really the wellspring of the approach and
practice that you have been telling me about?

Leithead: Yes, I think so.

The extent to which Whitehall wanted to claim PII is reflected
in minutes written by Coolican and Meadway at the DTI.
Coolican remarked that it was 'tempting' to claim PII on a
document which referred to a letter sent to Sir Geoffrey Howe,
the Foreign Secretary, in January 1988 by an anonymous Matrix
Churchill employee, which had warned that the company was
supplying Iraq with machine tools to make weapons. The letter
was distributed throughout Whitehall but ignored. Coolican,
however, said he was worried about proposing a PII claim on the
letter: 'the possibility that the information in it may well appear
across the front of the tabloid press during the course of court
proceedings, makes me somewhat diffident about suggesting it
[a PII claim]'.

Meadway's minute noted that the class of documents covered
by PII could be as wide as to cover papers relating to the
'discussion and formulation of policy advice', which would be
wider 'than advice given by officials to ministers in a narrow
sense would imply'.

Scott comments: 'These two minutes illustrate the approach
to PII that, in the understanding of two senior DTI officials, was
being proposed. There is not a word in either minute about
damage to important national interests that disclosure of the
documents might produce.'

A draft PII certificate drawn up for Peter Lilley, then trade and
industry secretary, for the committal hearings referred to sixteen
documents relating to 'meetings, discussions, and deliberations'
within Whitehall. They included evidence of the Government's,
notably Waldegrave's, knowledge that Matrix Churchill machine
tools were being used in Iraq to make arms. The prosecution,

including Moses, claimed that the documents should not be disclosed since they were not relevant to the prosecution case that the machine tools were 'specially designed' to make weapons. Scott describes that view as 'quite unreal'. Defence lawyers, he says, would have given their 'eye teeth' for them.

MI6 and Customs lawyers persuaded the prosecution that any reference to the sixteen documents should be removed from Lilley's PII certificate to prevent the trial judge and defence lawyers being alerted to their existence. Lilley later told the Inquiry that he was 'puzzled' about the way ministers were asked to sign PII certificates. Scott says, 'It was not his view that the sixteen documents, or any of them, would, if disclosed to the defence, have caused serious damage to the national interest.'

A draft PII certificate for Kenneth Baker, then Home Secretary, was drawn up in equally broad terms: he was responsible for both MI5 and MI6 as the latter had not then been 'avowed' by Government as officially existing. Scott notes that when Wally Hammond, the Home Office chief legal adviser, briefed Baker about the case, he did not tell Baker that Henderson had been an MI6 informer, and that the defence was expected to argue that the Government had been well aware of the intended use of the machine tools.

Scott points to two features of Baker's PII certificate: 'First, the certificate would, unless the [trial] judge ruled otherwise, have barred Mr Henderson from giving evidence describing the information he had given to the intelligence agencies. Second, the certificate would . . . have barred the prosecution from adducing evidence dealing with Mr Henderson's communications within the intelligence agencies.'

In June 1992, Henderson's defence lawyers – Geoffrey Robertson, QC, his junior, Ken Macdonald, with Kevin Robinson of the Sheffield-based solicitors Irwin Mitchell – repeated their request to Whitehall for documents, including minutes of the Interdepartmental Committee (IDC) which had been set up to monitor exports to Iran and Iraq. Customs claimed that 'no formal minutes were kept' by the IDC. This was not true. Scott describes the response as 'unsatisfactory'.

In response to the request from Henderson's lawyers for records relating to his contacts with MI6, Customs said: 'It is not conceded that any or all of the material . . . is relevant.'

Scott comments: 'The relevance of this material was, in my opinion, beyond dispute.' In response to their request for a report prepared by 'Martin Ford' – the MI5 contact of Mark Gutteridge, Henderson's former Matrix Churchill colleague – the prosecution said: 'So far as is known no such report was prepared or exists.' Scott remarks: 'The answer would, to anyone who knew all the facts, appear disingenuous. There were at least two sets of material which . . . matched, in substance, the description given in the request . . .' Scott says that 'the leading candidate for possible disclosure was the intelligence report of 30 November 1987, the starting point for the whole Matrix Churchill saga.' The importance and relevance of that report, he says, 'should have been beyond doubt'. He also discloses that an MI6 weekly digest of intelligence, sent to Thatcher in March 1988 – and initialled by her, confirming that she had seen it – had been based on the 30 November 1987 report. 'Whatever the reason,' says Scott, 'the relevant extract of the report was not disclosed at the Matrix Churchill trial,' and he describes the prosecution's reply to Henderson's lawyers as 'highly unsatisfactory'.

Whitehall appeared preoccupied in the summer and autumn of 1992 with drawing up PII certificates for successive ministers to sign for the trial which opened in October 1992. By now Kenneth Clarke had taken over from Kenneth Baker as Home Secretary. While Baker's PII certificate, signed for the committal hearings, would have barred Henderson's MI6 contact's evidence as being 'likely to cause serious and unquantifiable damage to the functions of the security and intelligence services', Clarke adopted a different wording, saying in his certificate that he was happy for the MI6 agent to give evidence – albeit strictly limited to giving the prosecution case. 'The incongruity' between the two certificates, says Scott, 'seems to have occurred to nobody.'

Moreover, the witness statement of Henderson's MI6 controller had already been disclosed to the defendants – without the authority of the Home Secretary. That was not all. An MI5 agent – Gutteridge's contact – signed a witness statement, and gave evidence at the trial, without the authority of any minister. This flew in the face of the *Makanjuola* judgment, quoted as a tablet of stone by Sir Nicholas Lyell, which ruled that such evidence should never be disclosed, and certainly not without a ministerial PII claim having been first put to the trial judge. Clarke told the Inquiry that he was simply 'exercising his discretion' – a discretion that Lyell, quoting Bingham, said he did not have. Scott comments: 'Mr Clarke's justification and explanation are, in my opinion, inconsistent with the proposition that it is not open to ministers, when considering material that falls within a class qualifying for PII protection, to authorise the disclosure of material . . .' It was a matter to which Scott was to return.

There was a further point. If Clarke's PII certificate had been upheld by the trial judge, any attempt by Henderson's lawyers, through cross-examination, to elicit evidence from his MI6 contact, about how the Government knew that Iraq was using Matrix Churchill equipment to make weapons, would also have been banned. The MI6 agent could give evidence, but only on the Government's terms. The issue, says Scott, places another question mark against the use of PII certificates: 'If the prosecution can, without requiring the blessing of a minister or a judge, introduce evidence that falls within a recognised PII class – i.e. intelligence agency operations – the so-called "duty" of a minister to claim PII and his inability in a suitable case to waive PII looks, as between the prosecution and defence, very one sided.' In other words, one rule for the prosecution, another for the defence. And, as Scott points out, Clarke's approach conflicted with the assertions made by Lyell on PII and his interpretation of the *Makanjuola* case.

Tristan Garel-Jones, Waldegrave's successor as FCO minister of state, also signed a PII certificate, in place of the Foreign Secretary, Douglas Hurd, who was abroad. He was given the certificate and accompanying papers on 3 September 1992 and told by officials that he had to sign it by the following morning. As a result, as Scott points out, he 'had to sit up into the small hours reading the papers, a time-scale about which he was understandably aggrieved'. Garel-Jones was not told of the likely lines of defence. (And neither Garel-Jones nor Douglas Hurd was told about Henderson's links with MI6. Both said they should have been.) But that did not influence Garel-Jones's willingness to sign his extraordinarily wide certificate. He told the Inquiry: 'You can pick out any document and say: "How does that damage national security?" That is not my point. My point is that every single one of these is part of the process of giving advice and implementing policy . . . in my view, all that is confidential.' His certificate claimed that the release of *any* information about the security and intelligence services would lead to 'unquantifiable damage'. That phrase, he told the Inquiry, covered damage that was both 'unquantifiably large' and 'unquantifiably small'. He said: 'It could be a mixture of both. I mean there could be some information where the damage would be unquantifiably large and may be leading to someone's death, and another instance where the damage could be unquantifiably small.'

'Minuscule, in other words?' asked Scott.

'Yes,' replied Garel-Jones.

Scott describes the former FCO minister's argument as 'risible'.

Malcolm Rifkind, then defence secretary, also signed a PII certificate. It, too, covered a wide range of key documents, including civil servants' advice to ministers recommending the refusal of Matrix Churchill ELAs on the grounds that they would be in breach of the Government's own export guidelines.

Rifkind signed his PII certificate after Jonathan Aitken, then Minister for Defence Procurement, had baulked at doing so. Aitken told Rifkind: 'I raised questions about the blanket nature of the immunities but was assured that in effect a minister's duty to sign was absolute . . . This was said to be the Attorney-General's advice. I fretted about this requirement, asking my private secretary at one stage, "Am I just a postman, then?"' Aitken said also that he wanted to distance himself from the prosecution because of a possible connection that might have been made between Matrix Churchill and his directorship of BMARC, a subsidiary of Astra, for merchant banking reasons. He said: 'I thought that this indirect connection could be attacked either by defence barristers or by journalists if it came to light as a result of my signing the papers.' Rifkind, a QC like Kenneth Clarke, had no qualms about signing a PII certificate.

Michael Heseltine, however, did have qualms, despite having been told by Meadway that he could not waive PII. Faced with Heseltine's reluctance to sign a PII certificate, Meadway told his minister: 'We have been careful hitherto . . . to avoid appearing to discourage Customs from proceeding with the case; the danger is that we would be accused of doing so to avoid political or administrative embarrassment.' Meadway's minute was dated 2 September 1992.

The following day it was read by Peter Smith, Heseltine's private secretary. In a handwritten note on the first page of Meadway's submission, Smith wrote: 'This is potentially troublesome. In the short term it appears that we have no choice but to claim [PII] immunity. But if it comes to court the press will have a field day.' It was another prophetic warning.

Heseltine, meanwhile, read the advice given to his predecessor, Peter Lilley, the previous year by Michael Coolican. It proved an illuminating exercise. Against the sentence 'the case against the defendants is not that the goods were used for manufacturing military equipment, but that the defendants lied as to whether the machines were "specially designed" to manufacture munitions', Heseltine wrote, 'Why not?' In his oral evidence to the Inquiry Heseltine explained: 'If the real crime was the export of this equipment, why were they not prosecuted for that as opposed to just the fact that they filled in a form inaccurately?' Against the passage, 'The case for the prosecution is a good one and it is the right one, but unfortunately the more closely it is argued and the more it focuses upon the fact that the individuals are being prosecuted simply for lying, the more it may appear for the uninformed reader that the Government did not and does not care that Matrix were selling equipment for manufacturing weapons of war, only that lies were told while in the process of so doing,' Heseltine placed two question marks. He told the Inquiry: 'This was exactly the point which had made me put the, "Why not?", five lines above, because that was exactly what people would say.'

Against a sentence referring to the contact between MI6 and Paul Henderson, Heseltine placed a line and question mark. He explained: 'This was telling me . . . that the security services at that time were in touch with Matrix Churchill. If they were in touch with Matrix Churchill and we were prosecuting them for lying about forms and not for the manufacture, at this time, I began to be preoccupied that we knew more than the superficialities of the submission would indicate.'

Heseltine placed three lines in three places, and five in

another, against a passage describing how, following a story in the press about the involvement of machine-tool companies in supplying equipment to Iraq, a Matrix Churchill employee had written to Sir Geoffrey Howe at the FCO telling him that the company was making tools for Iraq to make weapons. Against the sentence saying that the employee's letter was sent to the MoD, the export licensing branch of the DTI, and the security services, Heseltine marked two sets of three lines. 'It told me that everybody knew,' he told the Inquiry later.

As for the final sentence, which warned him that the employee may write to the press, Heseltine told the Inquiry: 'This attracted five lines, and the reason it attracted five lines is because it became apparent to me that, if this series of events unfolded at any stage, I would have to go and try to indulge in the process of – what is the word? – incommunicative answers, to which the document referred, and I was not prepared to do that.' He went on: 'So that was where we were when I first read this submission. I said: "Up with this I will not put."'

Heseltine called a meeting of his officials to discuss the issue, on the evening of 3 September, at which he said he was not willing to sign the PII certificate. He explained to the Inquiry: 'It could not be right to suggest [the evidence in the documents covered by PII] was not relevant to the defence.' In a note of the meeting, Philip Bovey, a DTI lawyer, recalled: 'I indicated that I did not expect the President [Heseltine, as President of the Board of Trade] to wish to sign a certificate. Counsel and the other lawyers said that it was his duty and pressed hard for me to so advise him.' Bovey added that, after being warned that the trial judge would order the disclosure of the documents despite the PII certificates, Heseltine said: 'It would look as though he [Heseltine] had been engaged in an attempted cover-up and had been overruled by the judge.'

Bovey suggested that the PII certificate could be rewritten to make it more palatable. On 4 September, Juliet Wheldon, a lawyer in the Attorney-General's office, told Sir Nicholas Lyell: 'I gather [Heseltine] is unhappy about the Customs prosecution and does not want to be a party to the suppression of documents which are helpful to the defendants.' Three days later, Lyell wrote to Heseltine: 'It would be quite wrong for you to make assertions which you believe to be untrue. As I understand it, however, you accept that the documents covered by the certificate fall into two recognised classes normally immune from discovery and moreover that it is in principle contrary to the public interest to disclose these classes of document in litigation.' Lyell attached passages from the *Makanjuola* judgment, though he also admitted he had not read the documents relating to the Matrix Churchill case, which, as Scott points out, he had still not read when he gave evidence to the Inquiry in late March 1994. He gave Heseltine a redrafted PII certificate. It contained the words: 'In making this certificate I emphasise that my concern is only with the question whether the documents to which I have referred fall within classes of documents which are prima facie immune from production. Whether in fact all or part of any individual document or documents should be disclosed is a matter for the court . . . The ultimate judge of where the balance of public interest lies is not the person asserting the immunity, but the court.' This last phrase, Heseltine told the Inquiry, was 'the clinching part as far as I was concerned'. On 11 September 1992, Heseltine wrote to Lyell saying: 'I am glad that a way has been found of reconciling the fact that I am under a legal duty which I cannot waive to claim immunity from disclosure of certain documents on grounds of public interest with the fact that, in my view, at least some of them ought to be disclosed in the public interest.'

Scott drives home the point that Heseltine was not told that, if he took the view that the case for disclosure to the defence was 'a clear one' (a reference to 'exceptional cases' in the *Makanjuola* judgment), he could have agreed to disclose the documents and refused to sign a PII certificate. Scott also notes that the documents covered by the certificate Heseltine eventually signed included the text of the revised guidelines secretly approved by ministers in 1988.

Official papers subsequently given to the Inquiry provide another insight into why Whitehall was so determined to get Heseltine to sign a PII certificate: his refusal to do so would have undermined the stand taken by other ministers and Whitehall departments. On 10 September 1992, Lyell met Moses to discuss how to handle the Matrix Churchill prosecution. Asked by Scott whether Lyell raised Heseltine's concerns at the meeting, Moses replied: 'No.'

In a damning indictment Scott concludes: '(i) that Mr Moses was not made aware of Mr Heseltine's opinion that the DTI documents ought to be disclosed to the defendants; (ii) that Mr Moses was not expressly asked by the Attorney-General about the contents of the documents . . . whether in the light of all the material available to the prosecution the continuance of the prosecution was fair.'

As we have seen, Moses was kept in the dark about key documents until after the trial was under way. Had he been aware of their existence he would have advised that the prosecution be dropped. Scott records Moses' frustration before the trial: 'Mr Moses asked repeatedly to be supplied with copies of the flagged documents.' A Customs note, dated 29 September 1992, refers to Moses 'crawling up the wall' at his lack of adequate instructions.

The PII Certificates: Summary

Scott first makes the point that while Kenneth Clarke had said he had discretion to authorize evidence by a prosecution witness, when asked if he had the same authority when it came to evidence needed by the defence, Clarke had said he did not know enough about the defence to be able to do so.

Heseltine had been told he had no choice but to sign a PII certificate. He had not been told of the 'exceptional case' ruling in the *Makanjuola* judgment. Scott says: 'If he had known he had discretion to authorise disclosure of DTI documents if he considered there to be a clear case in the interests of justice for such disclosure, he would have exercised it. If he had done so, however, he would have deprived of credibility the comparable PII claims being made by Mr Garel-Jones and Mr Rifkind.'

Lilley, Garel-Jones and Rifkind had different views about the type and extent of documents that should be protected by PII. Guidance given to the ministers, says Scott, was 'self-evidently insufficient to enable them to come to a consistent view about the scope of the class of documents they were protecting'.

The instructions given to Moses for hearings about PII with the trial judge, Judge Smedley, were designed to 'avoid the disclosure of the documents covered by the various Public Interest Immunity Certificates'. Scott notes that Moses' brief made no mention of Heseltine's view that DTI documents should have been disclosed to the defence.

In the event, Moses told Smedley that Heseltine's view was no different from that of other ministers – this despite Lyell's written assurance to Heseltine, more than a month before the trial opened, that the drafting of his PII certificate was 'unusual and the judge and defendants will be alert to its limited scope, which can if necessary be emphasised by counsel for the Crown orally'. It also sits uneasily with the Attorney-General's statement in the Commons on 25 April 1994, around the time he gave evidence to the Scott Inquiry, that 'the special nature' of Heseltine's PII claim was 'expressly drawn to the attention of the judge by counsel – it leapt from the page'. Scott remarks: 'Neither the brief to Mr Moses nor Mr Moses' submissions to the Judge on the PII issues were consistent with the views of Mr Heseltine, on whose behalf, along with others, the brief had been delivered and the submissions were made. In his oral evidence, Mr Heseltine underlined this point on a number of occasions, saying that, although he had understood that the Judge would be made aware of his views, the submissions made by Mr Moses did not satisfy the assurance given to him [Mr Heseltine] by the Attorney-General's letter of 7 September . . .' Moses did not know that Heseltine had been assured that at least some of the key DTI documents should be disclosed to the defence. 'Nor,' says Scott, 'did he know that Mr Heseltine held the view that no rational person who had looked at the files could have said that the documents should not be disclosed.' Moses told Juliet Wheldon after the trial: 'I did not understand and neither did the Judge that the other ministers were taking a different stance to that taken explicitly by Mr Heseltine.' Moses said that no one had suggested to him that his prepared statement to the court about PII – where he did not mention Heseltine's concerns – did not properly reflect Heseltine's position.

A copy of Moses' brief had been faxed to Leithead at the Treasury Solicitor's department. Leithead had also seen a copy of Heseltine's letter to Lyell. Scott says that Leithead 'knew, therefore, that it was Mr Heseltine's view that "at least some of [the documents] ought to be disclosed in the public interest".' And Leithead was not alone. DTI officials failed to pass on

Heseltine's concerns to the prosecution lawyers, and Philip Bovey, the DTI lawyer, told the Inquiry that Heseltine 'was not entitled' to put to the court his view that the documents ought to be disclosed. To that Scott retorts,

> This argument illuminates the absurdity of the notion that a minister who believes justice requires documents to be disclosed is nonetheless obliged to recommend to the Court that they be not disclosed. I have no hesitation in rejecting it. If a minister believes documents ought to be disclosed, he is entitled to say so and should say so. If he is uncertain whether or not the public interest requires them to be withheld from disclosure, he should share his uncertainty with the Court. Mr Bovey's argument overlooks the fact that judges who adjudicate on PII claims rely on the ministers making the claims to make known to the Court their concern, or their lack of it, that the documents should be withheld from disclosure.

A Treasury Solicitor's note, which related to the brief that was to be given to Moses, said in part: 'Mr Moses should be instructed to use such arguments as are available in respect of each document to persuade the Judge that they are of minimal relevance to the issues in the case . . . We know relatively little about the detail of the case and Mr Moses is in a far better position than we are to decide what arguments to employ.' Of this Scott says: 'There was, in my opinion, no justification, at least as far as Mr Heseltine and the DTI were concerned' for saying this. 'The proposed instructions to Mr Moses were inconsistent with the views of Mr Heseltine.'

Andrew Leithead told the Inquiry that because Heseltine could not have made a properly informed decision as to whether disclosure was in the overall public interest without being informed in detail of the views of prosecuting counsel, the reasons for those views and the details of the case, it would have been inappropriate for him to instruct Moses not to argue against the disclosure of DTI documents. Scott says:

> I reject this contention . . . There is no warrant in principle or in authority for the ministerial emasculation that underlies the argument. A minister is . . . entitled to have views on disclosure, and, if he does, is not only entitled but ought to inform the court of them. [And] if lawyers are drafting a brief to counsel on behalf of a department, it is, to my mind, an unacceptable presumption

for them to include instructions which are contrary to the known views of the ministerial head of the department.

Scott notes that Lyell accepted in evidence to the Inquiry that the brief to Moses was 'inadequate'. Lyell conceded that Moses 'was entitled to fuller instructions'. In damning criticism of Lyell, which was seized on by the opposition after his Report was published, Scott says:

> Major responsibility for the inadequacy of the instructions to Mr Moses must, in my opinion, be borne by the Attorney-General. In his evidence to the Inquiry, the Attorney-General drew a distinction between his constitutional responsibility and his personal responsibility. He said this: 'I am a Minister of the Crown. The Treasury Solicitor's Department is one of the four departments that fall under my responsibility and therefore I have ministerial responsibility for them. I accept that I have overall ministerial responsibility. If one comes to the detailed handling of individual matters, whilst, as I say, I am responsible in that constitutional sense and would not dream of seeking to evade that in the slightest, if one is going to the nitty gritty, I would not accept . . . anybody in my small team, to start jumping in and . . . "second-guessing".'

Lyell, says Scott, should have taken steps to see that the brief to Moses adequately reflected Heseltine's concerns. Scott accepts what he calls 'the genuineness' of Lyell's belief that 'he was personally, as opposed to constitutionally, blameless for the inadequacy of the instructions sent to Moses'. But he adds:

> I do not accept that he was not personally at fault. The issues that had been raised by Mr Heseltine's stand on the PII Certificate did not fall into the category of mundane, routine, run-of-the-mill issues that could properly be left to be dealt with by officials in the Treasury Solicitor's Department without the Attorney General's supervision. Mr Heseltine had taken his stand, not as a result of any legal analysis which he was not equipped to make, but as a result of an apprehension that justice might not be done if the documents were withheld from the defendants.
>
> Such an apprehension on the part of a senior minister, charged, as is the Government as a whole, with the taking of decisions regarding the maintenance of national security and the promotion of the public interest, raised very serious issues, constitutional and legal, as to the role of PII Certificates in criminal cases. If the responsible Minister does not regard the withholding of the

documents to the defence as being in the public interest, what is the function of the PII Certificate that he has, so it is said, a duty to sign? Is it proper for counsel to inform the Judge that the Minister believes the documents should be disclosed to the defence? What is the position if another Minister believes that his department's documents, not distinguishable in character, should not be disclosed to the defence? This point highlights the absurdity of Lyell's expectation that Moses could tell the trial judge that three of the PII certificates had to be upheld, but that Heseltine's certificate wasn't worth the paper it was written on.

Scott adds,

> These are difficult questions. The answers are not obvious, either in principle or on authority. I would not have expected Mr Heseltine, a non-lawyer, to have articulated them. But I would have expected the Attorney-General to have done so. I would have expected him to recognise that important constitutional and legal issues were raised by Mr Heseltine's stand and to have ensured that Mr Moses, whose responsibility was to place the issues fairly before the Court, was adequately instructed so that he could discharge that responsibility. So far as the preparation of Mr Moses' brief and the instructions to Mr Moses were concerned, there was, in my opinion, an absence of the personal involvement by the Attorney-General that Mr Heseltine's stance and its implications had made necessary.

11 · Economical with the *Actualité*

'If we had known then all we know now, I believe that the
Matrix Churchill prosecution would not have been brought.'
Valerie Strachan, chair of Customs and Excise

At the beginning of the Matrix Churchill trial Alan Moses told
the judge that he, and his junior counsel, had read the documents covered by the PII certificates. 'We do not consider . . .
they assist the defence in relation to any foreseeable issue,' he
said. He read out the terms of the certificates to the judge and
then asked the judge to read them for himself.

Scott notes that the judge made no comment on the difference
in wording between Heseltine's certificate and the others. He also
says that Moses' claim that the Whitehall documents relating to
policy-making were not relevant was 'fundamentally unsound'.
their value to the defence in preparing to cross-examine
Government officials and ministers on the issue of Government
knowledge and their attitude to the export to Iraq of machine
tools intended to make weapons was 'so obvious as to be hardly
worth stating'.

The documents were of value to the defence 'in seeking to
establish the true nature of the Government attitude to the
machine-tool exports . . . it was Mr Moses' failure to recognise
the value to the defence of documents that fell short of patently
demonstrating innocence that was, in my view, the flaw in his
approach'.

Among the documents Moses asked Judge Smedley to
read were many that ministers who had signed PII certificates
had never seen. This was further proof, Scott says, of the
extent to which Government lawyers treated a minister's role
as 'merely a mechanical one'. Smedley overturned the PII
claims on documents about general policy-making in Whitehall

but upheld those covering MI5 and MI6 files.

Then, on 6 October 1992 – the jury had still not been called – Geoffrey Robertson, QC, Paul Henderson's counsel, disclosed that his client's defence would include 'evidence that the security and intelligence services – the agents of the Government in this matter – were supplied by Paul Henderson himself . . . with information about all the Matrix Churchill dealings with Iraq, including details of the true nature of the Cardoen and ABA contracts'. Furthermore, said Robertson, Henderson believed that the information he (and Mark Gutteridge, Henderson's former colleague) had supplied to the intelligence agencies had been passed on to the DTI and to ministers.

At this point, says Scott, Moses made 'an important inter-jection'. Moses said: 'My Lord, might I interrupt . . . If the case be that either Mr Gutteridge or Mr Henderson told the security services . . . It could not be right to go on if that may be the case . . . ' Moses added that 'in light of what has been said by Mr Robertson today, we can well see . . . how the balance tips clearly in favour of the defence seeing the records of those meetings [between Henderson and Gutteridge] and their security and intelligence agency contacts'.

At this, the trial judge overturned his earlier ruling and said that all relevant MI5 and MI6 documents, as well as documents held by Whitehall departments referring to their contacts with the security and intelligence agencies, should be disclosed to the defence. The DTI and the MoD accepted his ruling without demur, raising the question as to what all the fuss had been about in the first place. The FCO, however, was less relaxed. Anthony Aust, one of its legal advisers, told his colleagues: 'We need to identify any documents which we could in no circum-stances agree to disclose. Such documents would have to be of EXTREME SENSITIVITY since the penalty for non-disclosure may be that the prosecution would have to be abandoned.' He warned Douglas Hogg, Garel-Jones's successor as FCO minister of state, that a refusal to go along with the judge's ruling would lead to the dropping of the prosecution and 'might be seen as covering up the embarrassment of an FCO Minister'. Hogg replied: 'Despite the fact that the disclosure of these documents will almost certainly cause embarrassment to the FCO and to the Government as a whole . . . it would be prudent at this stage for the Crown to persist with the prosecution.' He added: 'The prospect of embarrassment to ministers is not a good or sufficient reason for withholding the documents and thus sinking the prosecution.'

Hogg was referring here to the possibility that the Attorney-General, on the advice of ministers, would drop the prosecution rather than have further embarrassing documents released to the court. (In the event, crucial intelligence documents were still withheld and only emerged after the trial had started. Moses said later that if he had seen these before the trial began, he would have advised dropping the prosecution.)

Scott comments that the reaction of Whitehall departments at this point in the proceedings contrasted 'very strongly with the assertions in the PII certificates that it was "necessary for the functioning of the public service that the documents should be withheld from production" or that disclosure of evidence about MI5 and MI6 would "substantially impair the work of the security and intelligence services in protecting the United Kingdom and its allies from threats from hostile foreign powers"'. He adds: 'The sensible pragmatic reactions of the departments to the Judge's PII rulings go a long way, in my opinion, to deprive of credibility the basis on which the certificates had asserted the PII class claims' in the first place.

The defence lawyers asked for the disclosure of more documents, including Cabinet Office and 10 Downing Street papers. At the FCO, Aust again expressed concern that the prosecution might have to be dropped and that ministers might have to sign fresh PII certificates. Hogg commented that, like Heseltine, he would be reluctant to sign one, which prompted Scott to compare Hogg's approach with the different attitude of his predecessor, Garel-Jones.

On 8 October 1992, Customs told the Cabinet Office to look for papers concerning: 'a. Government policies on exports to Iraq; b. Policy towards the export of machine tools; c. Matrix Churchill in particular'. This involved searching the files of the Joint Intelligence Committee in the Cabinet Office. The following day, Moses, accompanied by Gibson Grenfell, his junior counsel, and Peter Wiltshire from Customs, were presented with what he later described as 'a vast array of documents', which he and his colleagues 'attempted to sort out'.

Moses explained: 'We were shown into Sir Robin Butler's room . . . There was a very big conference table . . . The table was covered with those files. There was a far table on the right with a box of individual documents, some of which were Cabinet minutes. There was nobody else there. We were just left to get on with it. I was furious. The big mistake I made – this is important. I should have walked out and made it abundantly plain these were not the circumstances, as it was the last day before the trial was due to start, for me to look at anything sensibly; but I did not . . . Nobody has any doubt that that was not a proper opportunity to look at documents.'

Scott, who describes Moses' comments as 'entirely understandable', notes that the documents flagged as relevant did not include the minutes of John Major's meeting with Alan Clark on 3 December 1990 – following newspaper allegations about Clark's conference in 1988 with machine-tool companies – which was among the files in Butler's private office. Asked why they had not been made available, Butler later told the Inquiry: 'I have no knowledge at all about what papers are necessarily admissible in legal proceedings. That is a matter for the prosecution and defence.' That, comments Scott, was 'beside the point'. Sir Robin had known for some time' that what was said at that meeting would be an important issue in the prosecution. Nearly a year later, in November 1991, Butler expressly told Major in a note that what had been in Clark's mind at the meeting with the MTTA companies was 'central to the case'.

At the Cabinet Office, Moses flagged sixteen documents for potential disclosure. Customs lawyers fobbed off a request by Henderson's counsel to see them. Pauline Neville-Jones, a senior Cabinet Office official, told Butler that asking the defence for 'further clarification' about what papers they wanted to see 'should buy a day or two'. The Customs lawyers' response made no mention of the sixteen documents – conduct, says Scott, that did not 'measure up to the standards to be expected of a prosecuting authority'. He adds: 'The trial was in progress. Potentially relevant documents had been identified by Moses. At the least the defendants should have been told that documents had been identified . . . '

The documents at issue included intelligence briefings for Waldegrave, minutes of the Cabinet committee meeting to discuss a further relaxation of export controls to Iraq, chaired by Douglas Hurd on 19 July 1990 – less than two weeks before Saddam Hussein invaded Kuwait – and papers titled 'Trade with Iraq'. Judge Smedley rejected a request from Henderson's lawyers to order Moses to search once again through Cabinet Office and also Downing Street files. Yet it was clear, Scott says, that in making the ruling the judge did not know about the sixteen documents already identified by Moses. He comments: 'I do not understand how Mr Moses could have allowed the judge to proceed under such a misapprehension.' He adds: 'The defence was kept in ignorance of the fact that their request for Cabinet Office documents had led to a search . . . ' But what he calls 'the saga of discovery' did not end there. On 29 October 1992, when the trial was well under way, a copy of the crucial 30 November 1987 MI6 report was shown for the first time to Moses and subsequently to the defence.

Meanwhile, solicitors representing Trevor Abraham, one of the three Matrix Churchill defendants, requested evidence from William Waldegrave, Douglas Hurd and the former FCO minister David Mellor. Andrew Leithead replied that Waldegrave had no first-hand knowledge of Matrix Churchill's ELAs and that any evidence he would give 'would be inadmissible as hearsay'. That assertion, says Scott, is 'difficult to follow . . . Mr Waldegrave's evidence of the discussions, meetings and correspondence that led to the grant of export licences to Matrix Churchill would have been first hand, not hearsay.' Leithead subsequently told the Inquiry that 'with hindsight' he should have appreciated the defence interest in Waldegrave's evidence and that he had 'never intended' to say that it would have been inadmissible.

In Moses' opening speech to the jury the prosecution's case identified the defendants' crime as having given false information in order to obtain an export licence – 'pretending that items are for civilian use when in truth they are specially designed for military use', as Moses put it. Scott remarks that the case of deception did not need to involve 'special design'. If Moses had simply said: 'Pretending that items are for civilian use when in truth they are for military use', the case would have been no weaker and much easier to understand. This was not a semantic point: the prosecution asserted that the Matrix

Churchill machine tools were 'specially designed' and therefore should have been placed under the Military List in the export regulations, which required a much stricter regime of supervision and scrutiny, not the Industrial List. But machine tools had always been considered dual-use equipment and, as such, placed on the Industrial List. Scott notes: 'Mr Henderson, certainly, was confused. He had never heard of "specially designed" machine tools. He knew the Matrix Churchill machine tools to be standard, off-the-shelf items.'

The MTTA exporters who had attended the meeting with Alan Clark in January 1988 were not concerned that the export of dual-use equipment *per se* might be prohibited. They were concerned that their ELAs might be revoked because the Government believed they were to be used for military production.

Eric Beston, a senior DTI official and key prosecution witness, told the court that he 'was not aware that there was conclusive evidence' that the company's equipment was to be used for military purposes. That evidence, says Scott, 'was not consistent' with the 30 November 1987 intelligence report, which Beston had seen. In 1991 Beston had himself told his DTI colleagues: 'Cross-examination could prove tricky. In the earlier period [1987/8] departments were aware that machines . . . were destined for munitions manufacture . . . ' He had also told government lawyers: 'I intend to do my best to avoid causing . . . embarrassment.' Scott comments: 'It is difficult to avoid the suspicion that Mr Beston's evidence . . . was designed to avoid giving what he may have thought would be a damaging admission, namely, that Government had been aware at the time the Cardoen licences and ABA licence were granted that previous Matrix Churchill machine-tool exports had gone to munitions factories to be used in producing munitions.'

In contrast to his evidence at the trial, Beston admitted at the Inquiry that he was 'quite aware that the intelligence showed that [the 1987/8 machine-tool orders from Iraq] were going to manufacture munitions'. He said of the trial: 'I fully accept that I got myself into quite a tangle about the difference between intention and actual use . . . I quite simply misled myself on what I thought the situation was.'

Scott points out that Beston had chaired a meeting in June

1989 where MI6 had reported that Matrix Churchill machine tools were intended for project 1728, an Iraqi missile programme. In evidence at the trial Beston said he could not 'recall' that information. Scott says in his Report: 'I have reached the conclusion that Mr Beston's evidence given at the trial as to the state of Government knowledge of the use for military purposes of Matrix Churchill machine tools licensed for export to Iraq was not frank evidence but was overly conditioned by a desire to avoid answers that might prove embarrassing to senior officials and ministers of his department.'

Scott notes that after he was shown a draft of the Report with this conclusion, Beston denied any intention of giving evidence that was not frank. Scott makes no comment.

Among the array of witnesses, none attracted so much media attention in a trial largely ignored by journalists as Mr T, Henderson's MI6 contact, known to him as 'John Balsom'. This was the name the agent had given to the gate attendant – to whom he described himself as a DTI official – during his visits to Henderson at the Matrix Churchill plant in 1989 and 1990. He told the court that while Henderson had given him information and drawings about the ABA project, he had not disclosed that Matrix Churchill was directly involved – which was just what the prosecution wanted to hear.

Mr T was cross-examined by Geoffrey Robertson, QC, for Henderson, who asked him if he accepted that Henderson had taken personal risks in providing MI6 with information about his trips to Iraq. Mr T replied: 'Absolutely. Mr Henderson was a very, very, brave man. There are few people I have met who would take such risks and take them so much in their stride, with all the pressures on him.'

The prosecution was horrified. Moses was desperately worried about the effect this would have on the jury. The next day, 4 November 1992, Sir Brian Unwin, Customs chairman, wrote a stiff letter to Sir Colin McColl, chief of MI6. 'We were extremely surprised, to say the least,' he thundered, 'at the nature of the testimonial that your officer gave to Henderson.' He complained that MI6 had never told Customs about the extent of its involvement with Henderson, a complaint which, Scott says, was 'unwarranted': Customs investigators had known since October 1990 that Henderson had been an MI6 agent. He adds: 'The value of the information provided by Mr Henderson is quite beside the point. The point is that Mr Henderson had, over a period, obtained and supplied information to MI6 at "great personal risk". That Mr Henderson had been at great personal risk should have been blindingly obvious to Customs and to anyone else who considered the matter.' The fate of Farzad Bazoft had 'demonstrated the fact'.

McColl rejected Unwin's complaints in a forthright letter. He referred to the known 'Iraqi ruthlessness in dealing with spies . . . Whilst I can quite see why this [Mr T's testimony] was less than welcome to prosecuting counsel, I myself see no cause for criticism where a witness speaks sincerely and impartially on such a matter.' Scott comments: 'I am in full agreement with Sir Colin's remarks . . . The need for the Matrix Churchill prosecution to be successful ranked higher in importance with Sir Brian Unwin than the need for Mr T to give fair and balanced evidence in his answers in cross-examination.'

But it was Alan Clark's evidence about his January 1988 meeting with MTTA companies that led Moses to advise Customs that the prosecution could not continue. Robertson asked Clark in cross-examination: 'You knew the Iraqis would not be using the current orders for general engineering purposes but would be using them to make munitions?' to which Clark replied: 'The current orders, yes.'

Robertson: If you had said, of course the Iraqis will be using the current order for general engineering purposes that could not be the case to your knowledge?

Clark: I do not see that the fact that they are using them, were using them, for munitions, excludes them using them for general engineering purposes more than the other way round.

Robertson: But here the writer of this minute [i.e. the DTI note of the MTTA meeting] is attributing to you a statement that the Iraqis will be using the current order for general engineering purposes, which cannot be correct to your knowledge.

Clark: Well, it's our old friend being economical, isn't it?

Robertson: With the truth?

Clark: With the *actualité*. There was nothing misleading or dishonest to make a formal or introductory comment that the Iraqis would be using the current orders for general engineering purposes. All I didn't say was 'and for making munitions . . . '

Clark then said it was a matter of 'Whitehall cosmetics' to keep the records of the meeting ambiguous. He had agreed that the companies would help by 'keeping quiet, stating nothing military'. He did not think the companies needed his advice.

Robertson: But they got it?

Clark: Not quite, in so many words, I do not think I said 'nothing military'.

Robertson: They got it by implication?

Clark: Yes, by implication is different. By implication they got it.

At the end of Clark's evidence on Thursday 5 November 1992, Moses asked the trial judge for an adjournment until the following Monday. He told Unwin: 'The evidence of Mr Clark read as a whole leads to the conclusion that those present at the [MTTA] meeting were being advised that they need not make frank and full disclosure as to the use to which the machines were to be put. Once that is the position, on the evidence, it seems to me wrong to continue to ask the jury to convict . . . ' Moses, according to Scott, 'then commented on some of the factors that had in his view contributed to the débâcle'. Moses said that 'One of the problems in this case was the total lack of any sensible investigation or inquiry by the DTI as to the precise nature and detail of the equipment the exporters were going to supply.' He described the DTI's system for checking export licences as 'porous'. Scott adds that Moses also admitted to Unwin that 'he had already received an intimation that the judge would stop the proceedings himself at the end of the prosecution's case, in the light of the evidence heard so far'. Nevertheless, in his final statement to the court, as Scott puts it, Moses 'tied the decision to abandon the prosecution firmly to the evidence that had been given by Mr Clark', a conclusion that Scott rejects.

Unwin reported the collapse of the trial to Sir Robin Butler. One of the problems, he said, was 'the equivocation of DTI, FCO, and MoD in relation to the policy on the enforcement of sanctions'. For Scott, one of the problems was the state of the law, which was then based, and still is, on the 1939 Emergency Powers Act, whose provisions were determined not by strict application of a specific law but by Government policy on exports 'open to shifts and changes depending on the flow of international relations in general and on the state of the UK's relations with the country in question in particular'. Scott adds:

> In the post [Iran–Iraq] war ceasefire, August 1988 to August 1990, Government policy on lethal weapons was clear enough. But what was Government policy on dual-use machine tools? What was Government policy on machine tools intended for the manufacture of conventional munitions? A prosecution policy directed to the enforcement of Government policy on the supply of machine tools to Iraq was bound, in my opinion, to run into difficulties.

Matrix Churchill: A Post-mortem

Scott says he does not subscribe 'to the simplistic view that all that went wrong was that Mr Alan Clark gave evidence which was in certain respects inconsistent with his witness statement and was fatal to the prosecution'. His conclusions as to why the case collapsed are embarrassing not only for Customs. They challenge the Government's central claim that little had gone wrong in the entire arms-to-Iraq affair other than Clark behaving like a loose cannon.

In Scott's view, the Customs investigation was 'inadequate' from start to finish. Their interview with Clark was 'neither rigorous nor searching'. Protests by Matrix Churchill executives that Clark had encouraged them to sell arms-related equipment to Iraq were never taken seriously, despite his reputation for 'plain and sometimes idiosyncratic speaking'. Investigation of the anticipated 'Government knowledge' defence was inadequate. Scott places responsibility for 'the inadequate investigation and search for documents' on the 'whole prosecution team'. The investigation was also inadequate, he says, because no attempt was made to interview any of the FCO or MoD ministers and officials who had been involved in the export-licensing decisions. Customs investigators, says Scott, were 'led into a trap created by the apparent strength of the evidence of deception that they had obtained'. And the prosecution's concentration on the 'special design' point distracted attention from the kernel of its case, 'namely the false statements made to the DTI for the purpose of obtaining the export licences'.

And there was the Government's attitude to disclosure of documents. Throughout Whitehall, says Scott, the attitude was 'consistently grudging', although on this score he absolves MI5 and MI6 from blame. 'Resistance to any documents being provided to the defence, although their disclosure of the contents would do no damage to national security interests', he says, had not been an attitude adopted by the security and intelligence agencies.

Scott runs through a list of cases, all civil (one, the 1991 Osman extradition case, was a habeas corpus application) that the Government and prosecution had cited to support its case that PII certificates needed to cover a wide range of documents, including any relating to discussions between Whitehall departments and civil servants' advice to ministers. Both Lyell and Leithead had insisted in evidence that it was the legal 'duty' of ministers to sign PII class claims covering wide categories of documents regardless of their contents. The Government, for example, had seized on Lord Reid's judgment in *Conway* v. *Rimmer*, a 1968 civil case where the law lord had said that the disclosure of 'policy' documents 'would create or fan ill-informed or captious public or political criticism' .

Scott also returned to the 1992 *Makanjuola* judgment in which Lord Justice Bingham dwelt on the 'duty' point. Bingham had conceded that there were 'exceptional' cases where PII need not be claimed if the documents were obviously relevant to the case and to the defence. Scott makes the point that Bingham's judgment had been made in the context of someone – in this case a police commissioner – who claimed that disclosure would be damaging to the public interest. But what if a minister did not believe this, as in the case of Heseltine? 'If a minister does not believe that disclosure to the defendant of the documents in question would be damaging to the public interest, how can it possibly be said that he is under a duty to claim PII for the documents?' Scott asks. Referring to Bingham's dictum that while people can waive rights they cannot waive duties, Scott responds: 'To decline to claim PII in circumstances where the minister does not believe that disclosure to the defendant would be damaging to the public interest is not a waiver of a duty . . . there is nothing to waive.'

Scott concludes:

The proposition that a minister is ever under a legal duty to claim PII in order to protect documents from disclosure to the defence notwithstanding that in the minister's view the public interest requires their disclosure to the defence is, in my opinion, based on a fundamental misconception of the principles of PII law. To the extent that the proposition is sought to be supported by reference to Lord Justice Bingham's judgment in *Makanjuola*, it is based, in my opinion, on a misreading of that judgment.

He also draws attention to the inconsistent way in which the Government had applied PII even according to its own criteria. In practice, ministers frequently decided which documents should be kept secret and which disclosed – to Parliamentary committees, for example, to journalists, to the Inquiry itself. Scott describes the 1985 Ponting official secrets case as an 'excellent example' in which a minister disclosed highly sensitive documents in a trial without any sanction by the judge: the MoD had been prepared to disclose a whole range of Whitehall documents 'which, in the Matrix Churchill case, produced a knee jerk reaction for a PII class claim to be made'.

In the Ponting case, the Government had volunteered to the defence and the jury unexpurgated intelligence material – the so-called Crown Jewels, relating to the sinking of the Argentine cruiser the *General Belgrano* during the Falklands War. 'The Ponting case,' says Scott, 'seems to me to illustrate the point that, in the context of litigation and outside it, ministers are well able in appropriate circumstances to conclude that government documents of a confidential character ought, in the broader public interest, to be disclosed to a particular recipient.'

In the Matrix Churchill case, the trial judge initially supported Kenneth Clarke's PII claims covering MI5 and MI6 documents. He overruled them only after Robertson, Henderson's counsel, disclosed his proposed defence. Yet it subsequently became clear that MI5's and MI6's own legal adviser, David Bickford, was quite happy to disclose the documents, provided that particularly sensitive and irrelevant contents were blacked out. Scott says: 'If the interests of the intelligence and security services do not require the protection of PII class claims, what possible justification can there be for PII class claims to protect documents [dealing with official advice to ministers]?' His conclusion is, again, damning: 'Mr Bickford's evidence underlines the point that the Matrix Churchill class claims were unnecessary for the protection of any legitimate public interest.' PII class claims, he says, were 'not warranted by authority and . . . ought to have had no place in a criminal trial'. He adds that Michael Heseltine's reluctance to sign a PII certificate showed 'an instinct for the requirements of justice that was fully justified' and, moreover, corresponded to legal principles. But Scott also refers to suggestions in the media that the ministers who signed PII certificates 'were seeking to deprive defendants in a criminal trial of the means by which to clear themselves of the charges'. These suggestions, he says, 'were not fair and in any case did not apply to Heseltine'. He adds: 'In relation to a legal issue of some complexity the ministers were entitled to rely on advice from their lawyers and cannot be blamed for following it.'

12 • Dunk and Co.

'I confess to innocent reluctance to connive at impeding the course of justice!'
       Patrick Nixon, FCO official

BSA Tools

Matrix Churchill was not the only machine-tool company charged with trying to evade regulations controlling exports to Iraq. In September 1991, Keith Bailey, chief executive of BSA Tools, based in Birmingham, was accused by Customs of selling goods to Iraq that were 'specially designed' to make weapons – the same charge that had been laid against the Matrix Churchill directors. But, Scott says, 'the complaint against Mr Bailey ought to have been that he failed to state that his goods were intended to be used for military purposes, not that he failed to state that they were specially designed for military purposes. There was no reason to suppose that Mr Bailey, any more than the DTI officials . . . would have regarded standard lathes as "specially designed".' (Some were used for car parts.) In one respect, the BSA prosecution was more cynical than the Matrix Churchill prosecution. In the latter case, the charges had related to licences that postdated the November 1987 MI6 intelligence report, which revealed the military destination of machine-tool exports. But the export for which Bailey was due to stand trial had been mentioned specifically in the MI6 report.

BSA's export licences were granted in January 1988 after the DTI had been told by ministers to approve them to protect an intelligence source. As Scott puts it: 'The incongruity of a prosecution being brought, on the ground of an unlawful export of machinery intended for use in the production of shells, where Government had consented to the export going ahead notwithstanding knowledge of that intended use, is striking.'

There was no alternative to dropping the prosecution of Bailey after the collapse of the Matrix case. But Scott emphasizes that Alan Clark's evidence in the Matrix Churchill trial was of 'minimal importance' in the decision. He adds: 'The emergence from its unmerited obscurity of the 30 November 1987 report was the definitive event.'

Euromac

On 12 June 1991, Ali Daghir and Jeanine Speckman, managing director and export executive of Euromac, a wholly owned Iraqi trading company based in Britain, were convicted of conspiracy to export to Iraq forty electrical capacitors – devices that store and release energy in high-voltage bursts – as Scott puts it, 'alleged to be specially designed for use in a nuclear warhead'. Their arrest had followed an elaborate undercover operation by US Customs after an American company received an inquiry in 1988 about capacitors which, it was suspected, were to be used in a nuclear device.

In March 1990 the capacitors arrived at Heathrow airport *en route* to Iraq. Daghir, Speckman and others were arrested and Euromac's offices in Thames Ditton, Surrey, searched.

After consulting the Atomic Weapons Establishment at Aldermaston, Barry Fletcher, an MoD scientist, reported that the uses to which the capacitors could be put were 'purely military'. He repeated the claim in a witness statement for the trial. The DTI said that if Euromac had applied for a licence to export the capacitors, it would have been refused. US officials and the chief executive of CSI Technologies, the Californian firm that had made the capacitors, insisted that the equipment was specially designed for nuclear weapons. This was to be the central theme of the prosecution case, part of which was held in camera, made by Alan Moses, the QC Customs later instructed in the Matrix case.

However, as Scott points out, the trial judge 'directed the jury that it was open to them to convict if they found the capacitors were specially designed for ANY military use'. Daghir was sentenced to five years in prison, Speckman to eighteen months. They subsequently appealed, and in May 1994 the Government suffered fresh embarrassment over the arms-to-Iraq affair when the Court of Appeal quashed the convictions. Lord Taylor, the Lord Chief Justice, ruled that the trial judge had misdirected the jury. He noted that Tony Tilford, managing director of Presto Flash, a Norwich-based high-speed photography firm, had said in evidence at the trial that the capacitors could be used in flash units for photographing explosives ballistics – 'the evidence served to rebut the prosecution's specific case that the capacitors were designed for nuclear weapons'. (Tilford said later that he had subsequently bought CSI capacitors with the same specifications as those in the Euromac case. 'They were supplied to me without hesitation,' he said, raising the question why action was taken against Euromac.)

Evidence at the trial revealed how, in the course of a nineteen-month operation, a US Customs secret agent, Dan Supnick, a recorder strapped to his back, tempted a reluctant Daghir to buy the high-grade capacitors, and discussed how they could disguise the end-user. In the space of two months Supnick made more than thirty unsolicited telephone calls to Euromac's offices. Scott says that the evidence available to Customs of an apparent attempt to smuggle the capacitors to Iraq justified a prosecution. He does not mention that the secret operation was run by United States Customs with the personal backing of the then Prime Minister, Margaret Thatcher. A US Customs document revealed that Operation Quarry – the code-name given to the undercover operation – was 'brokered' by CSI with the co-operation of British Customs and Excise and British intelligence. It adds: 'The British prime minister was advised of the status of this investigation and is very much interested in its progress and successful outcome.' The document is dated 4 August 1989, before the US-inspired operation got under way in Britain and seven months before Daghir and Speckman were arrested. After the arrests Thatcher wrote to congratulate British Customs. She did not refer to her involvement in the case when she gave evidence to the Scott Inquiry. Nor was she asked.

The Dunk Case

On Friday 18 February 1983, a shipment of two hundred Sterling sub-machine-guns was seized by Customs at Tilbury

Docks, London. The shipment was supported by export documents, including an end-user certificate signed by a senior officer in the Jordanian Army, which suggested that the destination of the guns was Jordan. However, Customs investigators reported that they 'had information to suggest that the goods were in fact destined for . . . Iraq'. Nearly three years later, in November 1985, Reginald Dunk, director of Atlantic Commercial, an arms-dealing firm, and a colleague, Alexander Schlesinger, pleaded guilty to evading export controls and were fined a total of £28,000.

Startling new evidence, which emerged at the Scott Inquiry, prompted Dunk to appeal. Scott notes that Dunk's lawyer had been told by the Iraqi embassy in London that the guns were a gift from Iraq to Jordan and the Sudan. The defence told the prosecution before the trial that it intended to call staff at the Iraqi and Jordanian embassies in London as witnesses. But when it tried to take statements from the staff, it was told that the ambassadors had withdrawn permission for them to do so. Senior Customs investigators and FCO officials had approached the two embassies to persuade them not to give evidence on behalf of the defence. In the course of the machinations in the FCO, Patrick Nixon, a senior official, admitted to Carsten Pigott, a colleague: 'I confess to innocent reluctance to connive at impeding the course of justice!'

When Scott asked Sir Stephen Egerton, former head of the FCO's Middle East Department (MED) and ambassador to Saudi Arabia, if he objected to the adjective 'disgraceful' to describe the activities of FCO and Customs officials, Sir Stephen replied: 'I would say it was a bad show.' Scott says in his Report: 'Expressions such as a "bad show" . . . fall, in my opinion, a long way short of adequately describing the degree of impropriety constituted by the steps taken in 1985 by FCO officials, at the behest of Customs, to dissuade the Iraqi and Jordanian embassies from calling embassy witnesses to give evidence at the trial. For the FCO officials to have lent themselves to this interference with the course of a criminal trial was, in my opinion, thoroughly reprehensible.' The actions of Customs, he says, were 'deserving of greater censure'.

In July 1994, the Court of Appeal quashed the conviction. In an unprecedented court indictment of senior Whitehall officials,

Lord Taylor said: 'In our judgment the machinations in this case to prevent witnesses for the defence being available, coupled with the non-disclosure of what had been done, constituted such an interference with the justice process as to amount to an abuse of it.' He added that the probability that a jury would not have accepted the evidence of the embassy staff was not the point. That should have been for the court to decide.

The officials named in the judgment have all since been promoted: at the time of writing Patrick Nixon was Britain's High Commissioner to Zambia, Carsten Pigott was deputy head of mission in Ethiopia, Patrick Wogan was ambassador to Qatar and Graham Boyce was ambassador to Kuwait.

Ordtec

The case with the most similarities to that of Matrix Churchill was the prosecution of Ordtec or, to give it its full name, Ordnance Technologies Ltd. Although the trial of Ordtec directors predates the Matrix Churchill prosecution, the dénouement came after the collapse of the Matrix case. Ordtec was formed in 1988 by a number of executives from Allivane, a Scottish-based arms procurement company (see p.87). When Allivane collapsed they relocated to Reading and, crucially, took with them a contract from the ubiquitous SRC to supply a fuse assembly line for the 'Al Fao Organisation, c/o Jordanian Armed Forces'. Paul Grecian, the firm's managing director, later acknowledged that from the start neither he 'nor anyone else at Ordtec dealing with this were in any doubt about the fact that the Iraqi Government was the intended end-user'.

The contract also involved Rexon, a US company, who would supply fuse components, and Astra, who were subcontracted to supply the booster pellets – a link that was to be Ordtec's downfall. In November 1988, Grecian submitted an ELA for the assembly line. Attached was an end-user certificate signed by the Jordanian Chief of Staff, Fathi Abu-Taleb. He certified that the equipment was for 'the sole use of Jordan Armed Forces'. The application was circulated around Whitehall, and landed on Lieutenant-Colonel Richard Glazebrook's desk at the MoD. He commented: 'We note the sale is via Belgium and so would like confirmation that Jordan is the real end-user.' Asked at the Scott

Inquiry to explain his suspicions, Glazebrook replied: 'It did not make financial sense. You need one fuse for each artillery shell. Artillery shells are extremely expensive things and therefore the numbers that you use in peacetime for training are very limited ... For a small country like Jordan to set up a special production line ... did not make financial sense.' He pointed to another curious aspect of the deal: 'Jordan at that stage was a very good customer of the UK and all the major UK defence manufacturers had contacts and indeed usually representatives available in Jordan, and under normal circumstances I believe that any orders would have gone directly from the Jordanians to the UK manufacturers, cutting out the middle man and thereby reducing the price. To have it coming via a company in Belgium ... did not make sense.' But the export licence was granted and Glazebrook's concerns, as Scott put it, were 'effectively ignored'.

The following month, February 1989, the order and Allivane's previous involvement in the deal were raised at a meeting of the Restricted Enforcement Unit (REU). The REU minutes showed that Allivane was suspected of supplying arms to Iraq and Iran, through various diverter countries. Yet no attempt was made to check for any connection between Allivane and Ordtec. In October, four containers with components for the assembly line were shipped from Felixstowe to Aqaba.

Here Scott notes that the Government was first warned about Ordtec in January 1988, when the company was discussed in the REU, and was alerted to its links with Allivane by two of Allivane's executives in mid-1988. In early March 1989, seven months before the Ordtec equipment was shipped to Iraq, the US Customs service in Newark, New Jersey, received an anonymous typewritten note warning of a conspiracy to sell US technology to Iraq. Also involved, said the informant, were the Space Research Corporation, manufacturer of the Iraqi Supergun, and a company based in Reading, England, called Ordtec. 'We hope,' the note concluded, 'you can stop illegal transactions ... ' It was immediately copied and sent to Customs investigators in Britain, who ignored it.

Customs officers told the Scott Inquiry that 'at the time the anonymous information was received', the Customs investigation team was 'particularly busy'. After pointing out that the information in the note was accurate 'in a number of very important respects', Scott adds: 'All that was necessary was for the DTI to have been asked whether Ordtec had submitted any [ELAs] to cover the export of the type of equipment referred to by the source. Neither the making nor the answering of such a simple request would have taken very long. The failure, in the light of such clear information, albeit from an anonymous source, to make enquiries of the DTI or to pass on the information to those concerned with export licensing was, in my view, an unfortunate error of judgment.'

Scott then reports that in August 1989 an MI6 note, based on information provided by Henderson, referred to the original contract for a fuse assembly line agreed between SRC and the Iraqis. A second MI6 report referred to SRC's involvement with Ordtec. Scott says: 'It was not copied to anyone outside the security and intelligence agencies.'

Paul Grecian, like Paul Henderson, provided information about Iraq's war machine to the intelligence agencies. He began doing so in 1985 or 1986 through his social contacts with Detective Constable Steven Wilkinson, who in 1988 was transferred to the Metropolitan Police Special Branch. Grecian first provided information about the Iraqi Supergun in September 1989. The pattern was for Wilkinson to pass on information from Grecian to MI5 who passed it on to MI6. Grecian insisted that Wilkinson kept his identity secret. It was not until December 1989 that Grecian, who was still anonymous, met MI5 and MI6 (Mr Q was the contact) face to face at a London hotel. The previous month he had told Wilkinson that Al Fao was a weapons plant. In January, GCHQ named Ordtec as one of six companies involved in a fuse assembly line at Al Fao. 'For reasons which are not clear,' says Scott, 'it was not copied to Customs [investigation department] until 19 July 1990, i.e. after the Ordtec licences had been revoked. It was also not copied to the DTI . . . If prompt action had been taken to follow up the information contained in this report, the export of the fuse assembly line may well have been prevented.' In evidence to the Inquiry a Mr K from GCHQ admitted the agency had failed to notice that Ordtec had applied for an ELA referring to Al Fao.

By December 1989 MI6 had identified Grecian's company as Ordtec, although it did not establish Grecian's identity until

3 April 1990 when it decided – in Wilkinson's absence – to question Grecian directly about the Ordtec contract. The presence of Wilkinson – a police officer who, unlike MI5 or MI6 officers, had the authority to make arrests – would have been embarrassing: Grecian's answers in response to MI6 questions might have revealed criminal activity on his part and thus obliged Wilkinson to arrest him. 'This,' Scott notes laconically, 'was considered highly undesirable given the presence of the intelligence officers and the social relationship between Mr Grecian and Mr Wilkinson.'

The day before the 3 April 1990 meeting when it was decided to question Grecian, Astra had alerted the MoD of their suspicions as to the true destination of the booster pellets Ordtec had asked them to supply. The warning was passed on to Mr Q at MI6 and to the DTI, which immediately told Grecian that Ordtec's export licences had been revoked.

Grecian was summoned to another meeting with Mr Q in mid-May, which was also attended, but only for part of the time, by Wilkinson. Grecian was told that Ordtec's ELAs had attracted the attention of the DTI and of the press. An MI6 note of the meeting adds: 'Throughout this "off the record" conversation, it was implicit (and was eventually stated explicitly by [Grecian]) that the fuses were to have gone to Iraq. [Grecian] said that the Iraqis had been able to obtain signatures at the highest levels of the Jordanian government to support false end-user certificates.' Scott comments that despite the earlier warnings by Wilkinson and MI6 'it would be understandable if Mr Grecian had left this meeting with the impression that he would be "assisted" by the intelligence agencies in relation to any subsequent prosecution'.

On 26 June, Grecian met MI6 for the last time. In August, Mr Q recorded in an internal MI6 note that Ordtec was 'standing into danger'. Customs was after the company. He added: 'If Ordtec ends up in court [Grecian] may be persuaded to keep quiet about his connection with [Special Branch] but there is the obvious risk he would try the "working for British intelligence" ploy. Perhaps this could be turned to our advantage if he could then be put on the witness stand in the Babylon [Supergun] prosecution . . . However, his personal future might be in some doubt if ever publicly identified as the man who blew the gaff on the Iraqi Babylon project. If we were not too squeamish we might use this point to ensure silence . . . ' It was a deeply cynical note.

Peter Clarke, Grecian's counsel at the Ordtec trial, later told the Inquiry about a meeting he had had with the leading prosecution counsel, Andrew Collins, QC, who has since been promoted to the bench as a High Court judge. Clarke said: 'One assertion which I distinctly recall because of the dismay I felt was that Andrew Collins commented that if the defendant chose to exploit his connections with the security services at a trial it might be difficult to keep secret that he had also given information about a highly active terrorist organisation . . . ' Scott subsequently asked Collins to comment on Clarke's evidence. Collins explained that Grecian 'ran the risk that we would have to cross-examine him to establish that he had not given any information about Ordtec. Once the issue was raised, there was an obvious risk . . . that the fact that he had been giving information could come to the notice of people, or organisations, who did not shrink from the use of violence.'

'On 16 August 1990,' Scott says, 'Mr Grecian telephoned DC Wilkinson to ask "if [the Security Service, MI5] would be prepared to contact Customs & Excise in an effort to forestall any further investigation." He was told by DC Wilkinson that the Security Service would not be prepared to intervene in this way.' In an extraordinarily cavalier abuse of their powers, Customs VAT officers tipped off their colleagues in Investigation Division (ID) that they were about to visit Ordtec's offices as a result of a 'pre-repayment query'. The ID had already told local VAT officers of their interest in the company. David Makin, an ID officer, accompanied the VAT inspectors on their visit in July 1990 when they seized papers relating to exports and the company's contract with SRC. At the Inquiry, Scott asked Valerie Strachan, who had taken over from Unwin as chair of Customs, to explain the role Makin had performed on what was ostensibly a visit to inquire about VAT payments. Despite concern expressed in internal minutes by Customs, that the company's documents could have been inadmissible under PACE (Police and Criminal Evidence Act) rules, Strachan insisted that the 'main purpose' of the visit was the VAT issue. Scott rejects her explanation, saying that

Makin's presence amounted to 'an abuse of power'.

On 2 August 1990, Customs investigators interviewed three Ordtec executives, Paul Grecian, John Grecian and Bryan Mason. Two months later, the three men were arrested and charged with conspiracy to evade export-control regulations. Here, the Scott Report returns to familiar ground: in spite of defence pleas, Customs failed to conduct a proper trawl of Government documents and the few that were provided were dismissed by Collins as 'irrelevant' to the defendants' case. 'There were a considerable number of documents held on FCO, MoD, Security Service and SIS [MI6] files showing the extent of Government knowledge of the use of Jordan as a diversionary route to Iraq,' says Scott. The failure of Customs to identify relevant documents was 'especially surprising' since key members of the Ordtec prosecuting team – Annabelle Bolt, Andrew Biker, Peter Wiltshire and Cedric Andrew – were also involved in the parallel investigations into Matrix Churchill. And just as in the Matrix case, the prosecution passed the buck. Collins told the Inquiry that whatever inquiries should have been made 'was not a matter for me . . . What enquiries the DTI should or did make, it was a matter for the DTI.' Scott notes tartly: 'Mr Collins took no steps to discover what inquiries had in fact been made or what the result of them had been . . . Customs should have been instructed to ask the relevant departments and agencies . . . for documents showing that a "blind eye" had been turned (which, if found, might have brought the prosecution to an end).'

Collins's argument that responsibility for supplying any relevant documents was up to the DTI is 'unsustainable', says Scott. Collins was 'clearly aware' that the FCO and the MoD were also involved in making decisions on export licences. Scott adds, in an astonishing attack on a senior QC and now a fellow judge:

> Once Mr Collins had accepted instructions to lead for the prosecution, it was, in my opinion, his responsibility to satisfy himself that adequate steps had been taken by Customs to identify any documents held by Government that were relevant to the prosecution or to the defence proposed to be run, so far as that was known. In the event, adequate steps were not taken. In failing to satisfy himself that adequate inquiries had been made of the

FCO, the MoD and the agencies, Mr Collins failed, in my opinion, to discharge that responsibility.

Meanwhile, in what appeared to be an insurance policy – or, in Scott's words, 'a long stop' – Peter Lilley, then Secretary of State for Trade and Industry, and Kenneth Baker, then Home Secretary, were asked by the prosecution to sign PII certificates. Baker's certificate covered evidence Wilkinson might have given under cross-examination. Lilley's certificate covered Whitehall policy documents and papers of discussions that revealed the extent of the Government's knowledge about illegal trade diverted through Jordan to Iraq. It was closely modelled on the one he had signed for the Matrix Churchill committal. But as Scott says: 'The principal factor responsible for the inability of the defendants to obtain the relevant documents in the Ordtec prosecution was not Mr Lilley's [PII] claim; it was the inadequacy of the steps taken to identify relevant documents and, in particular, the failure to request documents from the FCO, the MoD and the intelligence agencies.'

The prosecution's refusal to disclose documents and call key DTI witnesses prompted lawyers representing Stuart Blackledge, an SRC employee who was also subsequently charged with conspiracy, to demand that the case should be abandoned. Collins strongly argued against this, telling the trial judge that he would only consider advising a stay of the prosecution if there was evidence of any suggestion that the Government had turned a 'blind eye' or knew that the end-user certificate in the Ordtec deal 'did not mean what it said'. Collins had not seen documents which suggested that this was the case. As Scott points out, the Lord Chief Justice, Lord Taylor, at Ordtec's 1995 appeal, noted, in a reference to one of the documents Whitehall had suppressed at the trial: 'The very phrase "turned a blind eye" had appeared in an [MI6] telegram of August 1990 attributed to no less a person than the British Ambassador in Amman.' Taylor said: 'We cannot say that if all the material had been before them a jury would necessarily have acquitted, but we do consider that the documents would have enabled the defendants to present an arguable case along the lines they had already indicated well before seeing the documents.'

At the trial, Judge Spence ruled against disclosure. As a result, the defendants agreed in plea bargaining to a deal whereby if they admitted guilt they would receive suspended jail sentences. Paul Grecian, Mason and Blackledge received suspended sentences of between six months and a year, and Colin Phillips, director of EC Transport, a shipping company, was fined £1,000. The charge against John Grecian was dropped. At Customs, Douglas Tweddle noted: 'This is the first of a number of cases involving the illegal exportation of amunitions-related equipment to Iraq and it was important that a successful result was achieved.'

His satisfaction was short-lived. The Court of Appeal quashed the Ordtec convictions, ruling that the 'material irregularity' of withholding documents – and subsequent pressure on the defendants to 'go quietly' – made the convictions 'unsafe and unsatisfactory'. It was clear from the documents, the appeal court judgment said, that after 1988 the Government's export guidelines 'were more relaxed and lenient towards Iraq than they had previously been'. Documents withheld at the trial but disclosed at the appeal also showed that in 1988, before the Ordtec deal had been agreed, the British ambassador in Amman had had a meeting with senior Jordanian military officers who had admitted that Jordan was 'fronting' for Iraq.

Scott also contrasts the terms of Lilley's PII certificate at the 1990 trial and the PII claims made in 1995 by Michael Howard, the Home Secretary, and Douglas Hurd, the Foreign Secretary, for the final appeal hearing. Documents which Lilley certified would be 'injurious to the public interest' were voluntarily disclosed either in their entirety or with passages blacked out. The Inquiry's public exposure of the 'knee-jerk' response to PII had obviously shamed officialdom into reform. Scott notes acidly that the Ordtec appeal PII certificates were 'in marked contrast to the PII claims made in the Matrix Churchill case and [were] plainly inconsistent with the view expressed by many witnesses to the Inquiry that there was a duty to claim PII'.

Scott does not explicitly say, but the intimation is clear, that the four defendants charged with conspiracy had themselves become the victims of a Whitehall conspiracy. He omits from his Report evidence given at the Ordtec appeal that at a private hearing at Reading Crown Court Collins had made an extra-ordinary admission: 'It was known, of course, or should have been known, that one of the ways in which material was getting to Iraq was via Jordan.' He observed: 'I think it may be fair to say that the way it was dealt with by the DTI merely reflects the fact that at that time Saddam Hussein was not the bogeyman that he is now seen to be.' This had been exactly what the defence had wanted to argue. Despite repeated assurances from ministers – who included John Major – that official guidelines preventing exports of 'any lethal equipment' to Iraq were being 'scrupulously' adhered to, the Government was secretly turning a blind eye to the sale of weapons to Saddam Hussein.

On 16 June 1993, Collins was summoned by Scott to a private session of the Inquiry. The unpublished transcript of the hearing revealed a remarkable clash of views: Scott expressed astonishment at how Collins could say that the papers he had seen – notably documents in which Glazebrook expressed serious concern about exports ostensibly destined for Jordan – were irrelevant to the defence. Collins suggested that the Government may have taken the view that what Jordan did with the arms was not its concern. He told Scott: 'We are not talking about nuclear triggers or chemical warfare or anything like that. We are talking about things which blow people up which apparently are not considered all that unpleasant.'

Shortly before Christmas 1995, Grecian flew to Johannesburg to join his fiancée, Elizabeth Powell, for a holiday. He was immediately arrested at the airport under an Interpol extradition warrant requested by the US authorities. Grecian is wanted in the US for an alleged bank fraud relating to Rexon's involvement in the Ordtec deal with Iraq. He was initially refused bail: one of the arguments used by South African magistrates to justify this was that British intelligence might whisk him away in a submarine.

Grecian insists that he was given prior assurances by senior South African police officers that it was safe for him to visit the country. There were some suggestions that South Africa was keen to co-operate with the US, as a result of a continuing dispute between the two countries over sanctions-busting during the apartheid era: the US has accused South Africa's state-owned Armscor weapons procurement agency of acquiring American arms and technology in contravention of a mandatory United Nations arms embargo. Grecian was suddenly released in May 1996 and returned to Britain.

13 • Parliament Must Decide

'A denial of information to the public denies the public the ability to make an informed judgement on the Government's record. A failure by Ministers to meet the obligations of Ministerial accountability by providing information about the activities of their departments undermines, in my opinion, the democratic process.'
Sir Richard Scott, Report, Section K, Chapter 6, paragraph 3

After 1,750 pages that bristled with disapproval at the way in which ministers denied information to Parliament and tried to withhold Government documents from defence lawyers, it comes as no surprise that the principal subjects in Scott's concluding fifty pages of recommendations are ministerial accountability and PII law. He accepts that on occasion ministers should withhold information in the public interest, but he urges that the definition of the 'public interest' should be amended to make it impossible for ministers to shelter behind it if their actions are motivated by administrative convenience or the avoidance of political embarrassment. He also questions whether the long-standing convention of denying information to Parliament about arms sales is still justifiable. There are signs of change in ministerial practice, he says, but the time is ripe for the Government to clarify its intentions and stimulate a wide-ranging public debate on the subject.

On PII law, Scott insists that in criminal trials the Government should never again make PII class claims, which attempt to withhold documents from the courts simply on the grounds of the category to which they belong (such as 'policy advice to ministers') rather than on the grounds of their specific contents. He finds it hard to accept the Government's argument that class claims are necessary because disclosure of policy documents would hinder the proper functioning of the public service or prevent candid advice being offered to ministers by officials, and he says it is 'particularly bizarre and unacceptable' that ministers should use PII class claims to deny innocuous documents to people who are trying to prove their innocence in a criminal trial.

It is high time, Scott says, that the wartime powers made permanent in the Import and Export Control Act 1990 should be replaced. A new system must make it impossible for an export control order to be made without specific assent by Parliament. He also says there should be a wide-ranging public debate about whether it is acceptable – as two former Foreign Secretaries insisted – to continue to use export controls as tools of foreign policy, thus penalizing companies that happen to be trading with countries which fall out of political favour.

His other recommendations include greater supervision by the Attorney-General of prosecutions brought by Customs and Excise, improvements in the distribution of intelligence reports to relevant departments in Whitehall, a tightening-up of export licensing procedures and Customs and Excise law and procedures, and a new set of guidelines for conducting inquiries such as his own.

Scott's chapter on ministerial accountability starts by reiterating seven examples of the 'apparent failure' of ministers to conform with the requirement in their code of practice, *Questions of Procedure for Ministers*, that they should give Parliament as full information as possible about Government policies, decisions and actions and should not deceive or mislead Parliament or the public.

The existence of the amended 1984 Howe guidelines was deliberately not disclosed, the defence aspect of export credits to Iraq was excluded from a Parliamentary answer, and 'commercial confidentiality' was given as the reason for blocking two Parliamentary questions about export credits: 'Government statements made in 1989 and 1990, both in answers to Parliamentary Questions and in letters intended for members of the public, consistently failed to disclose either the terms of the adjustment to the Guidelines that had followed the ceasefire or the decision to adopt a more liberal policy on defence sales to

Iraq.' The other three examples were 'a deliberate concealment' in 1991 from Tony Banks, MP, of the circumstances in which David Hastie, a BAe executive seconded to the MoD, attended the Baghdad Military Exhibition in 1989; an 'inadequate' response to David Caborn, MP, on Government knowledge of the military implications of British pipeline equipment destined for Iraq; and the refusal to allow two retired civil servants, Roger Harding and Robert Primrose, to give evidence to the Trade and Industry Select Committee (TISC). Scott concludes that the withholding of such information was a neglect of the duty of ministerial accountability and undermined the democratic process.

The Government's response in July 1995 to the first Report of the Nolan Committee on Standards in Public Life said that it accepted the recommendation that 'Ministers must not mislead Parliament'. But Annex A of the Government's response contained an amendment to *Questions of Procedure for Ministers*, which read: 'Ministers must not knowingly mislead Parliament . . .' In a Commons debate on the report, Roger Freeman, the public service minister, said that when information was withheld in the public interest, the public interest would be determined 'in accordance with established Parliamentary convention, the law and any relevant Government Code of Practice'. The insertion of 'knowingly' does not, says Scott, make any difference to the substance of the obligation on ministers: it must always have been the case that ignorance of the facts was not regarded as breach, although questions might arise about why a minister was ignorant. And it has always been accepted that some information, such as imminent changes to interest or exchange rates, should be withheld. But 'the withholding of information by an accountable minister should never be based on reasons of convenience or for the avoidance of political embarrassment . . . The interpretation of "in the public interest" in the new formulation should, in my opinion, adopt that approach.'

Established ministerial convention on withholding information includes refusal to give details of arms sales. But, says Scott, a proposal that led to a 1991 United Nations decision to set up a register of sales of seven types of weapons systems to foreign countries had come from John Major: 'So presumably, there will now be an abandonment of the bar on arms sales Parliamentary Questions and defence Ministers will be prepared to answer such Questions, at least to the extent of supplying the information required to be entered on the Arms Register.' The Register, he adds, destroys the rationale for withholding details of arms sales not covered by the Register, and the time has now come for a comprehensive review of this area of policy: 'Is it any longer satisfactory that Parliament and the British public are not entitled to be told to which countries and in what quantities goods such as artillery shells, land mines and cluster bombs have been licensed for export?'

It is clear, Scott adds, from the Government's response to the Nolan Committee that ministers intend to continue to withhold information about arms sales on a 'public interest' basis: 'Would it be said that, because a purchaser of arms or defence-related equipment from the United Kingdom would be displeased if the sale became public knowledge (and as a consequence might place elsewhere future orders), it "would not be in the public interest" for the British public to be informed of the sale? Past experience suggests that that might well be the Government response.' He calls for public debate and further Government clarification of its intentions.

Finally, he looks at the distinction between ministerial 'accountability' and ministerial 'responsibility', which was made in evidence to the Inquiry by Sir Robin Butler, the Cabinet Secretary. Butler said that while ministers could not evade accountability, they could not be held responsible amid the complexities of modern government for departmental failures in which they had no personal involvement. Scott says he finds it hard to disagree, but adds: 'If ministers are to be excused blame and personal criticism on the basis of the absence of personal knowledge or involvement, the corollary ought to be an acceptance of the obligation to be forthcoming with information about the incident in question. Otherwise Parliament (and the public) will not be in a position to judge whether the absence of personal knowledge and involvement is fairly claimed or to judge on whom the responsibility for what has occurred ought to be placed.'

Scott's views on PII, an area of the law which is entirely judge-made, begin with the assertion that there is no need for a specific statute on the subject to be enacted by Parliament. A sensible, practical guide, which any minister could follow, had been given, he says, in a 1994 House of Lords speech by Lord Woolf during judgment in a civil case, *ex parte Wiley*. Lord Woolf said:

> If a document is not relevant and material it need not be disclosed and public interest immunity will not arise. In the case of doubt as to relevance and materiality the directions of the court can be obtained before trial . . . If a document is relevant and material then it must be disclosed unless a breach of confidentiality will cause harm to the public interest which outweighs the harm to the interests of justice caused by non-disclosure.
>
> It has been said that the holder of a confidential document for which public interest immunity may be claimed is under a duty to assert the claim, leaving the court to decide if the claim is well founded. For my part I consider that when a document is known to be relevant and material, the holder of the document should voluntarily disclose it unless he is satisfied that disclosure will cause substantial harm. If the holder is in doubt he may refer the matter to the court. If the holder decides that a document should not be disclosed then that decision can be upheld or set aside by the judge. A rubber stamp approach to public interest immunity by the holder of a document is neither necessary nor appropriate.

The Government was accused in the Matrix Churchill case of having adopted the latter approach.

Scott then considers documents which have obvious potential to help the defence in a criminal trial, asserting that the interests of a defendant can never be subordinate to the greater public interest:

> The balance must always come down in favour of disclosure if there is any real possibility that the withholding of the document may cause or contribute to a miscarriage of justice. The public interest factors underlying the PII claim cannot ever have a weight sufficient to outweigh that possibility . . . In criminal trials, once it has been decided that a document might be of assistance to the defence, that should be the end of the PII claim. If that is so, then there is no real balance to be struck.

Where documents are concerned whose potential to help the defence is not immediately obvious, Scott concedes that there is a balance to be struck. If there is no real risk of injustice, documents could be withheld in the public interest; but they should be withheld because of the sensitivity of their specific contents, not because of the class to which they belong. 'Moreover, experience suggests that if PII class claims are sanctioned, Whitehall departments will inevitably seek to bring within the recognised classes an increasing range of documents. I do not believe that the instinctive Whitehall reaction to seek to withhold Government documents from public inspection is likely to change.'

Scott makes ten points summarizing what he considers to be the correct approach. He begins by saying that documents do not have to be disclosed unless they are relevant under a broad definition established in case law. PII class claims should no longer be made, and claims on a contents basis should not be made where it is obvious that the documents might help the defence. Where the help to the defendant is not obvious, the minister or person making a PII claim on a contents basis must believe that disclosure would cause 'substantial harm'. No claim should be made if the minister thinks that the documents, despite their sensitivity, should be disclosed in the public interest. Judges ruling on PII claims should decide if the documents are material and might help the defence, in which case they should not be withheld: 'There is no true balance to be struck. The weight of public interest factors underlying the PII claim is immaterial.' But existing authority is ambiguous, he says, and it would be important for a judge who decided to withhold a document to indicate whether this was because he considered it would not help the defence or because he thought it would help the defence, but the protection of the public interest by non-disclosure was more important. 'The latter conclusion would, in my view, be wrong in principle and contrary to authority.'

Scott's last two guiding points on PII are that defendants should specify their lines of defence to help determine whether a particular document might assist their case, and that a judge may allow the retention of documents that do not appear to be helpful to the defence.

In the Matrix Churchill case the prosecuting barrister, Alan Moses, QC, represented Government departments in a hearing to decide whether or not PII claims should be upheld. Scott says this put Moses in an ambiguous position because the departments, not the prosecution, should make their case over PII. He recommends that in future any similar situation should be avoided.

PII certificates in the Matrix Churchill and Ordtec cases described the documents they covered in very general terms, Scott says, and future certificates should give more detail, including the date, author and function of the documents. This would give the defence an informed basis for opposing their retention by the Government.

In the Matrix Churchill and Ordtec prosecutions, Customs failed to obtain highly relevant documents from other Government departments. Scott says that documents relevant to the defence case as well as the prosecution's should be asked for, that records should be kept of applications for documents, and that those records should be supplied to the defence. A list of documents obtained should be made and supplied to the defence, and the defence should be told if any details are withheld from it on the grounds of public interest or national security. By the time his Report was published, Scott says, new legislation in this field was before Parliament.

Of the Government's powers to control exports, adopted just before the Second World War, Scott calls for a comprehensive review leading to a speedy replacement of the present system, which allows the Government to impose whatever controls it wants for whatever purposes. If a new system of controls allowed subordinate legislation (ministers simply making orders), this should be subject to affirmative resolution in Parliament, which would allow an order to take immediate effect but to lapse after a given period, unless one or both Houses of Parliament considers and votes in favour of the order.

The 1939 Act, amended to become the 1990 Act, has, he points out, allowed a situation to develop where export restrictions have frequently been imposed for foreign policy reasons – for example, when Iran pronounced a *fatwa* on the author Salman Rushdie or when Iraq executed the *Observer* journalist Farzad Bazoft. 'Is it appropriate for the Government to be able to exercise such a power for foreign policy reasons? Why should the exporters of goods which happened to be export licensable at the time have had to suffer the burden of potentially serious and damaging interference with their businesses in order to enable the Government to provide a presentational response to the public outrage that was undoubtedly felt over the *fatwa* and the execution?'

Scott feels that there would be broad agreement that the purposes of export controls should include complying with treaties, protecting the armed forces, preventing terrorism, and combating human rights abuses, serious crime and aggression by foreign countries. In evidence to the Inquiry the Government argued that export controls were also a legitimate foreign policy tool in a wider sense, in that they were available to pressure other governments into changing their ideology. The Confederation of British Industry (CBI), however, argued that foreign policy should play a part in export controls only if national security is involved. Scott calls for a wide-ranging public debate on the issue, and on the question of continuing the strategy of curbing high-technology exports to former Eastern bloc or certain developing countries: 'This is an issue which, in the end, Parliament, not the executive, should decide.'

Most witnesses at the Scott Inquiry agreed that legally prescribed procedures should be adopted for ELAs, instead of the present *ad hoc* methods. Scott suggests an application form requiring a statement of the potential uses of the goods as well as the actual use intended by the recipient. (The absence of a statement of potential use in the case of the Matrix Churchill and other exports was one source of the difficulties the Inquiry tried to unravel.) Scott also calls for the Government to take steps to shed the 'unsatisfactory and . . . quite unnecessary fiction' that export licence decisions are always made by the DTI – which was partly responsible, he says, for the inadequate disclosure of FCO and MoD documents in the Matrix Churchill and Ordtec trials, and for the failure of Customs investigators in those cases to interview officials or ministers in those departments that had played a crucial part in making decisions. 'In respect of weapons and goods licensable under the Military List, the licensing authority ought, logically, to be the MoD, not the DTI,' he writes.

Turning to the role of Customs and Excise in policing and prosecuting export control offences, Scott concludes that this is an anomaly, but stops short of saying the job should be taken over by the police and Crown Prosecution Service. Instead, he says, the Attorney-General should superintend Customs export control prosecutions in the same way that he does prosecutions by the Crown Prosecution Service and the Serious Fraud Office. There should be regular reports from Customs lawyers to the Attorney-General on cases involving novelty, difficulty, interest or sensitivity, and he would become answerable in Parliament for the conduct of Customs prosecutions. (The Government accepted these proposals in June 1996.)

During the Inquiry, Scott found several cases in which the Customs Solicitor's Office was not sufficiently independent of the Investigation Division (ID) – for example, when important legal decisions on the Matrix Churchill and other cases were taken by the ID with little or no reference to the Solicitor's Office. He argues that the process of interviewing or re-interviewing witnesses, and locating relevant Government documents after a prosecution has begun, should be directed by lawyers, which had not happened in the Matrix Churchill and Ordtec affairs. He recommends that the Solicitor's Office should accept 'positive responsibility' for directing the ID in the gathering of evidence and documents, and that the ID should 'accept the discipline' of referring the conduct of pending prosecutions to the Solicitor's Office.

It was obvious from evidence to the Inquiry, Scott says, that Government departments were not receiving intelligence reports relevant to their work. He recommends that each 'departmental customer for intelligence' should review its requirement regularly and take up instances where it does not receive copies of reports it needs. There should also be a system of recording and retrieving intelligence in the sections dealing with export licences so that newcomers are not left ignorant of important earlier information. FCO officials should adopt a clear system, in writing, to make sure that their versions of intelligence infor-mation are accurate: 'It should not be possible for submissions to ministers from government departments to attribute to intelligence agencies views or opinions which the relevant agency does not hold and subsequently repudiates. Nor should it be possible for there to be a dispute, not capable of being resolved by reference to written records, as to whether a confirmation of the accuracy of the reference had been given by the agency.'

Scott's recommendations also cover the rules for inquiries,

perhaps because of the way in which his own Inquiry was challenged and scrutinized. Those conducting inquiries, he says, have to take account of the six cardinal principles laid down by the 1966 Salmon Commission. But the principles 'carry strong overtones of ordinary adversarial litigation', he argues, and most inquiries are inquisitorial: there are no litigants, there is no 'case' to promote, and the adversarial procedures of British civil and criminal litigation are not necessarily appropriate. Scott is most concerned about principles four and six. Principle four, which says that people giving evidence to an inquiry should have the opportunity of stating their own case at the hearing and answering questions from their own lawyer, would need 'some adjustment to be suitable for most inquisitorial inquiries. In particular, a requirement that an opening statement or supplemental evidence should be elicited in question and answer mode, by the witness's solicitor or counsel is, in my opinion, likely in most cases to lead to an unnecessary waste of time and money.' Principle six says that witnesses' lawyers should be allowed to cross-examine anyone giving evidence which may affect their clients, but Scott 'unhesitatingly' rejects a blanket right to cross-examination and recommends that it should be decided on a pragmatic basis, case by case. Cross-examination might be allowed if it was the only way to guarantee fairness, but other methods should also be sought: sending copies of adverse evidence to those affected, for example, and inviting written or oral responses.

Scott warns against hampering inquiries by the 'indiscriminate adoption' of the Salmon Principles, and puts forward five alternatives: (i) adequate notice should be given to witnesses about the subjects on which they will be questioned; (ii) damaging allegations by other witnesses should be drawn to the attention of those affected so that they can respond; care should be taken to avoid irrelevant damaging allegations, which should not be published if they come in written form; (iii) draft criticisms should be sent for comment or additional evidence to those criticized before the criticism is finalized; (iv) witnesses should have legal help when they give evidence and respond to criticisms; and (v) adversarial procedures, such as examination-in-chief, cross-examination and re-examination, should not be used unless fairness makes it necessary. He adds that if the subject of an inquiry is the performance of public officials, oral hearings should be open to the public. He also says that the Statutory Declarations Act 1935 should be amended to allow applications to the Lord Chancellor or Attorney-General for evidence at *ad hoc* non-statutory inquiries such as his to be given under oath: 'I would have made an application to enable me to take evidence on oath.'

By the time the Report was published, the Government had taken action on some of the more obvious or technical recommendations set out by Scott. The question was, how much ground was it prepared to give over the weighty political and legal issues of ministerial accountability and PII? It was fairly clear in advance to most observers that the answer was 'as little as possible'. But the precise extent of concessions in the short term depended crucially on how much pressure the opposition parties and the handful of Tory rebels could bring to bear now that the Report was out.

14 • All Things to All Men

'If this affair is to pass without correction and without
investigation and if we are to have so little control or interest
in what Ministers and mandarins do in our name, the rights of
Parliament will count for nothing. Certainly if we continue to
talk of our honour, anyone still listening to us will rightly start
counting his spoons.'
> Jim Cousins, Labour MP for Newcastle upon Tyne
> Central, House of Commons, 26 February 1996

When Ian Lang stood up in the House of Commons at 3.40 p.m.
on Thursday 15 February 1996 to talk about the Scott Report, it
quickly became clear that the Government had decided on a
strategy of simplification, aggression and no surrender. The
team of ministers, civil servants and spin doctors who had been
working on the Report for eight days had cherry-picked the
phrases and sentences that suited the Government's line, and had
put together a brief that mentioned only in passing the great
mass of critical material produced by Scott. It was not ministers
who should be apologizing to the Commons, Lang declared, but
opposition members who had spent the last four years attacking
their integrity. The bottom line was that William Waldegrave
and Sir Nicholas Lyell, the two ministers most at risk from
Scott's criticisms, were staying put on their padded chairs in
their departments. It was an audacious strategy, built along the
lines of 'Labour's tax bombshell' and 'Labour's double
whammy' – two campaigning slogans that stretched the facts but
helped the Tories to victory at the 1992 general election – the
guiding principles of which were: stick to your soundbites and
get your retaliation in first.

Earlier that day, the Cabinet had met for a full briefing on the
approach Lang was to take. By now any fainthearts, who had
argued that the way to survive Scott was to throw a couple of

bodies to the wolves and get it over with, had been cajoled into line. Ministers not directly involved were given a boiled-down, three-page document containing the nuggets that suited the Government's case and other snippets of useful material, including quotations from Labour's dim and distant time in power when ministers had behaved as Tory ministers were behaving now. The members of the Cabinet directly affected by the Report were even better prepared: their copies of it had already been weighing down their bedside tables for eight days.

When the starting gate went up at 3.30 p.m. on 15 February, MPs were given their copies of the Report in the Commons and journalists plunged into the DTI lobby to claim their brown cardboard boxes and stagger off with them to waiting taxis. By the time Lang was on his feet ten minutes later, newspapers and broadcasting offices were struggling with the impossible task of filleting the vast document and producing a coherent account of it for their public: no summary had been produced by Scott and his team. The Government had refused to allow the media even the limited advance access granted to the opposition parties, but it was forthcoming with an interdepartmental press pack, which contained thirteen brief documents summarizing the Government's case in bite-sized, quotable chunks. The phone numbers of twenty-three press officers were listed. Lobby journalists at the House of Commons were also fed a list of numbered sections in the Report on which the Government would be relying (Labour was later to do the same). It was not the first time, and it is unlikely to be the last, that the Government has used a strategy like this to minimize media criticism when potentially embarrassing material has to be published: give it to them late, feed them a line, and by the time they've read it properly it'll be old news.

As Lang embarked on his statement, he held most of the cards. He and his backroom team had been studying the report since the Wednesday of the previous week and could draw on the advice and experience of eighteen civil servants who had been working for three years in the 'Scott Units' of Government departments, steeping themselves in the detail of the affair and tracking the progress of the Report's production. Robin Cook had been looking at the Report for only three and a half hours, and MPs were riffling through its pages, searching for ammunition, and dropping the heavy green volumes on their neighbours' toes.

But even with the odds stacked in his favour, Lang was facing one of the greatest tests of his political career. Until the Tory leadership election of the previous summer, when John Major had put himself up for re-election in a pre-emptive bid to sideline the Euro-rebels, Lang had been Secretary of State for Scotland, putting in a smooth and competent performance on a brief that had its challenges but which was not central to the political agenda. In the post-leadership-election reshuffle when Michael Heseltine moved from the DTI to become Deputy Prime Minister and First Secretary of State, Lang was promoted into his shoes, inheriting not only the grand extra title revived by Heseltine – President of the Board of Trade – but also the poisoned chalice of the Scott Report. He was suddenly right at the centre of the big screen.

Lang began soberly, stressing that Scott had found no evidence of bombs and guns going to Iraq, acknowledging the judge's criticism of a lack of openness about the export of non-lethal defence equipment, but asserting that no impropriety had been found in the way ministers had signed PII certificates for documents relating to the Matrix Churchill trial. Then, as if remembering his instructions that attack is the best form of defence, he quoted criticism from members of the opposition front bench and demanded apologies from them. 'There was no conspiracy,' he stormed. 'There was no cover-up. Such charges are reckless and malicious and they should never have been made. The House will now expect to hear them withdrawn without reservation.'

The phrase 'no conspiracy, no cover-up' was to become the official mantra in the gruelling round of media interviews undertaken by Lang and his ministerial colleagues in the hours and days to come. It was an effective slogan, because it was true – Scott had not found that ministers had conspired to send the Matrix Churchill defendants to jail or covered up such a conspiracy. But the phrase 'no conspiracy, no cover-up' was also a clever piece of misrepresentation, tantamount to shouting from the rooftops that you've been acquitted of murder when all you were accused of was grievous bodily harm. The Government was able to get away with the misrepresentation partly because it could use Labour quotations that had alleged cover-up, if not conspiracy. Early in his statement, Lang brought out a remark by Robin Cook, who had said that ministers 'were trying to cover up their role in arming Saddam Hussein', and another by John Prescott, who had said they were 'prepared to send citizens to jail to cover their own backs'.

But the charges examined by the Scott Inquiry were that ministers had misled Parliament and the Government had failed to stop an unfair prosecution. These accusations, largely substantiated in the Report, were deliberately played down. (A few days later, the clever, effective but fundamentally misleading nature of Lang's 'no conspiracy, no cover-up' was seized upon by the dissident Tory MP Richard Shepherd. 'The Government,' he said, 'has put up a phoney case to exonerate itself, saying it stood accused of a conspiracy. This is not so.')

After his detour to attack the opposition, Lang moved on to the 'no surrender' sections of his statement, defending the Attorney-General, Sir Nicholas Lyell, and the Chief Secretary to the Treasury, William Waldegrave. Scott 'does not in any way question the personal integrity of the Attorney-General', he asserted, and said that Scott's criticism of Lyell for failing to pass on Michael Heseltine's reservations about signing PII certificates was 'a matter of opinion'. As for the ministers who granted licences to Matrix Churchill for the exports that led to its prosecution by Customs, it was not their fault, said Lang, because intelligence reports about the end-use of the exports had not reached them. The same techniques of aggressive over-simplification were applied in the case of Waldegrave. Lang quoted Scott as saying that the Chief Secretary to the Treasury had 'no duplicitous intention'. Waldegrave was therefore 'absolved of the charge that he intended to mislead Members of the House or anyone else'. Scott's judgment that the Matrix Churchill trial should never have gone ahead was made 'with the benefit of hindsight', and his call for greater ministerial openness would be debated, but with no guarantees. The statement was a pugnacious and crafty performance, and Lang rounded it off with another demand for apologies from Labour 'to my right honourable and honourable friends whom they have defamed'.

When Lang sat down, Cook went straight on the attack, reeling off the choicest of the conclusions he had gleaned from his three and a half hours in solitary confinement with the Scott Report: that the Howe guidelines on exports had indeed been changed, that Parliament had not been told about it for fear of a public outcry, that ministers had failed to follow the rules on accountability, that PII certificates had been wrongly deployed, and that the Attorney-General had been 'personally at fault'.

But the crucial contrast was in the style and rhetoric, and when Cook came to his peroration it was clear that the Commons was witnessing an outstanding Parliamentary performance.

> Are the Government really going to ask us to accept a Report that says that the current Chief Secretary signed twenty-seven letters to Members of Parliament that were misleading, and which he was in a position to know were misleading, then tell us that he can remain in office as if the Report had never been published? Is the President really going to ask the House to accept a Report that shows that the Attorney-General wrongly advised ministers and failed to tell the court that at least one minister signed under protest, and then tell us that the Attorney-General can also stay in office? Is the President really going to ask the House to accept a Report which, over five volumes, demonstrates how this Government misjudged Saddam Hussein, misled Members of Parliament and misdirected the prosecution, then tell us that no one in the Government will accept responsibility for getting it wrong? . . . The Report goes beyond the career of individual Ministers or the reputation of some officials. It reveals the price that Britain pays for a culture of secrecy in Government.

The Labour benches were triumphant; the Tories sullen and silent. Lang accused Cook of twisting and distorting the Report, and managed a little sally to the effect that he had blighted his Commons career and should apologize or resign. A former minister, Tim Renton, asked Lang a question, which gave him the chance to play the foreigner card ('My right honourable Friend might like to know that France was exporting Exocets and Mirage fighters to Iraq . . . '). Another former minister, Tom King, described looking in vain for British equipment among the hardware captured from the Iraqis in the Gulf War ('I found one Land Rover'). But no amount of friendly questions lobbed to Lang from the back benches could hide that, in Parliamentary terms, Cook had won the day, especially as Labour MPs were now coming up with quotations from Scott reinforcing the impression that Lang's gloss on the Report was unrealistically favourable.

Two vital aspects of these initial Commons exchanges were to set the agenda for the coming ten days between the publication of the Report and the full debate on it scheduled for Monday 26 February. The first was that MPs and others leafing through the Report were beginning to realize that there were crucial ambiguities in it which allowed the opposing parties to make contrasting claims on the same subjects: as the former trade and industry secretary Paul Channon was later to say, 'The real difficulty with the Scott Report is that it is all things to all men. We can all find quotations to suit the argument that we are trying to advance or rebut. It is a great pity that the Report has no conclusions so that we can find out exactly what was intended.' The second was that not all the Tory MPs who questioned Lang over his statement were friendly. Would the Government, with its overall majority already down to four and Westminster gossip predicting the imminent defection of another MP, be able to carry the day in the crucial vote?

The ambiguities in the Report were most apparent in the passages dealing with the role of Waldegrave in answering Parliamentary questions and writing letters about whether or not the Government's export guidelines had changed after the ceasefire in the Iran–Iraq war in 1988. On the one hand, Scott said Waldegrave knew that the information he was giving to MPs was incorrect and that the effect of his letters and answers would be to mislead; but on the other, he acknowledged that Waldegrave did not intend his letters to be misleading and did not regard them as such. How could someone knowingly give wrong information, people wondered, and yet not intend to mislead? It was a confusing situation, apparently illogical and impossible to unravel, spawning circular semantic arguments about the precise difference between words like 'intentionally' and 'designedly'. Some MPs, lawyers and journalists began to feel that the Government's sustained pressure on Scott in the build-up to the Report, especially at the stage when draft criticisms were sent to Waldegrave and others asking for their responses, had achieved the desired effect. Had Scott, in the end, been made to feel that he must bend over backwards to be seen to be fair and politically unbiased? Had he felt that it would go beyond his role as an inquiry judge to produce conclusions that could be portrayed by his enemies as resulting in the downfall of ministers? Had he felt unable to come to a decisive view over the apparent contradictions, and decided to leave them hanging? And, if that was so, had Scott 'bottled out', as some critics were soon saying, or merely presented both sides of the argument to let the public, the final jury in the matter, decide for themselves?

Scott offered answers to none of these questions: his press conference on the day of publication amounted to a repeat of the sentence in the Report which says that the Report, and the Report alone, represented his final conclusions. But ambiguities are undoubtedly there, and they contributed crucially in saving the ministerial skins of Waldegrave and Lyell: first, they denied the opposition the unequivocal 'killer punch' it needed to press home its calls for resignation; and second, they allowed the Government to claim that the two had acted honestly, with good intentions and in good faith throughout.

Yet ambiguities also caused problems for the Government because ministers tried to present the findings of the Report as if they were unequivocal, which was immediately apparent in some of the press releases contained in the pack distributed to journalists with the Report. The most striking example was in a paper from the Treasury – Waldegrave's present department – entitled 'Scott Clears Waldegrave of Intent to Mislead', in which Waldegrave is quoted as saying: 'I am grateful to Sir Richard for listening carefully to what I said to him, above all for accepting my good faith.' The paper includes four brief extracts from the Report under a heading 'Scott Clears Waldegrave of Lying to Parliament or in Letters'.

If the extracts are read within their context in the Report, it quickly becomes obvious how selection can become distortion.

The first extract reads: 'I accept that he [Waldegrave] did not intend his letters to be misleading and did not so regard them.' The full sentence in the Report reads: 'Taken overall, the terms of Mr Waldegrave's letter to Mr Sackville and his other letters in like terms were, in my opinion, apt to mislead the readers as to the nature of the policy on export sales to Iraq that was currently being pursued by the Government. Mr Waldegrave was in a position to know that that was so although I accept that he did not intend his letters to be misleading and did not so regard them.'

The second extract reads: 'I accept also that . . . the junior Ministers believed they were avoiding a formal change to the 1985 guidelines.' But the full paragraph goes on to say: 'But, however the agreement reached by the junior Ministers be described, if the substance of the agreement was to change the criterion that would be applied to applications for licences to export defence equipment to Iraq, they were, in any ordinary use of language, agreeing on a change of policy. I regard the explanation that this could not be so because the approval of the senior Minister and the Prime Minister had not been obtained as sophistry.'

But perhaps the most audacious example of this feat of selective quotation comes in the next paragraph of the release headed, 'What Motivated Ministers?' The paragraph states: 'The overriding and determinative reason' for not answering the Parliamentary Questions and letters in the terms chosen was to protect 'British trading interests' The full sentence in the Report reads: 'I have come to the conclusion that the overriding and determinative reason was a fear of strong public opposition to the loosening of the restrictions on the supply of defence equipment to Iraq and a consequential fear that the pressure of the opposition might be detrimental to British trading interests.'

None of the other documents in the press pack are quite as blatant in their attempts to present only one side of the picture as the one from the Treasury, with the possible exception of a two-page Government summary, which concludes with impressive *chutzpah*: 'The Government welcomes this clearing of its good name.' What all the documents share, however, is an approach in which the amount of information about what the Scott Report actually says is kept to a minimum and the maximum amount of space is given to a self-serving alternative account of the events that led to the setting up of the Scott Inquiry. Thus the Cabinet Office document, couched in smooth mandarinese, avoids most of the sticky aspects of the arms-to-Iraq affair and argues that the wording of Parliamentary answers about changes in the guidelines was not misleading because MPs would have read between the lines:

> The agreed form of response, adopted with minor variations in such responses, was: 'The Guidelines on the export of defence equipment to Iran and Iraq are kept under constant review, and

are applied in the light of prevailing circumstances, including the ceasefire and developments in the peace negotiations.' This form of words clearly indicated that the ceasefire and progress in the peace negotiations were factors being taken into account when applications for exports to Iran and Iraq were being considered, and that other 'prevailing circumstances' were similarly taken into account (and MPs in 1989 would readily have identified the *fatwa* as such a 'prevailing circumstance'). The answers given to Parliamentary questions therefore gave an accurate description of the Government's policy . . . at the time. There was no question of Parliament being deliberately misled . . .

By the next day, Friday 16 February, Labour had done its homework on the press pack and produced three retaliatory documents, the first headed 'Five New Tory Lies on Arms to Iraq'. Two of the lies, it alleged, were in the Government summary, two in the Cabinet Office paper, and one in the Treasury press release. Labour quoted extracts from the Scott Report to attack the assertions in the Government summary that ministers were required by law to sign PII certificates and that Britain had supplied no arms to Iraq (it had known that lathes sent by BSA in 1988 were to be used to make shells and had turned a blind eye to the use of Jordan as a diversionary route). Labour applied the same method in the case of the assertions in the Cabinet Office paper that Parliamentary answers were accurate and that there had been no change of policy after the ceasefire, and in the case of that in the Treasury press release which said that Waldegrave did not mislead Parliament. Labour also put out two documents pulling together all the criticism of Waldegrave and Lyell in the Scott Report and argued that they were not fit for office.

It was, however, too late to make much impact in the media, which had either extracted much of the criticism from the Report the previous night, decided that Scott was a bit of damp squib because of its apparent equivocations, or resolved to wait until the full Parliamentary debate before getting excited about it again. The Government strategy of striking hard and decisively with a simple, predetermined line – however partial and misleading it might have been – had, to an extent, paid off. A consolation prize for Labour was a grudging letter four days later from the Chancellor, Kenneth Clarke, admitting that the annex to the Treasury press release headed 'Does Scott Say

Waldegrave Misled Parliament? No', should have carried the word 'intentionally' before 'misled'. The other aspect of the Parliamentary exchanges of 15 February which lived on until the night of the debate – and caused the Government more trouble than any of the recriminations about its over-selective publication strategy – concerned the loyalty of Tory MPs. One of the most telling interventions following Lang's statement on publication day came from Richard Shepherd, who quoted in full the paragraph in the Report which said that the failure to inform Parliament about the export policy shift was 'deliberate' and motivated by 'fear of strong public opposition'. The MP for Aldridge Brownhills, with a track record of determined defence of civil liberties and open government, asked: 'Does that not go to the heart of democratic and accountable government? What is the Government's response to that statement?'

The other Tory who put the Government on notice that it could not necessarily count on his support during the debate was Rupert Allason, MP for Torbay, who has a parallel career in writing about the world of spies under the *nom de plume* Nigel West, and a history of occasional defiance of the Government Whips' Office. Most notably, he failed to vote for the Government in the confidence vote over the Maastricht treaty in 1993, and was punished by being deprived of the whip for a year, which meant losing all the inside information and privileges that go with filing loyally through the division lobbies outside the Commons chamber. During questions following Lang's statement, Allason was exercised by the Scott Report's verdict that the use of PII certificates to cover whole classes of documents in the Matrix Churchill trial was 'bizarre and unacceptable', and called for a statute to replace the existing judge-made law on PII and ensure that such class claims were never made again.

The Government's concern about Shepherd and Allason intensified on Saturday 17 February when Peter Thurnham, MP for the marginal seat of Bolton North East, was revealed in the press as the latest Tory backbencher thinking of deserting the Government – Alan Howarth had gone over to Labour the previous year and Emma Nicholson had joined the Liberal Democrats over Christmas. Thurnham's departure would reduce the Government's majority from four to two, and the Tory machine appeared to pop a rivet at the prospect: over the weekend, it was put about that Thurnham was merely piqued over his rejection as a candidate in a safer seat than his current one for the next election, but at the same time efforts were made to convince him that his discontent with the Government's performance was being taken seriously and an audience was arranged for him with John Major.

The uncertainty over the Government's majority was compounded by the delicate state of affairs in the Northern Ireland peace process, which was raising familiar doubts about how the Ulster Unionists would vote and new questions about the price they might try to exact in return for their support. Desperate efforts were being made in London, Dublin and Washington to get the process back on track after the shattering of the ceasefire by the huge IRA bomb in London's Docklands earlier that month, but the particular difficulty confronting the Government just now was the kind of election that should be used in Northern Ireland to determine how many people of each party would be represented at the promised all-party talks: should it be a single list system for the whole province, which would favour the Protestant Ian Paisley's hardline Democratic Unionist Party and the mainly Catholic Social Democratic and Labour Party (SDLP), or a poll of separate constituencies, which would favour the Ulster Unionist Party, led by David Trimble?

The Government struggled through a messy week, trying to preserve over the Scott Report the advantage of surprise, which had seen it through the first day. Tony Blair won on points at Tuesday's Prime Minister's Question Time when he told John Major that if no minister took responsibility for Scott's criticism the Tories would remain 'knee deep in dishonour'. Scott let it be known that he felt that the Government was misrepresenting his Report by the use of soundbites, and later extended his strictures to the press and the opposition. Two eminent judges weighed into the PII debate, one on each side.

The worst blow for the Government, however, came on the Thursday, when John Major's attempts to soft-soap Peter Thurnham failed and he resigned the Government whip. By Saturday it was clear that there were four more doubters. Sir Teddy Taylor, Southend East, and Christopher Gill, Ludlow, were familiar members of the awkward squad, both of them

among the group of nine Euro-sceptics who had been deprived
of the Government whip for their opposition to Maastricht. The
other two were more unlikely rebels: John Marshall, MP for
Hendon South and chairman of the British Israel Parliamentary
group, who wrote to the *Jewish Chronicle* saying that he was
unhappy about the Scott Report because it showed that arms-
making equipment from Britain was getting through to Iraq at a
time when all defence-related exports to Israel were blocked;
and Quentin Davies, MP for Stamford and Spalding, a former
merchant banker and diplomat, who told a meeting of the
backbench 1922 Committee that he was concerned at the Report's
revelations about low standards of ministerial accountability and
civil service ethics. It began to look as if the Government could
lose the vote in the coming debate on the Scott Report.

The suspense continued over the weekend, with Ian
Paisley's three MPs deciding to abstain, Robert McCartney, the
Independent Unionist, declaring that he would vote with
Labour, and the nine Ulster Unionists electing to meet and
decide on the day of the debate.

Monday brought a charm offensive from ministers, who
emphasized to their supporters how willing they were to accept
Scott's recommendations – if not his criticisms – and take or
consider remedial action. Allason, however, raised the stakes,
speaking on the Press Association's news wires during the
morning in defence of Paul Henderson, Matrix Churchill's
former managing director and MI6 informer. Spineless
Whitehall officials, said Allason, had conspired to jail a brave
and innocent man when they should have been trying to find
ways of giving him a medal for his services. 'What kind of
message,' asked the spy writer, 'does this give to other people
who wish to assist our security and intelligence services?'

Ministers filed into the Chamber for the crucial debate
wondering if the Scott Report was a bomb on a slow fuse. A
defeat in the lobbies would lead inevitably to a vote of no
confidence in a highly unstable political atmosphere.

As the debate got under way, most notable was Ian Lang's
change in tone. In some passages of his speech he repeated his
tactics of the previous week, saying that Scott had acquitted the
Government of conspiracy and cover-up and that the opposition
was guilty of libelling ministers; but the bulk of his words were

more emollient, and clearly addressed to Tory backbenchers who looked, for the most part, dejected and defensive. Mistakes had been made and there were lessons to be learnt, Lang said, and the Government was willing to take action to put things right. As he worked through Scott's recommendations, however, it became clear that there were few areas where change was guaranteed, and many where the most he could offer was debate, consultation and review.

His backbenchers might have been a bit perkier when Lang sat down, but it didn't last long. Robin Cook had been polishing his weapons all week and rose to deliver an attack even more deft and deadly than that of ten days earlier. He had at his fingertips the sections of the Report most damaging to the Government, displayed them with some fine turns of outraged rhetoric and beat off his attackers with a dry, spontaneous wit. The ever-combative David Mellor was lying in wait, primed with remarks that Cook had made on the subject in the past and now seemed extreme; but even he failed to make an impact.

'Secrecy made this scandal possible,' declared Cook.

> . . . The Government are fond of lecturing the rest of the nation on its needs to accept responsibility. Parents are held responsible for actions; teachers are held responsible for the performance of their pupils; local councillors are held legally and financially responsible; yet, when it comes to themselves, suddenly, not a single minister can be found to accept responsibility for what went wrong . . . Sir Richard returns a verdict of guilty. You can tell, Madam Speaker, the importance that he attaches to the conclusion because, like all his key findings, it is expressed as a double negative: 'It is clear that policy and defence sales to Iraq did not remain unchanged.' Three years ago the Prime Minister told the House: 'The suggestion that Ministers misled the House is a serious and scurrilous charge and has no basis whatsoever in fact.' The suggestion does have a firm basis, in the five volumes beside me. I agree with the Prime Minister that was a serious charge. Will he now accept that, far from being scurrilous, it was entirely accurate? [Calls of 'Answer'.] Suddenly, we have a row of limpets stuck to the Treasury bench.

Cook hammered home the Report's descriptions of Waldegrave misleading Parliament and Lyell's incompetence over PII, produced references to John Major having being told about changes to the guidelines, and dragged in his deputy,

Michael Heseltine. 'I have concluded that what would hurt him most would be to praise him,' said Cook. 'Let me now do so. I praise him willingly, because he was the first person to introduce the term "cover-up" to the discussion. Two years before anyone else thought of the term, the Deputy Prime Minister objected to the attempt to withhold documents because "it would look as though he would be engaged in an attempted cover-up".' It was described next day by many Parliamentary veterans as one of the best performances of the decade.

Conservative backbenchers were now so gloomy that few attempted to speak in the debate. Instead there came a long procession of former ministers criticizing Scott, justifying their own past actions and those of their colleagues, and trying to turn the tables on Labour. Douglas Hurd, former Foreign Secretary, said that Scott was 'disappointing' and gave a misleading impression of Government policy-making; Tim Sainsbury, former Minister for Trade, produced quotations from Scott to say that the guidelines were 'adjusted' rather than 'changed'; Richard Needham, another former Minister for Trade, argued that no government could be entirely frank about arms sales; David Mellor went on about how he, when at the Foreign Office, had prevented the export of some rubber boats; and Tom King, former Secretary of State for Defence, doggedly returned to the solitary British Land Rover found in the lorry park after the Gulf War.

But the big questions remained: what were the nine Ulster Unionists up to, and which of the Conservative MPs was going to rebel? The first was addressed in meetings elsewhere in the Palace of Westminster by John Major and David Trimble, and the answer lent more importance still to the second, which would be decided in the lobbies at the end of the debate.

When Trimble went into the meeting with Major and Sir Patrick Mayhew, the Northern Ireland Secretary, he suspected that the Government had done a deal with his rivals, the Democratic Unionists, guaranteeing them the single list voting system that they and the SDLP wanted for the forthcoming elections in the province. According to accounts that emerged the next day, the question of the elections was raised at the meeting but Major, who was in the middle of crucial manoeuvres to convene a summit on the peace process with the

Irish Government in two days' time, declined to say what form the elections would take: this would have to be thrashed out at the 'proximity talks', which were due to be part of the revival of the peace process. Trimble himself wanted to abstain, but some of his troops were determined to vote against the Government and he decided to go along with them rather than cause a split. In any case, he was unhappy at what Scott had revealed about the use of PII certificates.

All eyes turned on the Tory dissidents. It was already obvious that some of those who had made angry noises in the previous few days – Sir Teddy Taylor, John Marshall and Christopher Gill – were not going to allow their discontent to push them into the opposition lobby. On the other hand, Peter Thurnham was now out of the party and it was clear that Richard Shepherd was a lost cause: the speech he made now resonated with criticism, cited six examples from Scott of the Government misleading Parliament and called for a Freedom of Information Act – something that Ian Lang had explicitly ruled out at the beginning of the debate. Paisley's three Democratic Unionists were pledged to abstain, and Liberal Democrat and Labour MPs were on the premises in full strength – some of the seven sick or injured Labour members had arrived by ambulance. The logic of the numbers was that if the Government failed to get either Quentin Davies or Rupert Allason on side, it would be voted down.

Davies was the first of the two to rise, and his speech was more focused and effective than many contributions from the Labour side. With William Waldegrave shaking his head on the front bench, Davies read out three quotations from Scott, which said that the minister had misled Parliament, and remarked that there were only two questions which mattered: did the House accept Scott's criticisms, and if so, what would it do about it? Davies made clear that he accepted Scott's verdict over the changing of the export guidelines and the misleading of Parliament, and that Waldegrave should resign: ' . . . It must be made clear that someone is taking responsibility and that the principle has been restored that ministers remain fully accountable to the House of Commons.'

Since the Government had pledged that there would be no resignations, this meant that their only hope was Allason. He spoke soon after Davies: he wasn't concerned, he said, about the questionable exports or the 'disingenuous' Parliamentary answers; he was concerned with the brave intelligence-gathering activities of Paul Henderson and the way in which every possible obstacle had been put in the way of his defence. Like Douglas Hurd earlier in the debate, he wanted to get rid of 'the mess of judge-made law' on PII 'so we can all understand the criteria by which ministers can or cannot claim public interest immunity'. He went on: 'I hope that when he winds up, my right honourable friend will agree that PII certificates should never again be used in a criminal case to cover whole classes of document; I also hope that he will agree that there should now be a presumption of disclosure, not suppression.'

It was clear, therefore, that Allason was ready to negotiate with Roger Freeman, the Chancellor of the Duchy of Lancaster and Minister in Charge of the Office of Public Service, who was due to wind up the debate for the Government. Freeman, keenly aware of what was at stake, was only a couple of minutes into his speech when he reached the issue of the use in prosecutions of PII certificates. Virtually every MP who had spoken had raised the same issue, but Allason's interest, in the circumstances, was clearly exceptional. 'I know that my honourable friend the Member for Torbay has taken the issue very seriously,' said Freeman, and yes, he would give way to his honourable friend as soon as he had finished his sentence.

Would Freeman, Allason interrupted, 'give an undertaking that the presumption in future will always be on disclosure and not suppression? Will he give an undertaking that there will never again be such an abuse of public interest immunity certificates granted on national security grounds?'

Freeman had already gone further than Lang and pledged a future Commons debate on PII – which the Government had evidently agreed on the hoof in the hope of mollifying rebels. He now replied: 'The presumption should be disclosure, and when the judge read and interpreted the public interest immunity certificates in the Matrix Churchill trial, he made a positive decision on disclosure. I give my honourable friend the undertaking I gave a few moments ago – the Government will ensure that an opportunity arises in Government time for that matter to be considered further.'

Had Allason been accorded the undertaking he had demanded? In post-mortems the following day, Government sources admitted that Freeman, far from making concessions, had merely stated the current legal position, which, it was claimed, differed from the position at the time of the Matrix Churchill case because of the Law Lords' judgment in 1994 in *ex parte Wiley*. In this case the Attorney-General, Sir Nicholas Lyell, had argued – as he had over the Matrix Churchill case – that ministers had a duty to apply for PII over certain classes of documents and to leave the final decision on disclosure to the courts. The Law Lords had rejected this argument in *Wiley*, saying instead that ministers should give priority to disclosure of documents, look at them carefully and sometimes agree to disclosure without troubling the courts to make a decision. But the courts should still be the final arbiter and decide what to do about documents for which ministers claimed immunity.

To muddy things further, there appear also to be differences between the position established in *Wiley* and the preferences of both Allason and Freeman. Allason said in his speech: 'It is quite clear that only ministers can decide these issues. They should not pass the matter to the courts.' Freeman said: 'Whatever system is adopted, it should remain for the judge to decide on disclosure – if justice so requires – on matters of national security or other matters covered by a PII certificate.'

In the end, though, it hardly mattered whether or not Allason really got a concession out of the Government. The crucial thing was he could claim he had won an undertaking on PII, and after voting for the Government he went out on College Green to proclaim his achievement to the television cameras. His vote saved the day for the Government, who squeaked in by 320 votes to 319. Labour hid their bitter disappointment by claiming that they had won the argument hands down, while ministers smiled weakly at each other and admitted in private that they had been extremely lucky.

In the event, the best summary of the publication and

immediate aftermath of the Scott Report had been produced by William Waldegrave, Chief Secretary to the Treasury, in the *Daily Mail* three weeks before: 'It will be hairy for ten days,' he said. 'But that will be all.'

15 • A Sense of Depression

'I do not believe that the instinctive Whitehall reaction to seek
to withhold government documents from public inspection is
likely to change.'
    Sir Richard Scott, Report, Section K, Chapter 6,
    paragraph 16

After winning the crucial vote in Parliament, the Government
made perfectly clear it wanted to bury the difficult issues in the
Scott Report and stifle any uncomfortable discussion about its
broader implications. Ministerial documents about arms-sales
information and PII had been quietly placed in the Commons
library, and a debate on PII had been promised. But Scott's call
for a wide-ranging public debate on crucial questions such as
arms-sales information and export controls has generally gone
unheeded, and it has been left to Scott himself, disappointed by
the Report's reception inside and outside Parliament, to carry
the torch forward in speeches to universities and lawyers.

The recommendations of the Report that the Government
found most unpalatable were, of course, those concerning
ministerial accountability and PII, the two subjects on which it
has given least ground. There has been no sign of ministers
promoting Scott's proposals for tightening up their accountability to Parliament and public, and the fightback against his
views on PII has continued quietly in the background.

On accountability, the Government has pledged to give
evidence to a select committee of MPs but, at the time of writing,
it has avoided any mention of Scott's key recommendation that
Questions of Procedure for Ministers should be amended to
make it impossible for them to use arguments about 'the public
interest' to impose secrecy on administrative blunders or
political embarrassments. There has been some sign of flexibility
on Scott's call for reconsideration of the policy of denying

information on arms sales to MPs, with a promise from Roger Freeman, the Minister for Public Service, that he will 'bring forward specific proposals in due course'.

However, there has been criticism, ironically, for both Scott and the Government over the one area of accountability in which Scott declared himself in agreement with the official line. This is the principle, first put forward by Sir Robin Butler, that ministers can only be held personally responsible for mistakes in their departments if they know, or ought to know, about the subject in question. Accountability, according to Sir Robin, does not mean ministers resigning over mistakes by their civil servants, but is a 'blame-free word' to be used when a minister is simply accepting the traditional constitutional principle of accountability by telling Parliament what is going on.

Scott's acceptance of these definitions in the closing pages of his Report brought a burst of flak from senior civil servants and their union, the First Division Association (FDA), who argued that they have been left in an impossibly exposed position, conducting vast areas of Government business without any apparent lines of responsibility to democratic representatives. The new distinction between responsibility and accountability means, according to the FDA, that ministers can claim credit when things go well, and blame civil servants when they go badly.

The FDA canvasses the possibility of a Civil Service Act to lay out the responsibilities and duties of officials and give them statutory protection for providing information directly to Parliament and the public. But the Government has already poured cold water on that idea in written evidence to the Public Service Committee of MPs, which is conducting an inquiry into the constitutional implications of the Scott Report. The evidence, submitted by the Cabinet Office, says that an arrangement where civil servants were directly accountable to Parliament would 'give unelected officials more power than is warranted in a Parliamentary democracy'. The paper also argues, disingenuously, that MPs would be able to pass judgment on the conduct of individual civil servants, putting their reputations and careers at risk. The same paper also takes the opportunity to cock a snook at Scott's criticism that ministers failed to ensure accountability when they prevented two retired civil servants from giving evidence to the Trade and Industry Select Committee (TISC). 'It has been a broadly accepted principle,' it insists, 'that the minister decides which officials are best placed to represent them.'

Meanwhile, there has been no sign of any change in the Government's defiance of Scott's criticisms of Sir Nicholas Lyell and his approach to PII law. Ian Lang told the Commons before the crucial vote on 26 February that the law had moved on since the events in the Report and had brought a number of Scott's points into current practice. Beyond that, the Government would 'consider his recommendations in the light of developing case law – in particular, his view that the time is opportune for a collective reappraisal by Ministers'.

Later in the debate, as MPs were offered a Commons debate on PII as part of the push to square the rebels, Roger Freeman acknowledged the importance of the question of PII class claims, which Scott had said should never be used again in criminal trials. 'The real question,' said Freeman, 'is whether there is a need for class claims, or whether claims should be content-based . . . Whatever system is adopted, it should remain for the judge to decide on disclosure – if justice so requires – on matters of national security or other matters covered by a PII certificate.' It was hardly an enthusiastic commitment to change, and on 29 February a kind of long-distance sparring began between the Attorney-General's department and Scott himself, when a document called 'Public Interest Immunity: Government Response to the Scott Report' was deposited without fanfare in the Commons library. It was billed as a full analysis of the issue, but, like Lyell's press release of eleven days before, was actually a paper dedicated to the argument that Scott's view on PII 'differs fundamentally from the generally accepted position'. It takes issue in particular with Scott's repeated argument that Government documents must be disclosed in a trial if they might be of assistance to the defence. This broad principle is one that could have serious repercussions for many prosecutions, it says, and cases against serious criminals and terrorists might have to be dropped to protect sensitive sources of information and prevent informants' lives being put at risk.

The paper also took up Scott's pre-eminent question of PII class claims and was more specifically negative than Freeman had been in the Commons debate. The Government remained concerned, it said, that the quality of advice by officials to ministers might suffer if class claims were abandoned: the inner workings of the government machine 'should not be exposed to the gaze of those ready to criticise without adequate knowledge of the background and perhaps with some axe to grind'.

When Scott read this he said he felt 'a sense of depression'. In response to Lyell's document, in the annual lecture of the Public Law Project in March, he went on: 'What is the quality of civil servants or ministers who it is feared will temper their advice because of the possibility that the terms of their advice might later become publicly known?' It had never been suggested, he went on, that references in Lady Thatcher's memoirs to confidential discussions between ministers had prejudiced the candour of subsequent Cabinet meetings. As for uninformed criticism, Government should do what it can to make sure that its critics are not ill-informed. 'The secrecy with which Government chooses to surround its inner workings, with light cast only by designer leaks and investigative journalists, is not, in my opinion, a reason for perpetuating the sort of PII claims that were made in the Matrix Churchill case.'

Scott was not the only one to continue the battle with Lyell. The Attorney-General and other ministers, including Scott's white knight Michael Heseltine, had made much in the days after publication of the fact that two of the counsel in the Matrix Churchill defence were among the eminent lawyers who took Lyell's side in the argument. But the lead defence counsel, Geoffrey Robertson, QC, made it clear in an article in the *Guardian* that he thought Lyell should resign, and that his reading of PII law was not the main issue. Picking up Lyell's own earlier description of the office of Attorney-General as 'a lighthouse in a thunderstorm', Robertson argued: 'The case for his resignation as lighthouse keeper is not that he is lacking in decency or integrity, or that he misunderstood PII law. It is that, as the Matrix Churchill storm clouds gathered in September 1992, he failed to tend the beacon.' The duty to look at the facts in an important prosecution, weigh them with public policy considerations and decide whether the prosecution should continue ought to be engraved on the heart of every Attorney-General, Robertson argued, but Lyell had neglected that duty and had not even bothered to read the documents. He had not acquainted himself with the most extraordinary fact of the case, namely that the main defendant, Paul Henderson, had risked his life as an MI6 agent and that one consequence of prosecuting him would be to damage MI6 recruitment. In short, he never applied his mind, judicial or otherwise, to the facts of the case or to the public interest considerations at stake: he abdicated his office. 'He is found at fault for failing to take firm (or any) action after being told authoritatively of the likelihood that justice would not be done in an important trial. The "spin" now being put on Scott's clear finding of personal fault is that it is based on criticism of Lyell's legal opinion about PII certificates. This is false. Lyell is found at fault not for being a poor lawyer, but for being a poor Attorney-General.'

It was a straightforward condemnation that Scott had hesitated to pronounce, perhaps because the passing of such resounding judgments on ministers could be attacked as taking part in party politics. The nearest he came in the Report to Robertson's view was in recording that the Attorney-General was 'personally at fault' for giving inadequate instructions to Matrix Churchill prosecuting counsel as the result of 'an absence of personal involvement'.

While the Government drags its heels on accountability and PII, however, it has, to some extent, accepted several of Scott's recommendations, most notably that there should be a thorough review of the 1990 Act on export controls leading to a new system with greater Parliamentary control. Whether the consultation paper it promised to issue by the summer of 1996 leads to a detailed Act suitable for peacetime in a post-cold-war world remains to be seen. Since publication of his Report, Scott has used increasingly strong language, calling the continued use of the Act a 'cynical evasion' of the Government's constitutional duty, and 'outrageous'.

The Government has also agreed to greater supervision of Customs prosecutions by the Attorney-General, stating that, as Scott recommends, such supervision will be equivalent to that exercised over the Crown Prosecution Service and the Serious Fraud Office.

The Government has been more hesitant about two other recommendations, that the prosecuting counsel in criminal trials should be given the specific duty of seeking and listing official documents which might be of use to defence lawyers, and that the ground rules for non-statutory inquisitorial inquiries such as the Scott Inquiry should be revised. But on two of Scott's proposals – that intelligence distribution and export licensing procedures should be improved – it says it has already made substantial progress and intends to do more.

The recommendations and responses are summarized below.

1. Inquiry procedures
Scott: Establish five alternative principles (see page 168) and allow for people to give evidence under oath to non-statutory bodies.
Government: The Lord Chancellor will consider the views of Scott and others, consult the Council on Tribunals and report to Parliament.

2. The power of Government to control exports
Scott: There should be a comprehensive review of the Import and Export Control Act 1990 (which made permanent the Import, Export and Customs Powers (Defence) Act 1939), with public debate over using export controls as a policy instrument, and a new system where Parliament approves export restrictions.
Government: The DTI will produce a consultation paper by the summer.

3. Export licensing procedures
Scott: New legally prescribed procedures for export licences for restricted goods, and an end to the 'fiction' that the DTI takes the decision in all cases.
Government: Changes made include more detailed and rigorous licence application procedures, a new section to process sensitive applications and hear appeals, and better links between the DTI, the MoD and the FCO.

4. The role of Customs and Excise in export control
Scott: Tidy up Customs and Excise law and prosecution procedures, strengthen the role of the Customs and Excise Solicitor's Office in prosecutions, and the Attorney-General to superintend export-control prosecutions.

Government: Legal proposals are 'largely accepted', Customs will consider strengthening the Solicitor's Office, and there will be greater supervision by the Attorney-General of Customs export-control prosecutions.

5. Prosecution procedures
Scott: It should be the duty of prosecution lawyers in Customs prosecutions to ensure that relevant documents from other Government departments are sought and details supplied to the defence.
Government: The Home Secretary will consider putting this proposal into the Criminal Procedure and Investigation Bill, now being examined by Parliament.

7. Use of intelligence by Government departments
Scott: Departments should review their requirements for intelligence, there should be better systems of recording and retrieving intelligence in the export licensing system, and FCO civil servants should ensure that the versions of intelligence they pass on to ministers are accurate.
Government: The FCO, DTI, Customs, Cabinet Office, MoD, MI6 and GCHQ have all changed intelligence procedures and increased their use of information technology; progress will be reported to the Commons Intelligence and Security Committee. The FCO and the DTI are sending more intelligence to senior officials and ministers, Customs has set up a new intelligence 'cell', the MoD and MI6 are concentrating more on intelligence about nuclear proliferation, and MI6 is giving Customs more material.

8. Ministerial accountability
Scott: Any new formulation of accountability should make explicit that fear of inconvenience or political embarrassment should never be a reason for withholding information from Parliament. There should also be a comprehensive review, with a public debate, of the refusal to give information about arms sales.
Government: The Select Committee on Public Service is investigating ministerial accountability and the Parliamentary convention of secrecy on weapons sales. The Government will

give evidence on both subjects and publish new proposals on the second in due course.

A generous summary of the response to Scott's eight recommendations, then, is three 'done it's, one 'will do it', two 'will consider it's, and two 'almost certainly not's. On the face of it, this is hardly a spectacular result for an Inquiry that took four years, studied 200,000 pages of official documents, and cost nearly £4 million.

Postscript

'It is for me a matter of regret . . . that the Report is going to
be used as a political football'
          Sir Richard Scott

Sir Richard Scott's Report raises fundamental and uncomfortable questions about how Britain is governed, and about the
nature and legitimacy of its Parliamentary democracy. That is
why an unholy alliance of ministers and mandarins went to such
lengths to try to belittle the Inquiry and, after the Report was
published, to close down all debate.

Scott cast light into the darkest recesses of Whitehall,
exposing a machine whose protection from any proper scrutiny
had bred a culture of incompetence, arrogance and, above all,
secrecy. Secrecy, Sir Robin Butler told the Inquiry, was needed 'in
the interests of good government'. Public Interest Immunity
certificates, admitted Andrew Leithead at the Treasury Solicitor's
Department, were used for 'administrative convenience'. 'It is
damaging', he told the Inquiry, 'to have any decision-making
process exposed.' But Scott exposed much more than simply a
bureaucratic instinct for secrecy: he found a Whitehall culture
that was profoundly undemocratic. When Scott suggested to
Lord Howe that he was adopting a 'Government-knows-best'
approach, the former Foreign Secretary replied: 'It is partly that.
But it is partly, if we were to lay specifically our thought
processes before you, they are laid before a world-wide range of
uncomprehending or malicious commentators. This is the point.
You cannot choose a well-balanced presentation to an élite
Parliamentary audience.'

It was not so much that Howe and his colleagues in
Government could not be bothered to share policy-making with
Parliament, it was that they were frightened to do so. Once

Parliament was told the truth, all sorts of pressure groups – even members of the public – would start to ask awkward questions.

Whitehall has developed an ugly, patronizing attitude to Parliament. It is encouraged to do so by MPs themselves, the majority of whom either appear to have given up trying to scrutinize and challenge the power of the executive, or are interested only in party preferment, willing fodder for the whips.

On 26 February 1996, a majority of MPs voted, in effect, to be repeatedly misled by ministers and civil servants. They voted for the comfortable status quo. Asked by a clutch of Labour and Liberal Democrat backbenchers what steps the Government intended to take in view of Scott's conclusion that Parliament had been misled about the policy towards arms sales to Iraq, Jeremy Hanley, the FCO minister and former chairman of the Conservative Party, replied: 'We continue to take the view that the Howe guidelines were not changed. My right honourable and learned friend, the Foreign Secretary, does not consider that further action is necessary.' Ministers adopted a stance of astonishing complacency, dismissing out of hand Scott's two main conclusions. According to the Government, ministers are free from blame because Parliament was not misled. The Government rejected the documentary evidence amassed by the Inquiry, and insisted that there had been no change in Government policy on arms-related exports to Iraq. Ministers, including Lyell, are free from blame because, despite Scott's conclusion to the contrary, the law on PII was correctly interpreted and applied. Ministers conceded only that there had been some cock-ups, and that the fault for those lay with officials.

A deep chasm has been left in the whole question of democratic accountability, a 'responsibility-free' zone. Ministers say they cannot be held personally responsible for all the actions of their departments. It is an argument supported by Butler, and accepted by Scott. Ministers also distinguish between 'policy', for which they are responsible, and 'operations', for which they are not. (Michael Howard, the Home Secretary, notably made this distinction in the wake of prison escapes. Derek Lewis, dismissed by Howard in 1995 from his post as chief executive of the Prison Service, says that such a distinction cannot be made.) Ministers, meanwhile, insist that they alone – not civil servants –

are responsible to Parliament. A Civil Service Act is desperately needed to establish the principle that civil servants are responsible not, as now, merely to their ministers or the Government of the day but to the public, through Parliament. As the First Division Association (FDA), which represents senior public servants, said in evidence in March 1996 to the Commons Public Service Committee: 'A Civil Service Act . . . should set out the duties and obligations of the civil service to ministers, Parliament and the public as is the case in many modern Western democracies.' Civil servants must in future give evidence to Parliament, notably through Commons select committees, in their own right, and not simply on behalf of their ministers. There is no reason why that evidence should not include their advice to ministers. As Scott suggests, if that advice is rational and objective, there is no reason to suppose that the politically neutral status of civil servants would be undermined. Stimulating constructive debate is quite different from indulging in party politics.

A Civil Service Act could protect officials from abuse if a minister objected to a civil servant telling the truth to Parliament. The electorate, the entire country – not just Parliament – would benefit immeasurably from more information and thus a more healthy and better-informed debate. Party whips should no longer be allowed to stand in the way of a more effective Parliamentary democracy. MPs must stop abdicating their responsibilities if Parliament is not to become increasingly irrelevant. Perhaps nothing less than a Royal Commission is needed to consider the future of Britain's creaking system of Parliamentary government.

On 8 May 1996, Scott gave evidence to the Commons Public Service Committee. MPs, he said, should be far more assertive in forcing ministers to provide them with information. 'Ministerial accountability', he said, 'is a very important constitutional doctrine . . . The provision of information is the key.' He questioned the way in which ministers had unilaterally exempted whole rafts of information from their code of conduct on 'Open Government', and said that his experience during the Inquiry had persuaded him that the time had come for a Freedom of Information Act. He also suggested that Parliament should appoint a watchdog to monitor and challenge any refusal by ministers to supply information on the grounds that it was not in the 'public interest' to disclose it. The MPs on the committee seemed bemused.

Scott also told the committee that it was 'complete nonsense' to suggest that his Report had not come to any clear conclusions. Asked by the Labour MP, Tony Wright: 'Did something constitutionally improper happen?', he replied, 'Yes, I said so.'

'Did ministers behave in a way they shouldn't have behaved? 'Yes, I said so.'

'Was Parliament denied information constitutionally it ought to have had?'

'Yes,' Scott replied.

His answers could not have been clearer.

List of Terms and Abbreviations

1939 Act	Import, Export and Customs Powers (Defence) Act 1939
1990 Act	Import and Export Control Act 1990
ACDD	Arms Control and Disarmament Dept (FCO)
BAe	British Aerospace
CBI	Confederation of British Industry
COCOM	Co-ordinating Committee for Multilateral Strategic Controls
DESO	Defence Export Services Organization
DESS	Defence Export Services Secretariat
DIS	Defence Intelligence Staff
DTI	Department of Trade and Industry
dual-use	usable for civil or military purposes
ECGD	Export Credits Guarantee Department
ELA	export licence application
ELB	Export Licensing Branch (or Bureau)
EU	European Union
FDA	First Division Association
FCO	Foreign and Commonwealth Office
GCHQ	Government Communications Headquarters
ID	Investigation Division (of Customs and Excise)
IDC	Interdepartmental Committee on licensing of exports to Iran and Iraq
IMS	International Military Services
IWC	Integrated Weapons Complex
JIC	Joint Intelligence Committee
MED	Middle East Department (of the FCO)
MI5	The Security Service
MI6	The Secret Intelligence Service (SIS)
MoD	Ministry of Defence
MODWG	MoD Working Group, Iran/Iraq
MOU	Memorandum of Understanding
MTTA	Machine Tool Technologies Association
NBC	nuclear, biological, chemical
OD	Oversea and Defence Committee of the Cabinet
Ordtec	Ordnance Technologies Limited
PII	Public Interest Immunity
RARDE	Royal Armaments Research and Development Establishment
REU	Restricted Enforcement Unit
SEND	Scientific, Energy and Nuclear Dept (of the FCO)
SRC	Space Research Corporation
TISC	Trade and Industry Select Committee
WGIP	Working Group on Iraqi Procurement

Index